THIRD TIME'S A CHARM

Linda Kay Silva

Spinsters Ink
2011

Spinsters Ink, Inc.
P.O. Box 242
Midway, Florida 32343

Printed in the United States of America on acid-free paper
First Edition

Editor: Katherine V. Forrest
Cover Designer: Linda Callaghan

ISBN 13:978-1-935226-44-4

This Time is dedicated to those who spend Time making my life the fun place it is. . . AND YOU TWO ARE MOST CERTAINLY INCLUDED IN THAT! YOUR FRIENDSHIP MEANS A GREAT DEAL TO ME . . . I HOPE YOU KNOW HOW MUCH!

Love,
Erin

Acknowledgments

Lori—for being brave enough to get on the back of my Harley and for being so incredibly supporting all these years of my writing. You are, quite simply, the best.

Gita, Sharon, and Julie—for riding the wind with me and being such good friends.

Fay and Karelia—for laughing with us and being the Gold Standard of friends.

Donna and Debbie—for honking, waving, laughing, and just being uber cool.

Billie—for being my go-to IT guy, my answer man, and my problem-solver. You rock!

Sandi—for your fast fingers, quick mind, and fantastic editing skills.

Katherine V. Forest—for your attention to detail and awesome support as my editor. You turn coal into diamonds, my friend.

Sunnie and Kelley—for growing up to be the two coolest chicks on the planet. I love you both very much.

Kim Jacobs and Bill Overton—for being the two best bosses in the world. I love what I do and you both make APUS such a great place to be!

Sherry, Bernie, Mary, Diane, Suzie, and the rest of my tennis world—for giving me a place to play even though I am a little scary.

And finally, to the production staff at Spinsters/Bella—for working tirelessly to bring readers quality fiction. Thank you.

"So, what are you saying?" Jessie Ferguson asked as she sat down at the small table in the kitchen of Madame Ceara's boathouse. Ceara lit patchouli incense and the smoke hung in the air like LA smog. Jessie fanned it away so she could see more clearly the visitor she'd met only a few hours ago.

"Now, now, my dear," Ceara said, scooting in next to Jessie. "All in good time." Ceara's two dozen bracelets jangled as she moved, and the layers of colorful silk she wore fluttered slightly. Although at least fifty years older than Jessie's twenty, Madame Ceara was one of Jessie's dearest friends, and it had been Ceara who had set up this unlikely meeting between Jessie, a history student/time traveler, and Ben Davidson, ghost hunter.

"What I'm saying," Ben replied patiently, "is your little brother is experiencing a haunting." He opened a coffee-stained folder and pushed it toward Jessie. His ringless hands were white, smooth and almost too feminine for his size. "But it is a haunting of a very different nature."

Jessie glanced up from the file at Ben and nodded. This didn't surprise her. Since they'd move to New Haven, a small tourist town on the Oregon Coast, she had had her fair share of strange and life-altering events happen to her within the confines of the decrepit Victorian Inn her parents had renovated. Those events had transformed her previously chaotic life and booze-filled world into something…magical.

Prior to moving to the Inn, Jessie Ferguson believed in

nothing; a morose, moody and sullen teenager, she had made some incredibly poor choices in San Francisco, which prompted her parents to move her away from the fun and fog to the even grayer mists of the rocky Oregon coast.

Daniel had been hearing voices in his room since the first night they moved in. For the past three years, he had been studying up on poltergeists and hauntings so he could communicate with the ghosts who had become more and more active in his bedroom. Finally, when he could stand it no longer, he asked Jessie if Madame Ceara would help him figure out just what it was these poltergeists wanted from him.

"I'm not one of those people you have to convince, Mr. Davidson. Believe me, there are paranormal activities present in my life even *you* would have a hard time believing. I just want to know if there is something you can do for my brother. These...spirits are beginning to get under his skin."

Ben cut a look over to Ceara, who smiled softly and said, "As I explained to you this morning, Ben, Jessie is well versed in metaphysical matters. Don't talk down to her or she'll walk. We want to know what they want from Daniel."

Ben was a tall, pencil-thin man who reminded Jessie of a person who spent too much time indoors. His skin was pasty white, his hair was cut in an earlier version of a Ken doll, and his eyes were the color of melted milk chocolate. Jessie thought that with a little more food and a touch of sun, he might even be handsome...for a ghost hunter.

"As this was just a cursory examination, I can't answer that yet. I would need to set up my equipment for a few nights in order to fully understand the situation. Every ghost hunt, like every ghost, is different." Retrieving the folder, he closed it and looked over at Jessie. "You say they only haunt Daniel."

She nodded. "There are times when I think I hear them, but just like that, they're gone. I never really know if I heard them or if it's just the old bones of a Victorian creaking away."

Ceara folded her hands on the table. She had been the town's most prominent medium for as far back as anyone could remember. Her clientele included actors and athletes, musicians and writers, many of whom would call in for a tarot reading over the phone. She had made quite a tidy profit with her business.

She also protected a secret only Jessie and one other person knew.

"You say these ghosts are not haunting the inn, but are only haunting Daniel. How can that be? It's not like they know him."

Ben wiped the corners of his mouth. "There are different types of hauntings, but from what I can tell without examining your ghosts, is that they've chosen to communicate solely with Daniel. It's a bit odd because most individual hauntings are directed toward young females, but there have been reported instances when young men have experienced what your brother is going through."

Jessie leaned forward. "Can they hurt him?"

Ceara and Ben both shook their heads, but it was Ben who answered. "Their intention isn't usually to hurt anyone. They're obviously trying to communicate with him and feel he's the best choice to hear them."

"But why him?" Jessie cut her eyes over at Ceara. They had had this conversation a few times before. As the one in the family who could send her soul back into her past lives, it seemed more likely that ghosts would contact Jessie instead, but they hadn't. They'd targeted Daniel and made his nights almost unbearable with all their chatter and histrionics.

"Could be any number of reasons. Maybe he was receptive to them. Maybe they are confined only to his bedroom. No one knows why ghosts do anything, Ms. Ferguson. All we know is they act up, and when this happens, ninety-nine percent of the time, they have a reason. It's up to us to ascertain what that is."

"Isn't their reason obvious? They haven't moved on." Jessie leaned forward a bit. "I have a pretty good knowledge base about souls and reincarnation, Mr. Davidson. It's pretty clear to me the spirits in the inn have yet to move on and they want Daniel to know why."

Ceara nodded. "That could be what's making them so irritable. He isn't getting it."

Ben shook his head. "Hauntings are different from

poltergeists. Poltergeist activity is probably the most misunderstood form of paranormal activity, at least in conjunction with haunted houses. The word *poltergeist* literally means 'noisy ghost'. The earliest known reports of poltergeists date back to the ancient Romans."

Jessie held her hand up to stop the lecture. "And this is different from hauntings in what way?"

"Well, hauntings involve the ghosts of deceased human beings in certain places and times, such as the inn, where poltergeists may not be ghosts at all." Ben held up a second finger. "In hauntings, activities are continuous over time, concentrated in the same general area, such as near your brother's bedroom. Poltergeist activities build up over time to a climax and then start over. Poltergeist energies can travel anywhere with anyone, yet your brother told you that he only hears them on the same floor in the inn. The good news is that hauntings are not violent by nature, whereas when a poltergeist nears the climax of the energy cycle, they can become dangerous, inflicting both mental and physical terror in extreme cases." Ben lowered his hands. "I didn't get the feeling these spirits are threatening to Daniel."

"Maybe not right now. We need to find out why they haven't moved on."

"Exactly. Souls really don't want to hang around the living. They *want* to move on. Usually, something happens to prevent this…some unfinished business, perhaps, so they linger, not really dead and certainly not alive. Trapped, as it were."

Jessie shivered even though it was early July. "Sounds like a form of Purgatory."

"For some, it is."

Jessie leaned forward on the already cramped table. "So, can we get them out? Send them on their way?"

Ben shrugged. "We can certainly try. I'll have to set up my equi…"

Jessie shook her head. "No can do. My parents are only now recuperating financially from the remodel. If word got out that the inn was haunted, it would ruin them. You have to find another way."

Ben leaned away from the table and locked eyes with Ceara. "Well, there may be a way, but it involves your brother and direct communication with the spirits."

Jessie looked at Ceara, who nodded. "My dear, it's the only way to find out what they want."

Running her hands through her short brown hair, Jessie stared out the porthole that looked directly out to the sea. No matter how often or how badly she had messed up in California, Daniel had always been her staunchest supporter. He believed in her and loved her even when she was forced into a drug rehab program. He stood by her and loved her even when she could barely stand to look at herself. Never judging her, never questioning her, Daniel possessed faith in her when she had ceased believing in anything. If spirits were beginning to torment him, if something from the underworld was attempting to reach through death in order to contact him, she would make sure it was safe for them to do so. "Will hypnosis work?"

Ben cocked his head. "Quite a brilliant young lady you have here, Ceara."

Ceara beamed. "Yes, she is."

"Hypnosis is a good first step prior to an actual communication with these spirits."

"My little brother means the world to me, Ben, and I'd rather spare him the trauma of talking to spirits if we can help it. I'd like to exhaust all other alternatives first."

Ben nodded. "Understandable. You are wise to be cautious. Hauntings, though not typically dangerous, can go sideways on you just as rapidly as poltergeist dealing."

"And you're sure they can't harm Daniel spiritually or emotionally, right? I mean, hypnosis won't let them in or anything."

Ceara placed her hand over Jessie's. "I would never let anything happen to your brother."

Turning back to Ben, Jessie nodded. "If it's okay with Daniel, I say we give it a go. He's been obsessing over these voices for a long time now. I think it's time we find out what it is they want from him."

14th Century BCE

Sakura rose from the shrine of Aset after her period of prayer and played with the plait hanging over her shoulder. She knew she needed more than prayer to save the Goddess she had sworn to serve, but nothing and no one seemed capable of stopping Akhenaten from creating a new and Goddess-less religion.

"Is there nothing I can do?" Sakura whispered as her deep brown eyes lingered over the relief of Aset, Goddess, and consort to the king, and mother who called herself the most clever and august of the gods. "I must be able to save her somehow."

"Can she not save herself?" came a deep voice from behind Sakura, who turned to find one of the Pharaoh's guards looming in the shadows, darker than the darkest corner, only his eyes gave him away. "You do that too well, my love," she said, walking silently across the dusty cavern floor to where he stood in near darkness. "For such a big man, you are so quiet and invisible." Sakura placed her hands on his bare and broad chest and splayed her fingers.

"It is what I do best," he said, wrapping her up in his long arms. He smelled of cloves and musk.

Sakura slid her arms across his chest and over his broad shoulders. She had to stand on tiptoe to lace her fingers together behind his neck. He was so stoic; hard, smooth muscles, cool to the touch like a statue. She loved the girth of his chest, the ripple of his stomach. He was a God of a man—confident, strong, loyal. He was what was best in all men. "I beg to differ, my love. You do many things well, but you are at your best when you are not on your feet."

The guard grinned now and wrapped his arms tighter around her waist, crushing her to him. "Only you know that, woman." Lowering his face, Tarik pressed his lips softly to hers as she felt the rest of him turn hard as well.

"Mmm...indeed. Though, I hear the princesses find you rather...delectable."

Tarik laughed, his white teeth brilliant against his Nubian skin. "Forbidden fruits, Sakura. My king has eyes and ears everywhere. It does not bode well for one to meddle with the king's daughters."

Sakura pulled slightly away, her hands still threaded together around his neck. "And what does the mouth report that the eyes have seen and the ears have heard?"

Tarik looked around before answering. "There is a rising movement against Aten. The Pharaoh is sending his men out to unearth these heretic groups and bring them to justice. They are organizing now against all religious change. It is at these times you and your priestess must be very careful. My king is looking to make an example of someone."

Sakura released him. "Can he not see the futility in such a decision? It has been six years since he purified Aten as the only god but Re and still, there are movements against this. Will he never quit his madness? Will he ever see what a foolish mistake he has made?"

Tarik reached out and stroked Sakura's cheek with his large hand, a dark contrast to her much lighter skin. He had fallen in love with her when she was just a child praying to Aset at her mother's side. Tarik was a teen then, but he knew the moment he could have her, he would do so at any cost.

Years later, when Akhenaten came to power and introduced the idea of monotheism of the one god, Aten, he sent Tarik and his other guards out to destroy the temples and kill the priests and priestesses who were unwilling to adopt the new religion. Sakura, whose mother was a high priestess to a goddess variously known as Ament, Mnehet, Usert and Isis, refused to accept the new religion, choosing, like many other priestesses to go underground with her followers in order to build secret temples dedicated to the "lady of words of power." Where Tarik stood now was one such temple, located within the rocky labyrinth on the outskirts of Akhentaten. It was here, where one of his own men had followed Sakura one day, that Tarik chose the path of love and rebellion over the wishes of his beloved pharaoh. That soldier died at the end of Tarik's sword before he could be a threat to Sakura.

"He will never stop trying to destroy the old ways, Sakura, madness or not."

"He is a fool."

"And good that he is, or his wife and you might not have lived this long."

Sakura studied her lover's face as the candlelight flickered behind them, casting shadows across his square jaw. She had never expected to find love in the arms of a soldier, but the moment his sword ran through his counterpart, she knew she would love this man for the rest of her life; a life that would not last long if either of them were caught worshipping Aset.

Sakura's mother had explained to her there were those who were part of their Ka, or soul, and that nothing that happened in this present life could change the feelings two Ka shared for each other. Tarik's job may have been to bring down the temples, but he would not do so, for the woman who held his heart was at the very center of this heresy. Instead, he allowed her and others to worship unmolested in this cavern deep within the labyrinth beneath the outskirts of the city.

"She must come see me at once, Tarik."

Tarik lowered his head. "It is not safe now."

"It is never safe, but I have seen things she needs to be made aware of...things I am not sure I can fully explain." Sakura walked over to several of the tapers and blew them out, leaving them in the relative darkness of the cave.

Tarik's eyes grew wide. "The last vision you had..."

Sakura nodded sadly. "Mekataten died. I know. That is why I must see her. You must tell her it is vital I see her as soon as can be arranged."

Tarik nodded and caressed her cheek with the back of his hand. "I will be sure she gets your message."

Sakura stepped up to him and wrapped her arms around him once more. "I would also be pleased if *you* would hear my message, my handsome soldier. You are so worried and preoccupied that I feel as if I must throw myself at you to get your attention."

Tarik chuckled and drew her closer. "I am here now, my little priestess. What is your message?"

Not long after he spoke those words, the message was received.

21st Century AD

It had taken Jessie's parents 2.2 seconds to accept Jessie's invitation to treat them to dinner and a movie while she and Daniel ran the inn for the evening. Three years ago, Rick and Reena Ferguson would have been suspicious of Jessie's motivation behind such a gesture, and they would have had every right to be. Jessie had spent the majority of her high school days stoned, partying and sleeping with any boy who had even remotely been interested in her. Try as she may, she couldn't fill the gaping void in her soul, so her parents had packed their bags and moved the family to New Haven to rebuild what was a pretty run-down painted lady. Three years later, Jessie was a junior at the University of Oregon majoring in history. She had cleaned up her act, found a passion that had grabbed her, and walked the straight path of sobriety.

She hadn't done any of this alone, nor had she done it with anyone who was alive in the twenty-first century. She had done it with the help of a woman who had called her back in time—a woman whom Jessie had once been two thousand years ago; a woman whom Jessie had once been, and was now friends with.

Once her parents left, Ceara and Ben came in and set themselves up in Daniel's room.

"How you feeling about all this, sport?"

Daniel blinked a couple of times before answering. At thirteen, he was finally taller than she was and it was strange to look up at her little brother. "I'm good, but who's going to watch the front desk?"

"Tanner's coming over. You think I'd let you go through this alone?" Jessie mussed up his already messy strawberry blond hair.

When they first moved into what the townies called The Money Pit, or The Pit for short, it didn't take Jessie long to figure out why. Her parents had had to sink thousands of dollars into the old inn just to make it habitable. Now, it was one of the premier bed-and-breakfasts on the coast with a waiting list for all special holidays and three-day weekends.

One of the bonuses of Jessie's travels back to the first century AD was that one of her former selves, Cate McEwen was a Druid and had a knack for anything that grew. As a result, Jessie had created one of the most incredible flower gardens of any bed-and-breakfast for miles around. It was so gorgeous, it was booked for weddings for every weekend during the short summer months. Now, the inn was at half capacity, which was great for midweek.

Once Ceara got herself situated in Daniel's room, she motioned to him. "Sit where you usually do when you hear them."

Daniel sat at the foot of his twin bed. His bedspread had pictures of the Milky Way on it, and when he sat down, it collapsed like a black hole. "I've spent tons of time trying to find the best place to hear them, and this is it," he said, looking up at the ceiling as if he expected to find someone there.

Ben nodded and patted Daniel's back. "That's excellent, Daniel. You're going to make a very good subject." To Jessie, Ben said, "Do you want to explain it to him or shall I?"

"I've explained most of it already, but I'll brief him again." Kneeling down Jessie leveled her gaze at Daniel. Gone was the little freckle-faced boy who constantly asked questions like what made stars stay in the sky. That little boy was replaced by a young man who now sought most answers for himself. Today was no exception.

"Ceara will hypnotize you to see if you can recall anything they may have said to you. Sometimes these spirits whisper to us when we sleep, and it's possible you just can't bring what they've said to the forefront of your mind."

Ceara looked down at Daniel. "You know there's nothing to be afraid of, right?"

Daniel nodded. "They've never scared me, Ceara. They're just trying to tell me something. I don't need verification they exist. I *know* they exist. I just don't know what they *want*." Daniel looked back to Jessie for confirmation.

Ceara closed the blinds to Daniel's room and lit a white and a black candle. "Comfortable, Daniel?"

He nodded.

"Will you know if they are here or not?"

"I've lived with them long enough to know when they're hanging around. They don't always talk to me. Sometimes, they yak at each other like someone or something has pissed them off. They get irritated pretty quickly."

Ceara asked Jessie and Ben to stand in the doorway. "When I put you under, you will not be afraid, you will not be unconscious and you will not be asleep."

Daniel nodded. "I'm ready, really." He looked over Ceara's shoulder at Jessie and gave her the thumbs-up.

"Then close your eyes and focus on the sound of my voice."

Less than three minutes later, Daniel opened his eyes. He did not smile, he did not look over at Jessie. He just stared hard into Ceara's blue eyes.

"Would you like to tell me more about the visitors you have in this room, Daniel?"

Daniel nodded. "Lately, they've been pretty agitated. They've started moving things around, acting up like that."

"When you say *they*, how many are there?"

"Three. There's always three. The same three."

Ceara nodded. "Good. So, what can you tell me about them?"

Daniel frowned in thought, two large freckles disappearing in the crease. "One is always mad and she yells the loudest. She really wants me to hear her and I think she's frustrated I can't."

"But you try."

His blue eyes grew larger. "Sure. I've left notepads, tape recorders, Post-its, you name it, but I haven't had any luck understanding them. It's like they're speaking a foreign language."

"What about the other two?"

"The other two aren't that bad. They're not as loud and not nearly as pissed off."

"Can you recall anything they might have said to you?"

"Nope."

"Are they here now?"

Daniel put a finger in his mouth and chewed on the nail. "She's just listening. She can hear everything."

Ceara shot a glance over to Jessie, whose eyebrows rose. "How do you know?"

"I feel her even when she's not saying anything. I'm sure she will later, though."

Ceara's eyes scanned the room as she tried to get a sense of these spirits, but they eluded her. She may have the ability to send her soul to the past, but she was out of her element where spirits were concerned. It was a bit unnerving. "Say something to her."

Daniel nodded and swallowed hard. "It's okay. They're here to help me hear you. I know you're getting frustrated and everything like that, but you gotta give me a break here. I'm doing the best I can."

No one moved or said a word for a full minute, and then, Daniel shook his head. "She's gone. She's like that. Moody."

Ceara asked a few more questions, none of which amounted to anything earth-shattering, and then she brought Daniel out of his trance.

"Did it help?" he asked.

Jessie sat next to him on the bed and patted his leg. "We learned a little, sport, but you don't remember one single word."

"Shoot. You know I want to help them. You'd think they'd help me out."

Ben stepped back into the room. "Spirits have all sorts of reasons for doing what they do. I imagine she will tell you in good time."

"It's been three years. What do you think she's been waiting for?"

Ceara, Ben and Jessie all shrugged.

"Don't you worry. We're not going to give up." Rising, Jessie turned to Ceara. "I suppose we can bring him back here if he wants to wor—"

"Wait!" Daniel said, leaping off the bed. "What did you just say?"

Jessie shook her head. "I said we could bring him back here if—"

"That's it! That's what she keeps saying! She keeps saying she wants me to bring *him* back!"

All three of them stared at Daniel.

"Who?" Jessie finally asked. "Who does she want you to bring back?"

Daniel shrugged and fidgeted with the pillow sham. "I have no idea. I just know that that's what she keeps saying...it's what she wants me to do."

Jessie glanced over at Ceara, who nodded. "There is much more for us to do before we can move forward on this. In the meantime, Daniel, do not get wrapped up in the lives of the dead. I suggest you continue living your own life and keep having fun while we figure out just what it is we need to do to let these spirits move on."

"Can't I help?"

"It would be best if you left it to us. We're used to dealing with the bizarre. We don't want this to become the center of your life."

Daniel nodded. "You don't want me to obsess."

"Bingo."

Nodding, Daniel looked over at Jessie. "Okay. I won't help, but you're going to help them, right?"

With a feeling of trepidation washing over her, Jessie nodded and laid her hand on his head. "Absolutely."

After Ben left, Jessie and Ceara headed straight for Del's Coffee Shop, their usual hangout. Del made the best cinnamon rolls on the coast and he also knew everyone in town.

"You gal looks like you're up to something," he said, bringing over two steaming cups of coffee in their very own coffee mugs.

Jessie looked up at the balding man who had always reminded her of the Pillsbury Doughboy. "We need some information on our painted lady."

"*Your* lady?" he asked, leaning against the booth. Del's Coffee Shop was as retro as they came, and there were license plates from as far back as 1910 hanging on the walls. "What is it you want to know?"

"Anything you can tell us would be helpful. We're going to have Tanner add some of the more colorful history to the website."

Del nodded. "Well, let me see. The inn's been here as long as I have, and that's fifty-eight years. Rumor has it, and this is just rumor, mind you, that someone died in there. I remember the story being told to me by my grandfather, but he cautioned not to talk about it because spirits have a way of punishing those who meddle."

"So you never talked about it?" Jessie asked with interest.

"Truth to tell, I plumb forgot until now. It wasn't something the good Christian folk liked to discuss."

Jessie and Ceara looked at each other, a cold breeze shared between them.

"There've been over a half dozen potential owners since the Sixties, but nobody but your folks have been successful with it. A bunch of hippies tried turning it into a commune, but they up and fled in the middle of the night claiming it was haunted. The townies just figured they'd smoked too much pot."

"Haunted?" Ceara said.

"I think it's more a case of bad luck than being haunted." He turned to face Ceara. "Actually, Ceara, I'm surprised you never pronounced it cursed or something. It's certainly had its share of disasters."

Ceara cocked her head to the side. "More than those you mentioned?"

Del chuckled. "If you really want the dirt, check the county records. You'll get more than your share of history there, I'm sure. A lot has gone on up the hill."

Two hours later, that was precisely where they wound up, and when they finally reached the front of the line, Jessie handed the address over to the clerk. "Hi. We're doing a story on an old Victorian in New Ha—"

"Just a moment," the woman answered tersely, walking away. She returned with a three-by-five card. "We have all the historical homes on CD. Pay the user fee and then you have thirty minutes for your research. Any more than that and we charge for the second half hour." Now here was a woman who loved her job.

"You're actually charging us for the information?"

The clerk stared at Jessie with dull shark eyes. "Not for the information. For the research and the machines."

Jessie paid the fee and forced a grin. "Thanks for splitting that hair for us." A minute later, they were sitting at a computer with a shiny CD labeled 1900-2010. "They put one hundred years of Victorians on a CD?"

Ceara pulled up a chair next to her. "Can't be that many then, at least, not in Douglas County."

Jessie put the CD in and pulled up the menu, which allowed her to search by address, date built, county, original owner and even architect. She punched in the address of the inn and waited while the little hourglass on the screen turned over and over.

When the information came up, it gave the name of the Seaside Inn with Rick and Reena as the current owners. There were bits and pieces about the inn, such as square footage, taxes, if there were liens on it, but the piece most pertinent to Jessie came when she scrolled past the mundane.

"Start at the beginning, my dear. All of this scrolling is giving me a headache."

"Oh. Sorry." Scrolling to the beginning of an article about the inn, Jessie read it slowly, moving closer and closer to the monitor as she did so. She finished, reading it twice more before leaning back in her chair and running her fingers through her hair. She knew Ceara was thinking the same thing.

"Well, *that* was certainly unexpected."

Jessie stared at the monitor, which read in sixteen point bold Ariel font.

Building was moved to present location from San Francisco in 1922, and was purchased by the Raleigh family in 1924. For earlier references to this building, see county recorder in San Francisco County, California.

Ceara blew out a deep breath. "That's quite odd. You and the house both came here from the Bay Area. If I believed in coincidences, I'd think this was one."

Jessie hit the print button and stared at the pages as they printed out. As someone who'd met her past lives, Jessie did not believe in coincidences, either. "Looks like we need a road trip."

Ceara clapped her hands together. "I'll do you one better. Let's take the boat!"

1st Century AD

Thunder rolled across the darkened sky. Its companion, ever eager to lead once more, flashed brilliantly, illuminating the two hooded figures huddled together beneath a great oak. A small fire in a pit surrounded by rocks did not seem affected by the constant breeze rustling the dry leaves of the massive oak.

"You are not concentrating, Catie," the auburn-tressed woman said not unkindly. "Perhaps we should take a break from your lesson."

Cate nodded, pushing back the hood of her Druid robe; an act signaling to others it was safe to approach the Druid priestess. Although they were miles from the nearest town or village, the act was symbolic of having ended a ritual.

Maeve lowered her hood as well and lay her arm across Cate's shoulders. Though Maeve was only a few years older, she possessed a regal bearing of one much older and wiser. "You have been distracted since this evening when I woke you, yet you do not share with me the cause of this distraction. Would now be a good time?"

Cate stared into the fire, feeling the distraction she had been trying to push away gnawing at her, hovering. At two and twenty, she was at the onset of her Druidic training; a beginning that would take her ten more years to eventually master. It took every bit of mental power she possessed and every fiber of her being to absorb the wisdom Maeve offered her. "I had a dream last night that felt like a vision, but I cannot discern which it was."

Maeve reached into a brown pouch tied around her waist. The thunder spoke again as she tossed a light yellow powder into the fire, making the flames leap up once before splitting into two columns. "Look deep into the heart of the flames, my love, and describe these images preventing you from completing your task."

Cate did as she was told—not because Maeve had been her teacher for the past ten years, but because she respected the strength of Maeve's power and her ability to find the truth no matter where it hid.

"At first, I saw Jessie on a boat. I thought it was Spencer, but then I realized the boat was too small and not of his time. It was of her time, and she was not alone. It was she on the deck with another…another from a time before ours."

Maeve watched the fire as the two columns twisted around each other. "*Before* ours?"

"The other woman was dark and beautiful, and she was asking for Jessie's help, but there was a darker force wrapping its arms around her and preventing her from getting the aid she sought." Cate sighed loudly. "The woman struggled. That was when I awoke." Cate ran her hands through her short red hair—a characteristic she and Jessie shared.

Maeve closed the two columns with a wave of her hand. "Jessie has assumed a great mantle of responsibility since her first step through the Sacred Place. You will feel her more than you ever have."

Cate nodded, instinctively reaching for Maeve's hand. "She does not appear to be in any danger, though the other woman might be. I could not be sure."

Maeve's gray eyes sparkled as they always did whenever she looked at Cate. More than lovers, more than friends, they were soul mates and had been for many lives. "It is all right to admit you miss her."

Cate stared into the fire. "When you first sent me through the portal, I had no idea what to expect, what would happen. To land in the bleakness that is the twenty-first century was so frightening, but Jessie made it easy. She was so strong and brave."

Maeve squeezed Cate's hand. They had been *anam cara*, soul mates, since the moment Maeve arrived from the mysterious land called Gaul nearly ten years ago. During that time, Maeve and Chief Druid, Lachlan had taught Cate McEwen as much as a novitiate could learn. She learned quickly, soaking up every bit of knowledge they offered. When they realized Cate possessed the sight, they chose to send her through the portal, a place where soul quests begin and end. They sent her on the most urgent of missions to save their people from total annihilation at the hands of the Roman soldiers occupying their land.

What Cate McEwen found on the other side of that portal was Jessie Ferguson, the young woman carrying Cate's soul two thousand years into the future. In the quest that followed, Cate and Jessie worked together to release the Druids off the island of Anglesey, thereby keeping alive the Druidic tradition for many more years to come. If the revelation of befriending one's self that far into the future wasn't strange enough, the idea that Cate now missed her *friend* from the future was never lost on Maeve.

"It is more than missing her, is it not?" Maeve asked, running her hand through Cate's fiery red hair.

Cate turned and stared into those gray eyes she had loved since the moment she first saw them. "I wish her to be happy, but her world is so devoid of intimacy, of hope. I fear she will never find it."

Maeve's lips turned up slightly as she tipped Cate's face to hers. "What you truly want—"

"Is for her to find *you*." Cate rose and spread her arms. "Look at all we have, Maeve. Fresh air, the stars, our freedom, our love—"

"Each other." Maeve took Cate's hand and gently pulled her back. "Sit, Catie." When Cate did, Maeve asked, "What is it you struggle with?"

Cate did not look at Maeve, but stared out over the river's edge. "In my dream, something was not right. There was this black force...this oppressive and evil heaviness looming near her. Too near. I do not know the origin or if it arose from Jessie's world or from the Egyptian woman, but it was there."

Maeve said not a word, but waited for the mask of revelation to come down on Cate's face.

"*Egyptian*." Cate hesitated. "I did not say before she was from Egypt, did I?"

"No, you did not."

Cate touched her neck where an ankh she once wore had hung her entire life. She had received the ankh from her mother before she died, and had worn it until the day she buried it beneath an enormous rock in a far off field in Wales to let Jessie know she had made it off the island safely. That wasn't the only reason she sent the mystical necklace. The ankh was a special key to the Dreamworld where Jessie and Cate could meet as two individuals.

"The ankh."

Maeve nodded. "Yes?"

"The Egyptian woman was wearing one just like it." Cate stopped and turned to Maeve. "It's the very one, is it not?"

Maeve said nothing.

"That woman...the ankh...you and I..." Cate looked hard at Maeve. They had spent every incarnation since Cate could remember trying to find each other. It was the remembering that made them search, made them know there was someone out there searching as well. It was the remembering that transported the remnants of their soul's memory into the beings housing the souls in different times. Sometimes, the memories came flowing freely, and other times, there was a vagueness that made it nearly impossible to remember who they were and who they were looking for. "Oh...Oh my," Cate breathed softly.

Maeve nodded slowly. "The ankh is indeed the same. It is from Egypt a long, long time ago."

Cate blinked several times. "This would mean—" Cate folded her hands together and swallowed hard. "Sakura...the Egyptian woman in my vision...is *me*."

Maeve nodded. "Yes, my love, Sakura is you. I am quite impressed you remember her name."

Cate thought about the dark-skinned woman and how brave her spirit had felt. There was an almost regal carriage about her, as if she were royalty. "Unlike Jessie, however, Sakura is not alone. You are there. You are...strong." Cate studied Maeve's eyes. "This was where we began, isn't it? Sakura is the one who started us all remembering."

Maeve's smile was soft and loving. "I do not know when

we began as souls, my sweet, but I do know it was Sakura who first achieved assurance that we would be bound together for all time."

Cate studied Maeve's eyes. "What are you not telling me?"

Maeve tucked a stray hair behind Cate's ear. "Our past lives are not a thing that can be shown. They are something that we *know*. When your knowledge reveals itself to you, Catie, it means you are prepared to see the truth in its entirety. It is not for me to tell you what you know or do not know. It is for you to *remember*."

"And now that I have seen her, will I remember more?"

"Perhaps."

"Do *you* remember?"

Maeve nodded, folding her robe so it lay smoothly against her legs. "I do. That life is very clear to me. I knew it would be clear to you one day as well, but this is not a thing I can show you."

Cate thought back to her vision of the Egyptian woman on the boat with Jessie. "Do you think *Jessie* is remembering and that is why I am getting fragments of her memory? Jessie and I are very connected on many levels. If she is remembering…"

"That, I cannot say. You would do well to ask her yourself."

"But Lachlan—"

"Is not here. I know he forbade you to go back through the portal because of when Ceara went through and never returned, but our lives are different now. We have been touched by both the past and the future, so each of us must make our own decision about what is best to do. Lachlan may present an order, but it is for each of us to decide what is right for our own lives."

"You would have me disobey him?"

"I would have you remember who you are. You went through the portal, Catie, not him. He cannot make choices for you around that."

"You think there is something to be done?"

Maeve stroked Cate's cheek. "Oh, little bird, you are always so eager to fly into danger. If there is something you need do, all you need to do is remember and go from there."

Turning toward the fire, Cate stared silently for a long time, as if willing herself to remember. Finally, in a very small voice, Cate whispered, "Maeve?"

"Yes, love?"

"I want to go."

Maeve sighed. "I know you do, Catie. I have known for some time now. Ever since we helped Spencer Morgan, your soul has been restless. You need to see her once again."

Cate nodded. "I do."

"Then we'll leave at dawn."

14th Century BCE

At dawn, Queen Nefertiti and Tarik entered Aset's underground temple from one of several entrances well-hidden among massive boulders. Sakura was kneeling at the altar and quickly finished her prayers when she heard the approaching footsteps.

"My queen," Sakura said softly, bowing her head.

Nefertiti glided across the granite flooring and gently tipped Sakura's head back so she could look into her dark brown eyes. "Must I continually remind you of your place in my heart? You needn't ever kneel or bow to me, Sakura."

Sakura smiled softly. "And must I remind *you* of *your* place in Egypt's heart? I am still but a citizen of your royal palace. It is as it shall always be."

This prompted a chuckle from the queen that sounded more like the chimes of a small bell than a human voice. "Oh, Sakura, I do so miss our daily time together. Would that we did not have to be so secretive."

Sakura gazed into the deep brown eyes so much like her own, and saw youthful memories of long ago...before the city built by the pharaohs of days' past...before Akhenaten's frenzied attempt at transforming Egypt's glorious and ancient religion into something more self-serving.

Before.

Before the woman standing regally in front of her became Nefertiti, Queen of Egypt, she and Nefertiti had frolicked on the banks of the Nile beneath a harsh and unyielding sun. As little girls they shared their secrets, their dreams, and even their forbidden yearnings. They swam in the warmth of the Nile, ran in the hot sand, and enjoyed the freedom children feel when days stretch into nights barely noticed. It had been a wonderful time before Akhenaten chose her for his queen...before Egypt would be dealt a spiritual blow that would shake the entire kingdom, cracking its very foundation.

Before.

Nefertiti broke their gaze and strode over to the twin statues of Aset. Between the life-size statues sat a gaping hole in the side of the rock where Sakura so often left her offerings. Tapers flickered on various levels of stones that had been cut with the singular intention of holding the candles. The smoke coming from the tapers lifted straight up, like gray ropes, and erupted through the narrow shaft above. Lining the walls were prayers, stories and chants to and about their beloved Aset, as well as glyphs depicting Nefertiti in worship; the latter had been inscribed against Tarik's warnings that it opened up the queen to foul cries of heresy, but Nefertiti refused to cower. In public, she appeared to support her husband's religious obsession, but in the privacy of this temple, she assisted Sakura and her priestess in maintaining the old ways—the ways of the goddess.

"Tarik says you have need of me. I would have come sooner, but you know how difficult it is to get away from that accursed palace."

Sakura rose and took the queen's hands. In the whole of the kingdom, Nefertiti was known for her soft beauty and regal stature. What few ever saw was the incredible grace of her hands. She had alabaster hands, smooth, graceful, evocative. "I have visions I cannot explain and they worry me."

Nefertiti sucked in her breath. Sakura's last vision had been the death of her daughter Meketare, which occurred in the precise manner and time Sakura had seen. "It is not—"

"No, my queen, it does not involve any of your precious daughters...at least, not that I can ascertain. I would have come to you had they been." Sakura released Nefertiti's hands and pointed toward the altar. "Please give your prayers first, my queen. Tarik and I shall wait in the courtyard."

The courtyard was the name Sakura had given to the open space deep within the stone temple. Filled with a variety of plants able to feed off the small rays of sunlight forcing their way through the small fissures of the stones, the courtyard breathed life amid the desert. Tarik had built her a stone bench to sit on while she meditated among the greenery hanging from every nook.

"She is worried," Tarik said, sitting next to Sakura on the cold bench. He reached out and took her hand in his. "Her belief in you is second only to her faith in the goddess."

Sakura nodded. "Her loyalties have always been well-placed. Was it difficult getting her out of the palace?"

"Getting away from Akhenaten's newest priest gets more difficult every day. He clucks about like an old hen, hovering always. I do not know what he is looking for, but his eyes never stop moving. It is as if he is searching for something." Tarik shook his head. "It is never good to trust a man whose eyes never rest."

Sakura said nothing, but waited for Tarik to continue.

"He has the King convinced there is to be an uprising of what he is calling anti-Atenists of some sort."

"For what purpose does he tell such tales?"

"He believes they may come after the queen and is spending a good amount of time trying to convince the King that Nefertiti is in danger—"

"Oh does he?" Sakura's stomach became queasy. "Is she?"

"If she were, I would have already moved her out of danger. I have yet to discover the intent of his disclosures, but I will. I do not trust him, and the pharaoh ought not to, either, but you know how he has been since changing the old ways."

"Indeed." Rising, Sakura paced across the sandy floor and bent to put her face into a large orange flower. "Find out what you can about this priest. If need be, we will find a man to… remove him."

Tarik nodded. "As you wish. These are frightening times, my love. It is best to trust few and suspect all."

Just then, Nefertiti's soft voice entered the courtyard before she did. "And just what is it that is frightening you so?"

Sakura and Tarik turned in unison toward Nefertiti, who walked out of the tunnel's darkness and into the light of the courtyard. "We have known each other too long, Sakura, for you to try to protect me from something I do not see coming. You did not spare me when little Meke was called, and I do not expect this time to be any different."

"I will leave you two," Tarik said, rising.

"No, Tarik," the queen replied. "I would wish for you to stay. You are one of the very few I can trust within the palace walls. I would like you to stay."

Tarik bowed his head and resumed his seat. "Yes, my queen."

Nefertiti turned to Sakura."Now, what is it that worries you so?"

Sakura walked to the queen and took her hands once more. "The vision is incomplete, yet there is something there that truly scares me."

Nefertiti's smile was soft and gentle, and if anyone did not know differently, they might think she was gazing at her lover. "Come, Sakura. Have we not managed all these years to protect the goddess? Surely, she can do no less for us if need be. You needn't be afraid. Of anything."

Sakura looked over at Tarik, who nodded. "Tell her."

Sakura returned her gaze to the queen's. "There is a darkness near you more powerful than even Ma'at. It threatens you and those you love, and intends to whisk you away from Akhenaten, the palace and us."

"*Whisk me away*? Is that what your vision is?"

Sakura bowed her head and then looked back up at Nefertiti's strong gaze. "Yes. It shows an Egypt without you, and that is a very dark place indeed, but there *is* one who can help, perhaps even destroy this darkness."

"Then send for her. If there is one who can save the Goddess, then she must be called."

"She is...very far away."

Nefertiti's left eyebrow rose. "How far away?"

Sakura and Tarik exchanged knowing glances. "Lifetimes, my friend. She is far, far away into the future."

Nefertiti nodded slowly. "I see. And you believe she can help?"

"I believe she may know how, yes. I do not yet have a *clear* picture of her. I feel her courage, her bravery, her true powers. There is but one way to discover her potential."

Nefertiti glanced over at Tarik, then up to the lightening sky over the fissures, and then finally back to Sakura. Releasing a breath, she nodded. "Do what you must, but be careful. It has been a long time and you are unpracticed."

Sakura smiled softly. "Unpracticed is not the same as unskilled, my queen. I believe I can locate this woman and find out what we need to know to protect you and the Goddess."

Nodding, Sakura kissed the queen's hands. "I shall send one of my priestesses to you upon my return so you do not have to worry needlessly."

A slight smile played on Nefertiti's lips. "I prefer to experience my worry *needfully*. I will not live on this earth without you."

"I *will* return."

"You had better." Nefertiti lifted Sakura's chin and gazed into her eyes. "It is your *queen* who commands you to go. It is your heart and blood who implores you to return." With that, Nefertiti disappeared into the darkness of the temple.

21st Century AD

The boat ride down the Pacific Coast was one of the most relaxing and enjoyable times Jessie had had in the last three years, and she realized just how hard she had been hitting the books. In between rushing off to help one of her other selves, running the inn and studying for exams, she had had little time for any real fun. With the wind in her face, the sun on her back and Tanner Dodds at the wheel, life just seemed less complicated. Closing her eyes, she imagined what it must have been like for Spencer Morgan, sixteenth century pirate, and one of her past souls. What was it like to sail the open sea? To be free to roam the oceans standing on the deck of a huge ship? Bits and pieces of his memories wafted in and out of her mind, making her smile softly at the tenderness the pirate seldom showed, but existed nonetheless. Yes, she remembered having loved the salt air upon her face long ago. She remembered the freedom of the open seas, the rock of the ship, the peacefulness at the bow of the boat. Yes, she remembered, and they were wonderful memories.

"Thinking of Spencer, my dear?"

Jessie turned and nodded at Ceara. "How did you know?"

"How do I always know?"

Jessie laughed.

"Come. Sit. Tell me your thoughts and your memories."

Jessie sat next to Ceara on one of her green plastic Adirondack chairs at the front of the houseboat. "He's a natural," she said, motioning to Tanner at the wheel of the boat. Tanner had been the first person to befriend her when she first came to New Haven. Back then, his hair had been dyed jet black, he wore a black leather jacket and enjoyed making people think he was some sort of bad boy. Now, three years later, his hair was back to its natural blond, he dumped the black leather and he owned a fairly successful web hosting business. For all intents and purposes, Tanner Dodds had grown up.

"That, he is."

"I had no idea this thing ever left the dock."

Ceara chuckled. "It's a *boat*, dear. It's what it does. I taught Tanner a long time ago how to sail her. He'd love to take her out more, but I just never really got my sea legs. Is it as cool as when you sailed as Spencer?"

Jessie smiled at the thought. "I don't know...his boat was pretty awesome."

"Think you can drive it?"

Jessie stared at her. "This boat?"

"Yes. Do you think you can get behind the wheel and steer it?"

"Oh, I don't know...I shouldn't—"

Ceara held her hand up. "Let me rephrase the question into a statement. I want you to access Spencer's memories and drive the damn boat."

"Ceara, I can't—"

"Sure you can. Can and will. Now, go on. Relieve Tanner of the wheel and take her where we need to go. I trust you."

"But this is your home."

"And this is the sea! What are you afraid of? Crashing into something? Look around you, my dear, there is nothing near us. All you need do is access his memories."

"It's not that easy."

Ceara waved this away, her bracelets jangling. "We haven't really started practicing that yet." Ceara took a strong grasp of Jessie's hand and held it tightly. "It is now time to learn how to access your memories when you need to, not just when they come." Turning to fully face Jessie, Ceara smiled softly. "I was going to wait to tell you, but I suppose now is as good a time as any. When we finished with Spencer and Duncan, it became clear you were finally ready to begin your Druidic studies in earnest. I have accepted the weighty task not because I am your friend, but because you are the one."

"The One?"

Ceara nodded. "You were not chosen merely because the portal was in your house. You were chosen because *Cate* chose you."

"Cate chose me?"

"Yes. She has the sight, and when she finally found you, she managed to come to you unscathed. She was the best at using the portal. Her power is tremendous—her abilities not even to full strength yet. She will become a priestess of incredible power, and it is my job to pass as much of our old way knowledge on to you so that you, too, may one day be as powerful as she once was. You are the one strongest enough to take over the job others were too weak to take up. In short, my dear, it is up to you to carry on the old ways."

Jessie nodded. "I'm ready. I think. It's hard to say. How does one know when they are ready to be The One?"

Ceara patted Jessie's hand. "My dear, when I first came through the portal and was forced to remain in this old, decrepit body here in this depraved time, I wasn't merely cruising around because I had a curiosity or had nothing better to do. I came here in search of someone...someone who could stop the destruction of our ancient ways." Ceara sighed. "Yet, even being trapped here wasn't a coincidence. I was stuck here because *someone* needed to teach you. Someone needed to be here to catch you." Ceara squeezed her hand. "You are the one I came across time for, Jessie. The goddesses knew you would need help learning all you need learn. That is why I am here."

"You came for me."

Ceara nodded. "Just as Cate did, only *she* knew who she was looking for. *I* did not. I have been in this body for nearly thirty years now, and until I met you, I constantly wondered why. Then, we met, and I knew. I *knew* you would continue the knowledge, that you would continue the quest. I am here, my dear, to show you the way. At long last I have a purpose in this wretched world."

Jessie released Ceara's hands and stared out at the open water, her heart feeling both glad and heavy.

"It is a huge task for both of us, my dear. One that requires a commitment few people of this age are capable of giving."

Jessie nodded solemnly. "This is more than becoming a Druid priestess, isn't it?"

"Much, much more. For you see, there has been no greater attack on women than on the one against us as priestesses. Once we became disempowered as priestesses, we became disenfranchised as women. There is a lot to know, my dear. You must be stronger than even Cate ever was, wiser than Maeve and braver than Spencer. There is so much riding on your shoulders, my dear, in this time as well as the past."

Jessie stared out at the Pacific Ocean, with its vast array of blues and greens. The portal reminded her of the ocean; initially, the frothing, churning water made one hesitate before entering, but the true dangers…the real beauty lurked beneath the surface.

"I am to continue their work."

Ceara nodded. "More than that. You are being inscribed to re-empower women in your own time. It is a mantle that will weigh heavy at times, but with enough education, courage and insight, you will be the champion they believe you to be."

"Champion, huh?" Jessie's lips twitched. "And you're going to jockey me?"

Ceara chuckled. "Something like that. Maeve believes in you. You were chosen for this. This, more than anything else, will give meaning to your life. You will have a far greater purpose and need to understand that this is a lifelong quest, not a momentary blip on life's radar."

Jessie nodded. "I understand."

"Then it is time to begin your lessons in earnest. Grab the wheel, my dear. It is time to take control of your Fate."

Jessie had only been asleep an hour when she realized where she was. This stone circle surrounding a firepit in the clearing of an enormous oak grove was not a dream. This was the Dreamworld; the one she shared with Cate. Being here could only mean one thing: Cate had come across time to see *her*.

"Yes, I have," Cate said, walking out from behind a curtain of mist clinging to the oaks like ethereal bark.

"Cate!" Jessie ran to the smaller woman and hugged her tightly, sweeping her off her feet and spinning her around. "It is so good to see you again!"

Cate hugged Jessie with equal enthusiasm "And you as well."

Jessie released the tiny Druid and stepped back to examine her in her hooded robe. "Is everything all right? Are you safe and well? Do you—"

Cate readjusted her robe. "We are all quite well, and Maeve sends her love."

"No Roman soldiers? No worries? You guys are okay?"

"We are fine." Cate snapped her fingers toward the firepit and up jumped a flame. "You look well rested from our last quest."

Nodding, Jessie sat on her familiar tall flat stone. It had been almost a month since they had both been in the year 1567 helping Spencer Morgan. It only felt like a few days since they parted.

"I'm great. I've been busy with some ghosts where we live, but other than that, I am well."

Cate cocked her head. "Spirits, eh? Your life is never dull, is it Jessie Ferguson?"

Jessie watched as Cate reached into the brown leather bag hanging from her waist and withdrew some blue powder. "Are you trying to catch this spirit?"

"No. I just wish to talk with it. It needs something from us, but we don't know what. Don't worry. I'll figure it all out." Jessie stepped back. "It's so good to see you. I've missed you."

"As I have you." Cate tossed the blue powder into the fire, and when the flame jumped, it parted and revealed a dark-skinned woman praying at a stone statue of a goddess. "I wish I were here merely to visit, but I am here because of her." Cate pointed to the praying woman. "Do you...do you remember her at all?"

Jessie leaned closer to the fire and studied the woman on her knees. The walls were clearly inscribed with colorful hieroglyphs and the statuary obviously from antiquity. The woman was wearing Egyptian kohl on her eyes and some sort of grease on her long black hair. She wore blue and gold jewelry Jessie had seen in textbooks in her ancient civs class, and had the carriage and bearing of nobility. She was breathtakingly beautiful.

"I do not remember her," Jessie replied. "I wish I did. She is incredible." Jessie watched as Cate brought her palms together, effectively closing the fire pillars together, making the image disappear. "She is one of us."

Cate nodded. "She is. Maeve bade me to not reveal anything more except for the vision I had of the two of you. You must recall her on your own."

"But I remember nothing of her. Is she in danger?"

Cate nodded again. "There is an evil threatening to wrap itself around her, possibly choking the life out of her. It is a presence nearer to her than she knows. I tell you this so you will heed her call if she makes contact with you. She...Sakura...has the power to reach you should she need to. She is a far more powerful priestess than I. She is in terrible danger, Jessie. Be ready. Be open. "

"I am always ready, Cate."

Cate lightly stroked Jessie's cheek with the back of her fingers—to date, their most intimate gesture. "I know you are.

The more lives you can recall and invest with the power to save the Goddess, the greater our chances at keeping them alive in the hearts of all men."

"So…that's my charge."

Cate nodded. "Not all of us heed the call, Jessie, and few of us ever hear it, but you…you are special. You have heard it and you continue to come."

Jessie shrugged. "I cannot imagine not coming, Cate. I am invested in all of our incarnations. If you want me to come, then I will."

"Good. Then please stay prepared. Listen. Know I am with you no matter what you do or where you go. If you are unsure about Sakura's needs, Maeve will allow me to help you with this because she has a special place in her heart for Sakura." The mist around them fluttered a bit, as if a gust of wind blew upon them. "And remember you can always find your answers in nature. We are creatures of this world, you and I. Be not afraid to lean on it for guidance. When you cannot see, nature can do so for you."

Jessie held Cate's hand. "Whatever this Sakura needs from me, I will deliver. You know that."

Cate nodded. "Indeed I do. Our faith is well placed in you."

"I think of you often, you know. Every single day."

Cate took Jessie's hand in both of hers. "I do know. Though I do not understand much of your world that creeps into my soul, I *do* know you are a person of quality and honor. I am… proud to be you."

"Can you stay a bit and visit?"

"For you, Jessie Ferguson, I most certainly can."

21st Century AD

When the boat docked and they had filled out the necessary slip paperwork, Ceara, Jessie and Tanner headed for the county recorder's office in San Francisco. The fog had followed them in and it was beginning to get cooler.

Jessie said nothing as she stared out the window of the car as it rolled up and down hills which blended modern architecture with gothic and Victorian ambiance. It had been almost two years since she had been back to her old hometown, but few changes were visible on the streets of San Francisco.

"I forget how beautiful this city is," Ceara said softly. "It really is amazing, isn't it?"

Jessie nodded. The last time she had come here was for a graduation party. She'd realized just how far she had grown from her friends, who drank too much, partied too hard and generally acted like spoiled rich kids the entire time. It wasn't their fault. They weren't the ones who had changed; Jessie had, and the depth of those changes had made it impossible for her to participate in beer bongs, silly chatter and adolescent male humor. Her friends didn't want to hear about the peaceful woods behind the inn, or the way the ocean's waves could sing her to sleep. They didn't want to hear about how she had finally found her path. Instead, they wanted to know if she had "done it" with Tanner and was it true flannel was a fashion *do* in Oregon. She had been every bit as narrowminded as her friends were, but not anymore. As much as she loved San Francisco, it was no longer her home.

"It's one of the prettiest cities in the world," she answered Ceara. "There are so many different kinds of people and the architecture is second to none."

"You don't miss it anymore, do you, Jess?" Tanner asked, stepping next to her and taking her hand in his.

Jessie looked down at their entwined fingers and shook her head. "Not at all. New Haven is my home now. It feels like I lived here a lifetime ago."

Ceara patted her leg. "Maybe you did. One never knows, after all."

Half an hour and several lines later, Jessie was able to explain to a bored clerk just what it was they were looking for. Instead of being handed a CD like the other office had given them, she paid a fee and waited until the woman sauntered over to the printer and handed her a printout of the house's history.

"It says here," Jessie said, pointing to a line so the clerk could see it. "That the house was moved *first* and then sold?"

"That's what it says. Next."

"Wait. Isn't that a little odd? Isn't it usually the other way around?"

The clerk looked like she might slit her own wrists any second. "This is San Francisco, dear. Anything can happen. Next."

Ceara looked over Jessie's shoulder. "If you want more information, you're going to have to look for the family who sold it. There's not much here, is there?"

"Do you have a map or anything that might help?" Jessie asked, trying to keep her voice from sounding as frustrated as she felt.

The clerk pulled out a big spiral-bound Thomas's guide, looked at the address of the house, punched some numbers into a computer, and then flipped through the dog-eared guide until she came to what she was looking for. "That house used to sit on 134 Betty Lane, but the name of the street was changed in 1954." Taking a piece of scratch paper out, she scribbled the address and handed it to Jessie. "I'm afraid that's about all I can do for you. Next."

"Thanks. Next." Jessie started for the door. When they got to the street, she glanced down at the address and froze. "Oh shit."

"What?"

Staring down at the address in her hand, Jessie shook her head. "I know where this is."

"Where?"

"It's where my old house was."

"Wow, nice place," Tanner remarked as they exited the car. "No wonder you had such a hard time moving into the pit. This place is totally cool."

Jessie hadn't said two words on the way over. All she could do was stare at the address and wonder what Cate would say to this strange turn of events. Now, here she was, in her old neighborhood, pulling up to her old house, wondering what in the hell she was getting into.

"My dear, are you all right?"

Jessie blinked rapidly and swallowed hard. "If there is one thing I've learned in our travels together, it's that there are no such thing as coincidences. Getting out of the cab, Jessie stood in front of her old house feeling as if she were seeing it for the first time. The lavender color with white trim—a traditional Victorian house color— befitted the painted lady sandwiched between two restored houses that looked nothing like this one. "I never noticed this before, but it's not like the houses on either side of it."

Jessie watched as Tanner strolled down the sidewalk, looking at the house from another angle. She had not had many good memories in this house. As a troubled teen, she had spent so much of her time trying hard *not* to be in it. Now, it reminded her of a past she'd rather forget.

Ceara stood on tiptoe and whispered. "Remember."

"Remember what? I was stoned most of the time I lived here, and I—"

Ceara shook her head. "There are other things to remember as well. Look outside yourself, my dear. You, yourself, house the answers to most of your own questions."

Jessie inhaled deeply and closed her eyes. She mostly remembered running up the stairs and slamming her bedroom door after yet another fight with Reena. They'd fought over everything from hair color to holey jeans. She remembered listening to Daniel's electric race track for hours on end and the clack, clack, clacking of his train set. She remembered the smell of the fog as it rolled in and the way the baking cookie aroma wafted into her bedroom window.

"Mrs. Greenblatt's cookies," Jessie said softy. "Mrs. Greenblatt lives in that house. She was always trying out some new Martha Stewart recipe and the scent always drifted through my bedroom window."

Ceara looked at Jessie and tilted her head. Jessie knew what this meant. And half a minute later, was being crushed in one of Mrs. Greenblatt's bear hugs.

"If it isn't Jessie Ferguson? How are you?"

"I'm great, Mrs. G. Really, really good." Jessie smiled at the old woman who still wore her hair in a bun. She had a lime green shawl draped over her shoulders and wore a flower print dress with pink and lime green swirls on it. Unlike many woman her age, her shoulders were not stooped and there was no curvature of her spine. "And how are you, Mrs. G?"

"Baking my life away as Sam always said. Please, come in and try some of Martha's new peanut butter cookies."

Jessie made the introductions of her companions before following Mrs. Greenblatt into the house. The house reminded Jessie of her grandmother's home; there were photos hanging on every wall. Doilies under every bric-a-brac and knickknack, and the furniture looked like something out of a 1950's Sears catalogue.

When Mrs. Greenblatt returned from the kitchen bearing a mountain of cookies and four glasses of milk, she set the platter in front of Jessie and sat across from her. "You look much better than the last time I saw you."

"I'm not doing drugs anymore. I had a rough patch , which is why we moved. Now, I'm in my junior year at the University of Oregon as a history major."

Mrs. Greenblatt clapped her hands. "Then your tough teenage times are over."

Jessie nodded and reached for a cookie. "I suppose they are, yeah."

"I kept telling Reena she needed to hang in there with you because you were a special young lady who just needed to find your way. By the looks of it, you have."

Jessie glanced over at Tanner and Ceara. "Absolutely."

"So, what brings you back to the old haunt? Visiting old friends?"

Jessie almost spewed her milk over Mrs. Greenblatt's choice of words. "Excuse me," she said, wiping her mouth and swallowing the milk. "I'm doing a bit of research and was wondering if you remembered the old Victorian that used to be where our house is before ours was built."

Mrs. Greenblatt looked away. "Yes, actually, I do."

Tanner cut his eyes over to Jessie and she nodded. She felt it too. "Something happened in that house, didn't it?"

Mrs. Greenblatt turned back to them. "Yes. It was tragic, really. They were such a nice family."

Jessie leaned forward. "What happened?"

"Well, I was just a little girl when it happened. Did you know I grew up in this old house?"

Jessie shook her head. She'd been so out of it in high school, she barely knew there were houses attached to theirs.

"Yes. My parents left it in their will to me, and we moved back in shortly after they died. Anyway, I was a little girl when it happened. It was the only thing the adults around here talked about for weeks after. Well, not talk, really. It was more like that sort of whispering adults do when they're afraid and don't want to alarm the children."

"Afraid?" Tanner reached over and covered Jessie's hand with his.

"Of scaring the little children, of course. The Gibson family lived next door when I was a kid. They were such a nice family. I played dolls with their daughter...her name was...Mary something. Maryanne? Mary Kathryn? Oh, it was so long ago, I can hardly remember. It might not have been Mary at all." Mrs. Greenblatt nudged the cookie tray closer to Tanner. "Her father was an archaeologist of some kind and was seldom ever home. So Mary was over at our house a lot. She loved my father dearly, and who could blame her? My father was unlike a man of his time. He preferred playing with his kids to smoking cigars with the menfolk. He was a wonderful father and all the kids in the neighborhood loved him. When he finally got a car, he would wash it every Saturday, and every kid within ten blocks knew if they rode their bikes past our house, my dad would spray them." She sighed. "He was such a good man." Mrs. Greenblatt stared off into space a moment before returning her attention to Jessie. "Where was I? Oh, anyway, one morning, the police came to our house, and there was more whispering from the kitchen. My father would not allow the police to question his kids, so he politely answered their questions and sent them on their way."

Jessie inched forward. "What happened?"

"Apparently, in the middle of the night, some madman snuck

into the house and killed the entire family. I never saw my friend again. I do remember crying a lot that week. It was horrible, and all our parents made us play indoors for an eternity. I later heard from a teenage boy that the family had been hacked up by a psycho, but my father told me not to believe anything I heard on the street."

Jessie felt her blood run cold. "How many were killed?"

"Let's see, his wife, a son and Mary."

"What about Mr. Gibson?"

Mrs. Greenblatt shook her head. "He disappeared. The police suspected him for the longest time, but they never found him and I guess there was no evidence against him, so they stopped looking. I'm not even sure he was in town that weekend, as he was always traveling off to foreign lands in search of some ruin to dig up." She paused to sip her milk. "Not long after the murders, his oldest daughter, Kathryn, who was away at a boarding school, had the place boarded up and a for sale sign on it. Of course, no one would buy the thing as soon as they found out the truth about what had happened in it. Eventually, Kathryn had it removed and sold the lot for a nice, tidy sum. I imagine they destroyed the house."

Jessie looked over at Tanner, who gave a brief shake of his head. He didn't think Mrs. Greenblatt needed to know Jessie was now living in that very house. Some things were better left unsaid. "Would you happen to know anything about where Kathryn might have gone?"

"Oh, yes. She was a brilliant young lady. Mary was always raving on about how Kathryn was going to follow in her father's footsteps. He was pretty well known for his work in Egyptology. Wrote scholarly articles, gave presentations, that sort of thing. *More interested in the dead than in the living* is what my father used to say. He even spent time working with Howard Carter, the man who found King Tut's tomb. I remember because my father had the chance to meet Mr. Carter one evening when he came to see Mr. Gibson and his partner, Mr. Townsend."

"Oh. Wow. How cool was that?"

"It was *cool* for the men, but we females were relegated to the kitchen. Wait...except for Kathryn. She had come home for a break and she got to meet Mr. Carter as well. Made a big impression on her, from what I recall. I did receive a graduation announcement from her when she graduated from college. USF, or maybe it was San Francisco State. It was so long ago, you'll have to forgive my tired memory."

"You're doing great, Mrs. G."

She glanced back out the window. "They were such a nice family too."

"Do you remember anything else about Mr. Gibson?"

Mrs. Greenblatt thought for a moment before shaking her head. "Like I said, he was seldom home. I just know he was a man of some prominence in archaeology and that Kathryn did, in fact, follow in his footsteps." She smiled sadly. "After the house moved, life got back to normal and we never spoke of it again. I know my parents were thrilled when the house was being moved. It was creepy having it next door all boarded up like some haunted house."

Jessie licked her lips. "I can imagine."

"That's about all I can remember. Tell me what's been going on in your life."

For the next half hour, Jessie regaled Mrs. Greenblatt about her Oregon life, her work at the inn (minus the truth about where the inn came from), and her trip to Wales with Ceara. Mrs. Greenblatt listened with enthusiasm to every story Jessie told, often clapping with delight.

As they stood at the door to leave, Jessie promised she would write her and thanked her for the dozen or so cookies Tanner consumed.

"An old woman loves company, Jessie. The pleasure has been all mine. It was nice meeting your friends. You both are lucky to have such a wonderful young woman as a friend."

Tanner nodded as he handed Mrs. Greenblatt one of his business cards. "If you remember anything about the house or that story, feel free to contact me."

Walking to the corner to get a cab, Jessie threw her arm around Tanner's shoulders and pulled him to her. "Think you could have eaten a few more cookies?"

Tanner groaned and patted his stomach. "My grandmother

always told me old women love it when you eat their food. I was just trying to make her comfortable."

Ceara pressed the walk button. "That's enough prattling, you two. What on earth do you think about that horrible story she told?"

Jessie kept her arm around Tanner as they crossed the street. "The story fits. Daniel says there's three of them. It could be those three who are haunting Daniel."

"Think Mr. Gibson is still alive somewhere?"

Jessie shrugged as she held the cab door open for Ceara. "Who can say? He may not be, but I bet Katheryn is."

Jessie turned to Ceara. "So, what now? Where to?"

"The nearest Internet café. I want to know what happened to Kathryn Gibson."

14th Century BCE

When Tarik removed the two stones covering the peephole into the pharaoh's chambers, he was not the least bit surprised to find Efru in consort. The priest had become a reliable spy for Akhenaten, and his daily reports underscored just how much the pharaoh trusted him to sift the rumors from the truth.

"Your detractors are mounting some sort of rebellion, to be sure, your grace. They believe Aten should remain a minor deity since Egypt has not grown since you changed the religion. The murmurings grow louder, I'm afraid. The people are restless."

Akhenaten strode across the chamber with the regal bearing of a man used to ruling the most powerful kingdom in the world. His dark eyes were almost black as they glared into the courtyard below. "Bah. They have been saying so for such a long time, I no longer believe them capable of acting upon it. They are weak. I am not."

"Weak they may be, but they are beginning to speak out against your queen."

Akhenaten stopped and slowly turned, his eyes glowing embers, his chest puffed out. "What? Who? When was this? I'll have their heads before nightfall! Well? Speak! Do not waste my time with riddles. Why have you not brought these traitors to me?"

Efru bowed his head. He was much shorter than the pharaoh. "I apologize, Your Eminence. You asked that I merely observe and listen. I fear Nefertiti may be in danger. There is some belief they might take her and force you to renounce this new religion and return to the old ways. Everyone knows how much you love the queen. They want to use that love against you."

Akhenaten's face suddenly softened. "She is my guiding light, Efru, my beacon in the dead of night." His eyes immediately hardened. "If *anyone* so much as whispers a word against her name, I want them brought to me immediately. Do not think, do not question, do not judge. Do you understand?"

Efru nodded. "If I may be so bold. She may be your light, but she is also the weakest part of your armor. Forgive me my honesty, My King, but your love for her is seen as a weakness. She makes you...vulnerable."

"She makes me happy, damn you, and I'll not pander to such lunacy. Watch your tongue, priest, and do not overstep your boundary." Akhenaten turned and gazed out the opening onto the terrace. "Get Tarik. Get the whole army and bring me these cowards who would utter a word against my beloved. I will crush them like the vermin they are."

"I must strongly urge you not to do anything rash. You would not want to show them you are threatened by the or—"

"I shall show them who is threatening! I fear no man. All men need fear me! Now do as I bade."

"Yes, My King, but let us not rush into something until we have all of the information we need to crush them with one swift blow. You need a decisive victory over these anti-Atenists. Give them no room to breathe."

Akhenaten calmed himself. When he first came to power, the priests of Amun held most of the power in Egypt and did exactly as they pleased. By destroying the temples and proclaiming Aten as supreme god, Akhenaten had removed the power from the priests' possession and given it back to the throne; a throne he knew he would have to fight for if his people did not readily accede to the change of religions.

"If I may be so bold, My King, as to suggest that perhaps you spirit the queen to lower Egypt for a time. While she is gone, Tarik and his men can run the rats out of hiding once and for all. Make an example of them."

Akhenaten lowered his gaze to the priest. "You would see to her safety."

Efru bowed his head. "I would be honored to do so."

Akhenaten sat down heavily on the throne. "The death of our beloved Mekataten was difficult for Nefertiti. Perhaps a voyage to the lower kingdom might lift her spirits. I shall think it over. In the meantime, continue your vigilance and bring to me any report you feel needs my attention. Now, bring Tarik to me."

When Efru left the pharaoh's chambers, Tarik replaced the stones and removed himself to the antechamber of the queen's room. There was something odd about the exchange between the king and the priest, but Tarik could not discern what it was. Until he did, he would keep a closer eye out on Efru. The man was dangerous indeed, and anyone who was a danger to Sakura would need to be dealt with sooner or later.

Tarik hoped it would not be later.

21st Century AD

The Internet café on Market Street was cool and clean, and Jessie and company were seated at the only computer near the window so Tanner could sit and people watch. He was always people watching.

"There are going to be quite a few genealogy pages to look through, my dear. This could take some time."

Jessie nodded. "I'm not going to any of those. There's a new people-find site Tanner showed me and it kicks ass." Jessie typed up Kathryn Gibson and came up with one hundred hits in the Bay Area. She then typed in Albert Gibson, her missing father, and came up with information on the archaeologist right away. "Bingo. Looks like old Albert wrote two books on the subject of archaeological practices in antiquity." Jessie read the blurb before going to the next page. "Looks like he had a partner named Robert Townsend. There's a list of articles they wrote prior to 1922. Very prolific writers. They worked together for quite some time, but there's nothing in here about his family." Jessie shook her head. "Impressive. Seems they were in the Valley of the Kings around the same time Carter was."

"That *is* impressive. Did they know each other?"

"Doesn't say."

"Anything about Townsend?"

Jessie traced the words with her finger. "Just that he was British, was an excellent archaeologist who had a promising career before it ended abruptly."

"Sounds like a second fiddle," Tanner said from his perch by the window. "Maybe he was the details man."

"Maybe." She minimized the page and went back to the search engine with Kathryn Gibson's name on it and scrolled through the links. "Well, hello there," Jessie said, leaning closer to the monitor. "Says here her father was Albert, her mother, Olivia, and Mrs. Greenblatt's little friend was named Marybeth. All died in 1922." Jessie read more. "Looks like Kathryn married Samuel Leland in 1940 and they had Samuel Gibson Leland in 1942. Let's see—" Jessie scrolled down more. "That would make Samuel Gibson Leland Albert's grandson."

Ceara pushed her glasses further up the bridge of her nose as she leaned in. "No deceased date for her."

Jessie's heart was banging in her chest. "Kathryn must know more about the murders than Mrs. G."

"If she's still alive and has all her marbles. Try Samuel Gibson Leland first," Tanner said from his window seat. "See what sort of grandson he turned out to be."

Jessie did so and had fifty-three hits. She scanned the links and saw Professor Gibson Leland at Cal Berkeley. "Excellent. He's in the Bay Area."

For the next half hour, Jessie culled everything she could offline about the Gibson family and printed copies of every piece of information. "Our professor is much more prolific than his grandfather. He's penned dozens of articles and four textbooks over the years." Jessie turned to Tanner, who hadn't moved in some time. "What's going on in that head of yours?"

Tanner turned to her and smiled. "I've been sitting here thinking. We may be looking for answers in the wrong place." Hopping off the window seat, he stretched and yawned. "There's one place where there are people who know *who* the murderer is."

Jessie looked over at Ceara, who nodded. "The inn. If our ghosts are those from the Gibson family, my guess is they want us to know who murdered them. That's why they are so agitated. I think they want answers. They think Daniel has them."

"And do what?"

Ceara shrugged. "I guess we'll just have to ask them."

Back at the boat, Jessie and Ceara pored over the pages they had printed at the Internet café.

"This article I found online is perfect," Jessie said, pulling it out and placing it on top of the stack. "I'll read it out loud." Jessie cleared her throat. "*Last night, Carolyn Gibson, her son and daughter were found murdered in their home. There was no sign of a break-in, but they appeared to be victims of a burglary.*" Jessie looked up. "News was so different back then. No suppositions, no sensationalism, just the facts, Jack." Pulling the papers closer to her, Jessie continued reading. "*Albert Gibson, age 43, has not been located. Neighbors refused to comment, saying only that the Gibsons were a nice family who deserve respect. Blah, blah, blah.* Wait. Here. *His partner, Robert Townsend, appeared in a state of shock when told of the brutal nature of the crime, but he refused to comment.* The article ends with the line that Kathryn Gibson was unavailable for comment."

"Mrs. Greenblatt didn't say anything about a burglary. She must have forgotten."

Ceara shook her head. "Life was so different back then. People didn't always lock their doors. You weren't so paranoid back then. Someone could have waltzed right in and killed them."

"And besides, Mrs. G was just a little girl. There's probably a lot she doesn't remember. I wouldn't count on all of her memories even being correct."

"So, what's our next move?" Tanner asked.

"Tomorrow, we go to Berkley and see if we can't find the grandson."

"Think he knows anything?"

Ceara nodded. "There are some things in a family history one never lives down or forgets. Having a heinous crime happen is another. He may not know a lot, but he knows *something*."

"Maybe he won't be willing to discuss the bloody skeletons in the closet."

Jessie patted Tanner's arm. "That, my boy, is where you come in."

Summer was a quiet time on the UC Berkeley campus, which was situated among old Victorians and newer million dollar rebuilds where upscale hippies had transformed into dot.com yuppies, and finally landed as 21st century guppies. Sidewalks once filled with rollerbladers, scooters, walkers and skateboarders were now filled with tourists and locals enjoying the sun as they sipped overpriced mochas and ate expensive croissants. Berkeley liked to believe it was still flower power and New Age aware, but Jessie knew better.

When they finally made it to the administration building, Jessie let Ceara ask all the questions.

"Is Professor Gibson Leland working this term?" Ceara asked the young Asian clerk.

"Let me check." Running her finger down a list, the clerk looked up and nodded. "Yes, he is. What can I do for you?"

"Does he have office hours?"

The clerk turned the page. "You're in luck. You might still catch him. Proffessors don't hang around very long during the summer." She pointed a French manicured fingernail to a campus map. "It's in the Morgan Building, but you better hurry."

Ten minutes later, they were standing outside the office of Professor Leland. The aging sign on his office door said he was in a conference and not to knock. They didn't have long to wait. Two young men walked out followed by a gaunt, six foot, older gentleman wearing a rumpled short sleeved collared shirt with a tie that matched the light blue of the shirt and the light blue of his eyes. His hair was thinning on the top and graying on the sides, and he wore wire rimmed glasses that had seen better days.

Professor Gibson Leland stood at the door looking down at the three of them. "And I thought this summer term was going to die a slow death of boredom. Strangers calling always bodes interesting. Please, do come in."

The three of them entered his confined quarters and took a seat on the small, red leather sofa that had also seen better days.

"My name is Jessie and this is Ceara and Tanner. We've just sailed in from Oregon and have a few questions for you."

"About?"

Jessie hesitated. "Well...it's about your family."

He cocked his head. "My family?" His eyes scanned the area behind them. "Are you reporters?"

"No, sir."

Ceara cleared her throat. "We do not wish to take much of your time, Professor, but Jessie here, well...she currently lives in the house where your grandmother was killed." She paused and waited for a response that never came. "She was wondering if you have any information about what happened there."

Professor Leland tilted his head and looked slowly from Ceara to Jessie to Tanner and back to Jessie. "What does she mean you *live* there?"

"After the murders, the house was sold and then moved to a town called New Haven up the Oregon coast, where we all live. My family runs a bed-and-breakfast in that house. I'm doing a history project on it and we were hoping—"

Professor Leland held his hands up. "Whoa. This is about the *house*? I thought you said you had questions about my family?"

Jessie nodded. "Well, sir, it's a little of both. I need to know as much as you can tell me about what happened that night in the house."

He never took his eyes off Jessie's. "And what's so important about that horrible night that you would travel all the way down here to ask me about it?" Again, his eyes darted out the door. "And I would like the truth. All of it. Don't waste my time with lies of omission or prevarication."

Nodding, Jessie looked over at Ceara, who nodded for her to go on. Taking a deep breath, Jessie forged ahead. "I have a thirteen-year-old brother who is…well…to put it bluntly, he is being haunted by three people—people who used to live in that house. We need to know what it is they want and I was hoping you might be able to shed some light on that."

Professor Leland stared at Jessie a long time before rising from his desk. "Let me get this straight. You came all the way down here to see what I could tell you about the greatest tragedy in my family because you believe the house you live in is haunted by my relatives?"

Jessie nodded. "In a nutshell, yes."

He turned from the window. "Is this some sick joke? Did someone put you up to it?"

Jessie shook her head. "Please…hear us out. This is no joke and it isn't meant to be cruel. Something is happening to my brother and we've come here to see if you might be able to help us figure it out." Jessie pushed on. "I need your help, Professor."

He gazed hard at Jessie as if trying to determine the sincerity of her request. "Haunted, you say?"

Jessie nodded. "I know how crazy it sounds, but—"

"Almost as insane as having your family chopped up and no one ever being caught for it." Professor Leland tore his gaze from Jessie and returned to staring out the window as the cuckoo clock on the wall tick-tocked away. "It is not a history my family is proud of, so I'm sure you can imagine how something like this would only exacerbate matters. Your discretion is of the utmost, you understand."

"My grandfather was a consummate archaeologist and brilliant educator. His name is forever besmirched because the police were too inept to find the real murderer and bungled the entire investigation." He turned back around. "But that is beside the point. You came here because you think my ancestors are haunting your brother. Will this nightmare never end?"

"I'm so sorry, but they've been bothering him for three years now and it's getting worse. We have a profitable family business that does not need nor does it want a ghost. This isn't for sensationalizing, Professor. This is about the mental health and well-being of my brother."

He steepled his fingers and pressed his two index fingers against his lips. "I see. You're not joking then about any of this?"

"No sir, I am not."

He nodded pensively. "You said that accursed house is a bed-and-breakfast now?"

Jessie nodded.

Professor Leland turned his laptop toward Jessie. "Pull it up on the Internet. I take it you have a Web site of some sort?"

Jessie nodded and quickly typed in the URL. When the photo of the front of the house came up, Jessie turned the laptop back toward the professor, who gasped and covered his mouth when he saw it.

"That...that's the old house. I would know it anywhere." Leaning over, he pushed his glasses back on his nose and studied the house before clicking on photos showing the interior and many of the rooms. "It's far more beautiful than any of the old photos I've seen of the house."

Jessie said nothing for the five minutes he surveyed the Web site. When he finally rose, he blinked rapidly and then returned to his chair, like he didn't know whether to stand, sit or run away. "I don't know anything about ghosts or hauntings, Jessie, but I *can* tell you the house you're living in is definitely the one my ancestors died in. I had no idea they moved it. I assumed it had been destroyed."

"It was moved up the coast and now perches high on a hill overlooking the Pacific. It's beautiful, really, but it's had its share of bad luck. My parents have been the only ones capable of making a go of it."

Tanner added, "The townies have called it the Money Pit for years because it drains people of everything they own before they have to sell it. It's changed hands quite a few times."

Professor Leland nodded. "That doesn't surprise me. The mayhem that happened in that house was as horrific as it gets.

My ancestors didn't stand a chance against whatever madman killed them. He left them in pieces."

"Is there anything you can tell us that you think might help? We need to figure out what they want so we can give it to them and let them go wherever souls go."

The Professor blew on his glasses and wiped them off before putting them back on. "I'm not a man who believes in ghosts or spirits, or even afterlife curses, Jessie, so you must forgive me if I appear dubious. Are you sure your brother didn't somehow discover the murders and—"

"Is making it all up? No sir, he isn't. He's not that kind of kid. He doesn't do drugs, he's not an attention seeker. He's a straight-A student with a good head on his shoulders."

As Professor Leland started to bring the laptop back, he knocked a pen to the floor, and when Jessie knelt over to pick it up, her ankh fell from her shirt and dangled in the air. When she returned the pen to the desk, Professor Leland was staring at the ankh as it lay against her chest. "What a magnificent piece that is," he said, rising and leaning over the desk. "May I?"

Jessie lifted the ankh on its chain from her chest and handed it to him. He was so close to her, she could smell his spearmint gum.

"What a remarkable piece. This is from antiquity, isn't it? Have you any idea how much something like this is worth?"

Jessie carefully took it from him and leaned back. "It's priceless to me, Professor, so it doesn't really matter how much it's worth."

"Mind if I ask where you got it?"

Jessie warmed, thinking of Cate as she buried it beneath a large rock. "A dear old friend."

"From the looks of it, that's from around the 18th dynasty. It's in remarkably great condition. There are collectors everywhere who would give their eyeteeth for a piece like that."

Jessie tucked it back in her shirt. "I'd never sell it."

He studied her a moment, as if discarding every question coming to his mind until the right one settled in his mouth. "Do you know something of Egyptology?"

"A little. I am a history major at the University of Oregon specializing in ancient civilizations."

The change that came over Professor Leland was palpable as he realized he was speaking with a kindred spirit and not some silly girl looking into spiritual manifestations. "Okay then. Seems I underestimated you. I apologize for that. Let's start over, shall we? While your talk of ghosts and hauntings may not endear you to most of my academic colleagues, I *do* appreciate your candor about why you've come all this way. Why don't we get down to brass tacks and you tell me what it is you *really* wish to know."

"We've been doing our homework on the house and the murders, and, well, quite frankly, things aren't really adding up. We ended up with more questions than answers."

He nodded. "I can understand that. Living with that mystery my entire life, I've always come up with more questions than answers. That never sits well with someone used to providing both. I know what *didn't* add up for me. What isn't adding up for you?"

Jessie turned to fully face him. "First off, your grandfather was a renowned archaeologist with articles and photos all over the place and yet no one ever found him or saw him ever again after the murders."

Professor Leland shook his head sadly. "My grandfather was famous for a variety of things, not the least of which was his work with Howard Carter. He had so much potential—so much to offer the field."

"But?"

The Professor shrugged. "He angered a lot of people. Cut a lot of corners. He believed himself to be as great as Carter, when the sad fact is he was a lazy archaeologist who got lucky."

Jessie nodded. "And then not so lucky. I understand your mother was away at the time and that's why she survived.

"Yes. She hired a private detective when she got older to find the murderers, but life was different back then, and he came up with nothing."

"What did she wind up doing with her life?"

"Unfortunately for my mother, following in his footsteps

was nigh impossible because no one wanted to hire a woman connected to him, nor did anyone want anything to do with what would later become known as the Curse of Tut's Tomb."

Jessie studied him a moment. "I take it you don't believe in curses, either?"

"I believe in a good many things, Jessie, but the idea that my family somehow suffered at the hands of a curse for being present at the opening of the great tomb in the Valley of the Kings, well, I simply don't believe it."

"So what happened to Kathryn?"

"My mother became a collector. You see, she inherited all his share of money for his excavations and managed to parlay that into quite a tidy fortune. My mother was an incredible woman. She was an impeccable collector, a brilliant historian, and financially astute business woman. She put me through Stanford, but she won't talk about that night. Not with me, not with anyone."

"What happened to your father?"

"He died when I was nine. He was on a dig in Egypt when a boulder fell on him crushing him instantly. As you can imagine, that brought back the notion that my family was cursed and we would never rest because of something my grandfather did when he went into Tut's tomb."

Tanner leaned forward, enrapt by the unfolding mystery. "What did he do?"

Professor Leland took his glasses off and wiped them with the bottom of his shirt. "He opened it. Well, that's not entirely true. He was *there* when Carter opened it. Many of the people who were there for the opening suffered bizarre twists in their lives, and the press being what it is and was, thought a curse was the next hot topic. My mother and I have been living with the notion of that stupid curse our whole lives. That was why I decided to become a historian and not an archaeologist. I prefer reminding people about history, not finding it."

Jessie nodded. "Sounds like a good choice. So, what do *you* think happened to your grandfather?"

The professor inhaled deeply and blew a breath out loudly. "When I was younger, I spent months trying to piece everything together. Near as I can tell from the evidence at hand, he died the same night as his family."

"What makes you think that?"

"Because his body was found in the house."

"What?" This came from all three listening to the story.

He nodded. "My grandfather and Mr. Townsend were on the brink of a huge discovery of some sort when Albert suddenly took ill. My grandfather had just returned from Egypt believing he had come close to discovering Queen Nefertiti's tomb. I guess Albert started speaking of her as if she were alive and Townsend thought maybe he had hurt his head on the dig."

Jessie and Ceara exchanged glances, but said nothing.

"According to his journals, Albert told Townsend he had *the key* to ancient Egypt, as great a find as the Rosetta Stone, but he would not divulge the information until he had completed his research. Townsend then became angry and threatened my grandfather, but that did not dissuade him about revealing whatever he had found. As time went on, Albert became more and more delusional and so Townsend went back to Egypt to continue with the search for Nefertiti's tomb alone."

"Was it hers?"

"No. It might have been the tomb of a lesser queen, but not much more than that. Townsend wrote Albert several letters begging him to return to Egypt, but Albert never did. Instead, he fell deeper and deeper into a delusional state until the tragedy struck."

Jessie swallowed her questions and waited.

"When my ancestors were brutally murdered, Townsend came home. By the time he arrived, the dust had settled and life had moved on as best it could. He did help Kathryn clear the house, and eventually, he found a buyer for it."

"Why sell it?" Ceara asked. "Why not just demolish it? That would have been easier. Why move it?"

Professor Leland nodded. "Good question. I asked myself that a million times. The family myth is that Townsend actually bought the damn thing so he could look for whatever it was he believed Albert had. Those two might have been partners, but according to the few journal entries found in the house, there was no trust between them at the end. Albert had become withdrawn and delusional and Townsend became bitter and adversarial. He thought my grandfather had something of value—something he had kept for himself. What that was is anybody's guess. It was never found."

"So you think Townsend bought the house to look for it?"

"What other reason could there be? Townsend offered her the same price to have it removed as she asked to let it stay. Kathryn said Townsend searched every inch of that house, and when he found nothing, he sold it to a family who moved it up north."

"Creepy." Jessie looked over at Ceara, who did not look back, and Jessie knew she was thinking the same thing: whether or not the *thing* Albert had discovered was the portal.

"So he moved the house because—"

"Because he wanted to still be able to look for whatever it was he thought my grandfather had found. By selling it to a couple who wanted a Victorian for a bed-and-breakfast, he was keeping it public so he could continue to search."

"And did he ever find anything?"

"What few people know is that the house had been turned inside out when my family was killed. Nothing of value was stolen, so it was evident that whoever came in there was looking for something very specific."

"You're suggesting—"

"That Robert Townsend murdered my ancestors and got away with it? Yes. Yes I am, though I have absolutely no proof of that."

"But I thought you said he was in Egypt at the time."

"That was what everyone thinks, yes. This was 1922, remember, and he was never even a suspect. Law enforcement worked very differently than it does today. How hard would it have been for him to have someone else sail his passage? How hard was it to just knock on the front door and be allowed in?"

"What makes you believe all this?"

Unlocking the middle drawer to his desk, the professor pulled out a brown leather-bound book and set it on the desk. "They found this with my grandfather the day someone accidentally found his body."

Jessie felt Ceara shiver. "What do you mean, *accidentally*?"

Professor Leland pushed a bowl of Hersheys Kisses toward them. "Around Medford, Oregon, the house started leaning and crashed into a large tree. To the horror of the movers, my grandfather's decomposed body fell out of the hole torn open by a massive oak. Anyway, he and the chair he was in plummeted to the ground. This journal was still in his hands when the movers reached him."

Jessie inhaled deeply, not wanting to ask the next question, but not able to stop herself. "Was this wall on the back side of the house over the porch?"

"I have no idea."

Jessie nodded. "That's okay. What happened after they found the body?"

"They called Kathryn who managed to get to Medford, identify her father's badly decomposed body, and claim the journal. My grandfather was rather prolific, if not altogether sane in this journal, but from what we've gathered, the information, at least, is very accurate."

Jessie stared at the journal. It was dog-eared, thick, and looked the worse for wear. Stained leather covered yellowing paper. "What did he die of?"

Professor Leland shrugged. "No one knows. There were no marks on his body, no bruises, and his body was pretty well preserved, considering. That was pretty bizarre."

"So he wasn't a victim of the murderer?"

"Apparently not. We never knew what killed him or where his body had been before it fell out. The entire side of the house had a gaping hole, but the workers could never pinpoint just where it was his body had been. Kathryn quietly buried him in Medford as a way of keeping more scandal and shame away from the family. You see, she never cared for Townsend, and she knew if this leaked out, he would return for the journal and bring with him unwanted attention. She just wanted her life back."

"Can't blame her for that."

"No, no you can't. Albert was left in peace until my father took up the cause to find out more. You see, my family never believed Albert was the killer, but to bring him out as having been in the house…well…the case would have closed then and there, leaving my grandfather's name besmirched yet again. We just wanted it all to go away."

"And what of Townsend?"

"Oh, he had minor success as an archaeologist, but nothing compared to Carter or Albert. He died a bitter and broken man who blamed Albert for many of his failures. He was convinced Albert had discovered something earth-shattering that would unlock the doors to ancient Egypt and propel them both to fame. Townsend was never able to find whatever the hell it was my grandfather raved about. He died bitter and alone."

Jessie leaned forward. "What do you think Albert found?"

"Quite frankly, not a damn thing. One look at Albert's journal, and you see a man on the verge of either insanity or dementia. My grandfather's demise merely gave a mediocre archaeologist someone to blame for his failure at recognition in the field. He died penniless and had even written a scathing rant about Albert days before he died."

Jessie glanced down at the leather journal. The cover was soft and well oiled from the touch of human hands. "That's really quite a tale."

Professor Leland nodded and rose. "You have been a kind audience, and I hope I was able to answer some of your questions, but I am expecting a call from the curator of the British Museum. I hope this sheds some light on your ghost problem." He shook his head. "Ten years ago, I might have had security remove you, but I've learned one thing in this life— anything is possible where my family is concerned. It's up to each subsequent generation to either disprove the theories or protect our good name. My own son even changed his name because the archaeological world is a small one indeed, and he did not wish to suffer condemnation because of *the curse*."

Jessie rose. "Can I ask one more thing of you before we go?"

"Certainly."

"I know it's a lot to ask, but is there any chance you might send me a few of the pages from the journal? You have my word that—"

Professor Leland held up his hand. "As you can see, the journal stays with me always. It's sort of the albatross around my family's neck, but it's my family, and I'm going to protect it as much as I can."

"I understand."

"However, the whole thing is transcribed on the computer. I can e-mail it to you without anyone knowing it's from the journal of Albert Gibson. You would have no proof that it is his other than your word against mine. I'm sorry for sounding so defensive, but—"

"I totally understand. You have my word it would not be used for anything other than to help my brother out."

"Consider it done, then. And Jessie…I trust this won't come back to haunt me, pardon the play on words." Professor Leland swiveled over to the laptop and waited while Jessie recited her e-mail address to him.

"You have my word, sir." Rising, Jessie extended her hand. "And thank you so much for your time."

"My grandfather was a good man. My family deserved better than to be butchered by some criminal. They were innocents who never had a chance." The Professor opened the door. "Is your house haunted? I have no idea. If—and that's a big word—if my family is haunting your little brother, it would be interesting to see what it is they want."

"Thought you didn't believe." Jessie smiled at him.

"I don't. That doesn't mean I can't hope for the best for you and your family. I wish you the best of luck, Jessie."

When the three of them left the building, Ceara turned to Jessie. "That man can sure weave a tale."

Jessie nodded. "I think they found Albert's body near the room with the portal, if not in it. The only question is—"

"Did he go through?"

The three of them stopped and looked at each other.

"Internet café?"

"Oh yes. There's one way to be sure. Either Albert was a raving loon, or he had, in fact, been back to ancient Egypt."

14th Century BCE

Sakura stood in front of the two carved alabaster statues and stared into the gaping darkness she could barely squeeze through. The first time, she did not understand what had happened to her or where she went whenever she slipped between the two statues and into the crag of the rock. After a couple of times through, she understood Aset had given her the gift of glimpsing other places, other times. The wisdom she constantly prayed for was given to her by beings she knew nothing of, but experienced nonetheless.

The first time she went into the rocks, she lost her own personal awareness and discovered she was someone else; someone else in another time doing things she had no sense of knowing. She was only able to remember a tiny fraction of what had transpired that first day, but after more prayer and alms to the almighty Aset, the second time she went through, she was able to remain herself long enough to realize that wherever and *when*ever she was, this was not her, but a being like her; a priestess with so much wisdom and yet, like Sakura, yearning for so much more. She tried to remember her life in Egypt when she was away, but memory seemed to fade as soon as she became this other person. When she returned to her real life, she was always disconcerted by the lack of memories returning with her.

Sakura closed her eyes now and meditated. There was one on the other side who was a priestess as well, only this one was more powerful and she was learning from one who held more ancient wisdom and power within her than Sakura ever thought possible. The one she always went to was the one in the green robe. She seemed more receptive, more willing to entertain Sakura's presence.

For Sakura, wisdom was her drug, and the power that came with it, her euphoria. She was not willing to release either to the new male priests of Aten. She had seen enough to know a possible fate of her goddess, and if she could find a way to keep the power on the throne of Aset, she would do so at all costs.

This was what the robed woman believed. This was what

the robed priestess did with her own knowledge…she tried to keep alive the old ways…Sakura's old ways.

Opening her eyes, Sakura quickly sucked in a breath. Was it possible the red-haired one actually knew what was happening? Had she actually summoned her there or was that some vision Sakura alone held? More importantly, was this woman possessing her Ka, her spirit?

Wedging through the small fissure in the stone, Sakura found herself standing beneath a tree older than the two young women beneath it. The tree was unlike anything Sakura had ever seen and possessed more wisdom than—

"Catie? What is it? You have that look."

Cate looked down at her hands, at her robe, and then back up at Maeve. "It is that dark-skinned woman. The one who came before. She has returned."

Maeve rose and took Cate's hands, looking deep into her eyes. "Tell me about her."

"She is powerful. Strong. She came here not by accident. As with us all, she seeks."

"Can you tell what it is that she wants?"

Cate stared hard into Maeve's gray eyes. "She is a quester. She has come for a reason, but I cannot tell yet."

"Then let us ascertain what that reason may be. Come." Maeve took Cate by the hand and led her to a small grassy knoll, where she bid her to lay down. "You say she is powerful?"

"Yes. Very."

"We will take you to your Dreamworld where you can determine what it is she wants, but be very careful, Catie. Remember…she is not Jessie."

Cate frowned and then shook her head. "She is not…odd, though…"

"What is odd?"

Cate closed her eyes and listened. Slowly opening them, she sat up. "I believe she knows who Jessie is."

21ˢᵗ Century AD

Jessie, Ceara and Tanner hunkered down in the small dining area of Ceara's houseboat to read the journal information Professor Leland had sent.

"I feel like a voyeur," Tanner whispered.

"Shh," came the response from both Ceara and Jessie.

Nefertiti is as beautiful as the scant pieces of artwork paying homage to her. Not Nubian, but lighter, caramel-colored skin that has not one blemish on it. The kohl on her eyes is so perfectly orchestrated, it could be tattooed upon her. The artwork that remains of her does not adequately convey the length of her neck or the curve of her leg, and no artwork can, of course, show the grace of her movement when she ascends the stairs of her chamber. She is grace personified and all stop to stare whenever she walks by.

Jessie stopped reading and looked over at Ceara. "He did go through," she said softly.

Ceara nodded. "Apparently." Taking her glasses off, Ceara huffed on them and wiped them off. "I always wondered…but I think…I think this means the *house* is the portal, not the space in which it resides, and you, my dear, are truly the one. You and the portal were meant to be."

Jessie exhaled and ran her hands through her hair. "If I *am* the one, then what was he?"

"Merely a trespasser who fell in love with Queen Nefertiti. Perhaps going in and out of the portal drove him mad. Perhaps he found a way to stay there. We can't really know. Maybe his journal will shine some light on that point."

Jessie turned her attention back to the journal.

I believe I can take the priest, though I have not yet determined whether or not she has an affinity for him. There is a great deal going on here…more than the history books have ever conveyed. More politics, more love webs, more machinations. It makes me marvel at how little we know about Egypt's most famous queen.

"Cleopatra," Jessie whispered. "She wouldn't come along for almost fifteen hundred more years. I wonder what he was up to."

"By the sounds of it, Albert was a frequent flier of the portal," Tanner added, threading his fingers through Jessie's. "He used it as his own personal time taxi."

Jessie nodded. "Because he fell in love with Nefertiti, with the notion of time travel, with the very place he was excavating thousands of years after Nefertiti. It's almost hard to be mad at the guy. He fell in love."

"Falling in love is one thing," Tanner said softly, "but coming back sounding like a nutcase is another story. He wasn't just visiting, Jessie, he was up to something. In the professor's office, I left wondering what this key was he was talking about."

It gets harder and harder to come back, though I've yet to find a way to relieve the priest of his duties. That will certainly come with time, with planning, with every breath I take. The priest is the other key. With him, I can bend an ear, I can go places the peons may not. Speaking of peons, Townsend suspects nothing, but was impressed when he received a wire from Cairo acknowledging the necklace was precisely where I had told him it would be. That piece should keep the greedy bastard satisfied for a while. He sees me as a more viable partner now, not just a brilliant mind. He now needs me more than I need him, and once he receives the necklace, he will no longer doubt my contribution to the project.

The project. This has grown to mean so much more to me than a single-focus archaeological project. Since my introduction to Nefertiti, it has become my life's blood. It takes every ounce of energy I have to return and spend my life in the mundane. This world is so dreary compared to theirs. Our abodes, our cities, the very color of our skin is colorless compared to the grandeur of Egyptian society and culture. I cannot stay and yet, it becomes more difficult to return. I am a torn man.

Townsend came to see me this morning and urges me to return to Cairo immediately with him because another tomb has been discovered in the Valley of the Kings. He says Carter is acting strangely, as if he is close to some great discovery. I cannot imagine leaving here for even a day, but I feel I must. This will be my final trip to the dead country that was once a glorious, thriving Egypt.

"No wonder his relatives thought he was a loon," Tanner said softly. "If you didn't know about the portal, he sounds like some rambling crackpot."

Jessie read the piece again. "This still doesn't help us with our problem back home. Yes, he came and went, but that doesn't make him a murderer."

Ancient Egypt is more wonderful every time I see it. Modern day Egypt is so trite and dull, as the Nile is such a color now as to be unrecognizable back then. Dark, filthy, it is not the water of Cleopatra and Ramses. The buildings now reflect a poverty that did not exist during the 18th dynasty. The city stinks now of fear, of boredom, of the mundane, and yet the excavations outside of Cairo, Luxor and Thebes bring in priceless antiquities that the citizens will never see and would sell if they did. I have never seen a culture care less about their antiquities than the residents of Cairo. It is heartbreaking, really.

In modern day Egypt it is strange to see the near lifeless city that was once Akhentaten. Around every corner, I expect to see her, to hear the soft lilt of her laughter, but then I remember what era I am in and know that she is long past, sleeping the great sleep.

But oh, I know where she is, and I also know where to go to get Townsend those priceless baubles he is so interested in. I abhor the current archeological mentality of collecting. So much of the work is improperly handled, categorized with a dullard's imprecision, and much of it is unceremoniously stolen by grave robbers and men of letters alike.

I am tired and weary from the intense heat and dust that coats my lungs, so I will close now. The evenings give me pause and respite so I might reflect upon my life here. More and more, I wonder if, perhaps, I am living in the wrong time. I feel more and more out of place and less and less a viable being in this century. I wonder if I found this other Egypt because it is where I truly belong.

I wonder.

"Uh-oh," Jessie said, pinching the bridge of her nose. "Anyone else get the feeling he stopped wondering?"

1st Century AD

Cate peered through the mist and watched in awe as Sakura gingerly looked about, picking her way across moss-covered flagstones. She did not appear frightened or apprehensive. Just curious. Surveying the ring of stones, and empty firepit, Sakura ran her hand over the bark of one of the towering oaks standing watch over Cate's Dreamworld.

Cate watched Sakura intently, thinking about Jessie and how much she enjoyed their friendship. Could one actually be friends with one's self from another time? It seemed she and Jessie had answered that question. The thought made Cate smile, and when she did, Sakura stopped and cocked her head.

She knows where she is, Cate thought, watching Sakura take a seat on the stones, glad she hadn't chosen the stone usually reserved for Jessie. Bringing her arms up, Cate parted the mist and walked through it to where Sakura was sitting.

"You!" Sakura said, jumping to her feet. "Then it *is* you!"

Cate smiled softly. "Who else did you expect? You have traveled thousands of years to see *me*, have you not?"

Sakura nodded as she walked over to Cate and examined her with her intense dark brown eyes. "I have, but I never thought we would come face-to-face. I have...been within you, for moments at a time on and off for many years. I have traveled to places I do not understand, to times I cannot even imagine, but I have never had the chance to see what you look like or who you are. You are quite...young for a priestess, are you not?"

Cate shook her head. "I am still in training. My name is Cate McEwen and I am Druid priestess, Novate of Maeve, quester of souls and Guardian of the Gate."

Sakura bowed. "I am Sakura, Priestess to the great Queen Nefertiti and the almighty goddess Aset."

Cate motioned for Sakura to sit down and took a stone next to her. "And what a powerful priestess you must be in order to come here. It is not an easy journey and not all of us can do so."

Sakura glanced about. "And what is this place?"

"This is my Dreamworld. It is where I come to communicate with souls who have come to me from past and future. It is where we maintain our own separate identity when communing with each other."

"Ah. Then you have done this before."

Cate nodded. "Indeed. Many times."

Sakura nodded, taking it all in. "Then as I understamd it, you and I are one."

"Yes. You and I share a soul that traverses time."

Sakura nodded slowly. "The Ka does continue on," Sakura muttered this to herself.

"The Ka is known as the soul in my time, and yes, it does move on. *Ours* has moved on through time in many different incarnations, both male and female."

Sakura's eyes lit up. "Most excellent. How much later from my time is yours?"

Cate shrugged. "I live in sixty-four *anno domini*."

Sakura nodded slowly. "Ah, after the Christ. You are much further into the future than I expected."

Cate's eyebrows lifted. "How do you know this? Your language is not—"

"You are not the first I have journeyed to, Cate. I have knowledge of this man they call Christ, Son of God, but I was never quite sure how I knew it. I exist almost fourteen hundred years before your time in the beautiful land of Egypt."

Cate nodded. "That was so long ago and much has changed."

"And I see much has not. In our respective times, Cate, we have been charged with saving the goddesses, mine before the Christ comes, and yours, after. The goddess and our feminine powers, threaten man at the very core of his being."

"Not all men."

"Of course not, but the men in power? Oh yes. The goddess is peace, nurturing, harmony, birth, understanding and love. She is all that is good in people. Man cannot use his baseness as an advantage when those qualities prevail. Man can only be his aggressive, chest-beating, war mongering self in a competitive, chaotic, unharmonious and hate-filled society. Brute force is his weapon, his power, and there is no need of that brute force when the goddess reigns supreme. That is why we must fight to keep her alive, Cate, because if we do not, man will destroy the very planet upon which we stand."

Cate simply stared at this dark-skinned woman who held herself with so much poise and respect. Maeve would love her.

"Maeve already does."

Cate whirled around to see Maeve walking through the mist, her long robe flowing behind her. The mist closed around the trailing hem of her robe.

Taking both of Cate's hands in hers, Maeve brought them to her lips and kissed the backs of each. Then, she turned to Sakura and nodded. "It is good to see you again, Sakura."

Cate's mouth hung open.

"And you as well. It has been a long time." Rising, Sakura bowed low and then embraced Maeve in a manner much like Cate always did.

Maeve released her and turned to a stunned Cate. "Be not so surprised, Catie, for there is much for you to know and so much more for you to learn." Turning to the firepit, Maeve flicked her fingers at it and a tall blaze crackled instantly. Reaching into her pouch, she sprinkled an orange powder over the flames, which spit and sizzled.

"I know you are surprised, but we can discuss that later. Right now, we need to help Sakura." Maeve led Cate to the firepit and tossed a blue powder into the orange flames which leapt up and turned into one sheet of fire.

When Cate peered into the heart of the flames, she saw a very handsome, incredibly dark young man wearing what looked like a soldier's outfit from long, long ago.

"Catie, I did not come from Gaul just in search of you, though that was my main motive. I came to aid in our calling by enabling you to use the Sacred Places we have found thus far. It had always been my job to help you find your past selves. It is my vocation. It has always been so."

Sakura rose and waved her hand across the fire. The young Egyptian soldier was replaced by an island in a mist barely visible through the fog.

"Avalon," Cate murmured.

Sakura nodded. "When I was but a young girl beginning my studies, the Lady came to me. I knew not how, but I *did* know she was very real and had a plan for my life...for *our* lives. She came to me with a frightening vision; the state of the goddess and the fate of a world that no longer knew her. She showed me visions of a future where citizens of countries killed each other for centuries over a small strip of land called the Holy Land. She showed me a culture where children were killed because their parents did not follow all of the precepts of the one church. She showed me the mass destruction of whole societies by people called missionaries. In short, she showed me a world of death and decay because *She* is no longer the central part of our lives."

Cate reached for Maeve's hand, but said nothing.

"This Lady of the Lake bade me not only to become a powerful priestess in my own time, but to travel through time to bid as many of my incarnations as possible to keep alive the memory of a world where the goddess reigns supreme. For only in remembering can we save ourselves."

Cate gripped Maeve's hand tighter. "But how is it you met Maeve? You and she are not one."

"No, we are not. However, Maeve and Tarik—my loved one—are. The young man in the mist Maeve showed you is he. Before Tarik was a soldier, he was training to be a priest. His parents were powerful priests and when they foresaw his spiritual powers would pale besides physical prowess, they sent him through in order to determine the right path for him. Once there, he made contact with Maeve and told her his greatest desire was to be with me always. He would do anything to be with me for the rest of eternity. He showed Maeve there was someone who would love her forever and help in this quest if only Maeve was willing to leave home. That someone was you, Cate."

Maeve squeezed Cate's hand. "And for you, Catie, I was more than willing."

"That was when he and Maeve devised their plan."

Cate turned to Maeve. "You had a plan?"

Maeve nodded. "Of course. I apologize for never telling you, but all of this did not start with us, Catie. It began with Tarik's love of Sakura and their desire to please the goddesses."

"Actually," Sakura interjected. "It all started with the Lady. She came as far back as she dared. She may have gone further, but I have no memories to access. All I know is what *our* mission is, no matter what time we are in."

Cate nodded slowly. "Why did you not tell me sooner, Maeve?"

Maeve brought Cate's hand to her lips once more and kissed

it. "Catie, there is so much you do not yet know. There is a time and a place for all wisdom to be revealed, and now was the right time for Sakura to come here."

"Do you know Jessie?" Cate asked.

Sakura shook her head. "I do not. Traveling through the stones is not my main quest at the moment. The goddess and her followers have been forced underground. My job now is to keep them believing."

"Is that why you have come?"

Sakura nodded. "My people are at the precipice of losing their belief system forever. My queen wishes to help me, but at what cost, I know not. I have come to you, Cate, because I am afraid I am losing the battle even before it has begun. Tarik, who is now a soldier and the Chief of the palace guards, says that Akhenaten is planning to seek out any remaining believers and destroy them all. I would have sent Tarik through, but ever since he chose the sword, his spiritual powers have waned quite a bit and I will not lose him at this point in my life."

Maeve nodded and lightly touched Sakura's shoulder. "There is much to do and more to know, my friend, but I believe Cate can be of help to you."

Cate turned quickly to Maeve. "What of you?"

"I wish I could be of help here, Catie, but Lachlan has need of me north and I swore to him I would come if he should ever have need of my healing powers. Already, I have stayed too long. I am quite confident you can help Sakura. I have trained you well, my love. When you are done here, come to the garden so we might say goodbye." Maeve kissed Cate's lips softly before disappearing into the mist.

Sakura's eyes trailed after the priestess. "She is so much like Tarik, it makes my head spin."

Cate bit the inside of her mouth. "She has that effect on people. What I do not understand, however, is what it is she thinks *I* can do to help. I have not been questing for very long, I'm afraid, but if I cannot help you, I know one who can."

21st Century AD

"Jessie?"

Jessie glanced up from the final page of the journal. Ceara and Tanner both looked like she felt. The horror of the murders oozed off the page as she read.

I can hear them screaming...or perhaps that is all in my head. It seems I can no longer distinguish between what is real and what is not. Someone, I'm sure I know who it is...is coming after them...or me... or it...perhaps all of the above. A small part of me yearns to help, but I am afraid I would only wind up as a victim myself. At least this settles any issues about going back. Ah, I hear my wife calling for me. Her voice weak. Now, silence. I sit and listen as if a movie were playing in the hall. Now, chaos, as though the house were being turned inside out and is screaming because of it. I know what he is searching for, but he will never have it. No one will. The secret, the key, dies with me.

It is time to return for the final time. I am anxious and excited about beginning anew. The priest cannot stop me. Townsend cannot find me, and no one will ever truly know who I am.

I am coming, my darling.

"I can see why the professor was so defensive." Ceara offered. "His grandfather did nothing while his family was being butchered."

"How sad. Even knowing what we know, we have no idea if those ghosts have come from the portal, if they've chosen to stay with the house all these years, or if they're even talking about Albert, but this journal borders on nuts."

"You think they want Daniel to bring Albert's soul back to them?"

"That would not be possible," Ceara answered. "Albert died in 1922, or thereabouts, and this is 2012. That was ninety years ago. His soul could have reincarnated once or a dozen times since then, and if the soul could currently be inhabiting a body, it is already here in this time."

"Maybe we can't find him in *this* time, but I'm pretty sure we can find him in Nefertiti's." Jessie opened a search engine and typed in *Nefertiti*.

"The priest," Tanner said. "All that talk about a priest. Maybe he knows he was a priest in Akhenaten's court."

Jessie and Ceara stared at each other. "A priest in Akhenaten's court wouldn't be that hard to find."

Ceara laid her hand on top of Jessie's "You're thinking of going there, aren't you?"

Jessie looked up and blinked. "And doing what? Ask him to turn his soul over to me? You know I can't control when and where I go from the portal. I walk in, and I end up in the grove or on a pirate ship."

Ceara nodded. "Only because I have not yet taught you how. We would need far more information before you go anywhere, my dear." Ceara took her glasses off and wiped them on one of her scarves. "Let's assess this, shall we? What we have are three ghosts who may or may not be connected to the man who used the portal to traverse back to ancient Egypt. We *think*, we don't *know* for sure, mind you, but we *think* Albert left his body for good when he went to Egypt the final time. If we can make the spirits understand that, perhaps they will leave Daniel alone."

Jessie nodded. "And what if we're totally wrong?"

"Then we go back to the drawing board."

It was a little after one in the morning when Jessie finally put the last web page down in her mounting stack of research. Tanner had already gone to bed, and Ceara had taken her tea out to the deck…something she could seldom do at this time of night in Oregon.

"You have to love this California weather, eh, my dear?" Ceara said, when Jessie sat in the Adirondack chair next to her. "So, what did you find out?"

Jessie inhaled the warm salt air. "There's so much to know. Let's see, Akhenaten begins a new religion, which angers a lot of people. Nefertiti becomes queen and appears to help him with the transition from polytheism to monotheism, but something happens around the twelfth year of his reign. Nefertiti either died or disappeared, no one knows for sure. Now, here's a fascinating little tidbit in one of history's mysteries: Nefertiti, who is, by all accounts deeply loved by her husband, disappears. Now here's the weird part. His nickname for her was Nefernefraten. Well, not long after she disappears, a new name enters the history books. His name is Smenkhara. Guess what Akhenaten called him?"

"Smenny?"

Jessie laughed out loud. "Nefernefraten."

Ceara suddenly sat up. "What?"

"Uh-huh. Weird, huh? Not only that, but Smenkhara—"

"Smenny. I like that better."

"Smenny appears on the scene, and shortly after, serves as *co-regent* to Akhenaten."

"Wait. The Pharaoh agreed to *share* his power with Smenny, a complete newcomer to court? Why on earth would he do that?"

"Good question. The *real* question historians are asking is: was Smenny really a man? There are those who think not." Jessie rifled through her notes until she came to page five. "Two years after Nefertiti disappears from history, Smenny appears on the scene and is given the same nickname as Nefertiti. They think that Smenny was around sixteen at the time, but there are conflicting reports about his gender and whether or not Akhenaten was sexually involved with him or her. No one really knows who this person was or where he or she came from, but come on! The nickname alone is a dead giveaway."

"So what are your thoughts?"

"I think Albert went back to Egypt to save his beloved Nefertiti. After getting her out of danger, she returned in the guise of a young man."

"Very interesting," Tanner said softly as he poked his head around the corner. "So, we might very well have a twenty-first century man in the eighteenth dynasty of Egypt near the time Nefertiti vanishes from history replaced by a man or woman who acts as co-regent of Egypt."

Ceara rubbed her hands together. "This is just the sort of mystery you can sink your teeth into, my dear."

Jessie shook her head. "But even knowing all of that, we're still no closer to finding out what it is those spirits want from Daniel."

Ceara sipped her tea and then studied the tea leaves at the bottom of her cup. "No? You think there's a connection between our dead Albert and the missing queen, well, that means we have to consider everything that happened in that house."

"I don't know what to think. I am trying not to jump to conclusions."

"Then I suggest you sleep on it, my dear. The time will come soon enough for you to act."

"Act? You think I'm going to have to go back there?"

Ceara rose slowly from her chair and stretched. "Frankly, I don't know what to think, but I can guarantee you this...there's something you're *supposed* to learn...something you're *supposed* to be doing, and time will reveal what that is."

Staring out into the darkness of the Pacific Ocean, Jessie knew Ceara was right. It was only a matter of time.

When Jessie closed her eyes, she felt the familiar tingle at the base of her skull. This particular "nudge" told her Cate had come through wishing to see her.

"Coming," Jessie murmured, reaching deep within herself to the path to her Dreamworld. She had gotten much better at accessing it in the weeks past, as Ceara drilled her over and over again how to be more successful and quicker at travel.

As she relaxed into a state that would allow her to make contact with Cate, Jessie smiled. She loved going there, to the stone circle around the firepit and the sheet of mist separating the real world from the past. While she had been practicing with Ceara, Jessie often went there just to sit on the rocks and feel the energy...to remember times when her soul was doing other things with other people.

"You are getting better at remembering," Cate said, when Jessie was fully within the stone circle.

"Hey you." Walking over to the smaller woman with the flaming red hair, Jessie hugged her tightly. It wasn't until she pulled away from the hug that she saw the dark-skinned woman she had seen from the fire. "Well hello there. Who's your friend?"

Sakura bowed. "My name is Sakura."

"Sakura is from long ago in a land called Egypt."

Jessie studied Sakura and was taken aback by the intensity of the kohl-lined eyes, the hauteur of her demeanor, and the overall beauty of her face. Slightly taller than Jessie, Sakura was lean with a stomach that, in her terms, could only be described as a washboard. Her long black hair hung in single plait down her back and was adorned with various gold items. Her skirt, if it could be called that, had teals and reds unlike any colors Jessie had ever seen. Her feet wore leather sandals that laced halfway up her calves, sandals that were all the rage in California this year. Two thick gold arm bands in the shape of serpents clasped to her slender biceps, but the gold in them is not what caught Jessie's eye. Around Sakura's neck hung the ankh.

"It is an honor," Jessie said, her eyes fixated on the ankh. Reflexively, Jessie touched her own—a motion that did not go unnoticed by Sakura.

"I see the ankh has managed to find itself even further into the future than I would have imagined." Sakura grinned, and Jessie noted her flawless white teeth.

"Cate sent it to me as an answer to a question."

Sakura looked over at Cate. "Indeed?"

"Cate is an amazing Druid priestess, Sakura, capable of powerful magic. She represents us well in her time."

"As I understand you shall in yours."

Jessie blushed and shook her head. "I wish that were true, but at the moment, I am pretty much lower than a novice. I have so much to learn and often don't even know where to begin."

Sakura sat on a stone next to Jessie's and beckoned her to sit down. All three women took a seat and Cate bade the flames to rise, which they did in two precise columns that spun like twin tornadoes.

"Cate speaks very highly of you, Jessie, so you can do no less for yourself." Sakura adjusted one of her armbands.

"Sorry. It's just…as far as modernday priestesses go, I'm really an amateur."

"Cate tells me you helped her and her people escape complete annihilation. That does not sound like a novice."

"I answered Cate's call. I will always answer Cate's call. It's sort of what I do now." Jessie shrugged. She felt humbled in the presence of these two priestesses.

This made Sakura laugh. "Upon my word, I did not imagine you to be so lacking in pride. If what you do, Jessie, is protect the longevity of the goddesses, then you ought to be walking with your head tall and proud. It is a meaningful position you have, and not to be taken lightly."

"Oh, believe me, I don't. It's just…well—"

Cate finished for her. "The weight of the one male god has oppressed so many people for so many centuries, Jessie must learn how to shrug off those fetters and find a place for herself as a priestess in a world that denies their very existence."

Sakura nodded. "I see. It must be a dark, cold world you live in, bereft of the loving arms of the Goddess."

"More than you can even imagine."

Cate reached over and took Jessie's hand. "Jessie has a knowledge of a different type, and it has aided us not once, but twice. She is far more powerful than even she realizes."

"Then is it she I have ventured here for?"

"You came to me, Sakura, because I am an open vessel for any and all of us who wish to or need to pass through. It is my training that has enabled me to reach through and take your hand. Jessie is no different. She just does not yet know the extent of her own powers. The important thing is that she remembers. She remembers quite quickly, and the combined memories she receives from all she meets will make her far more powerful and greater than ever you or I could hope to be."

Sakura smiled at Jessie. "Then it would appear I have come to the right place after all. Let me show you why I have come." She motioned to the flames once more and they parted, showing a man sitting on a throne having a conversation with what looked like a priest. His long, white robe was different from the shorter kilt the king wore.

Sakura's voice was somber. "There is an evil threatening Egypt and our goddesses, but I cannot yet see it clearly enough to know how to stop it. Akhenaten, my queen's husband, has transformed our religion to only Aten, thereby raising himself to be higher than priests and even politicians. He has become so intent with his new religion, the whole of the empire suffers greatly beneath the weight of the change. Even now my beloved Tarik says Akhenaten is sending out soldiers to torture and destroy anyone speaking out against Aten."

"And that would be you," Jessie said softly.

Sakura nodded. "As well as his wife and queen."

"Whoa. Wait a second." This came as a surprise to Jessie. "Everything I've read said Nefertiti *aided* in the transformation from one religion to the other. There was even a stone block from an Aten temple used as filling in a pylon at the temple of Karnak. It *shows* Queen Nefertiti hitting unfortunate foes. Were those foes Atenists?"

Sakura nodded.

Jessie held her hand up. "So Nefertiti does *not* support her husband's new religion?"

"Outwardly, of course. She must. But make no mistake: Queen Nefertiti serves Aset and only Aset. Her actions are necessary to spare both her own life and the power of Aset."

Jessie recalled the page she had read about Aset. "The great Lady, God-mother, Queen of all Gods, Lady of Life..." Jessie looked over at Cate who looked perplexed. "You and I know her by the name of Isis. Nefertiti is a follower of Isis, and Sakura is one of her priestesses. The followers of Isis have had to go to ground otherwise Ahkenaten would seek them out and kill them. This is what you fear most, isn't it, Sakura?"

Sakura nodded. "Indeed. Ahkenaten has a single-minded goal of ridding his palace of heretics, and he has a great deal of help from his priests."

Jessie leaned forward, choosing her next words carefully. "Is there one priest among the court who might...be *in love* with Nefertiti?"

Sakura waved this off. "My queen is so beautiful men and women both fall in love with her."

"This man is...different."

Sakura's eyebrows rose. "Oh? In what manner?"

Jessie looked at Cate for approval, which she received in the form of a nod. "He is from my time."

Sakura's eyes narrowed and she pulled on her earlobe as she thought. "There is a vision I have seen...and in that vision, I saw you, Jessie, and a cold, dark evil spreading its arms around Nefertiti. This evil wants to take her away from us—away from court. Away. Could that evil be the man you speak of?"

Jessie silently reminded herself there was no such thing as a coincidence. "I'm pretty sure the evil you see is our guy. He left his time in order to be with Queen Nefertiti. All I can tell you about him is that he is a priest in Akhenaten's court who returned to your time because he is in love with her."

Cate was up now and pacing back and forth. "A man from the future dabbling in the past would have serious ramifications for us all."

"That's just it, Cate. He isn't dabbling. What he's doing could endanger more than just Nefertiti." For the next ten minutes, Jessie told Cate and Sakura all she knew about Albert Gibson and his obsessions.

When she finished, Sakura cracked her neck to one side and pulled herself up to her highest height.

"This would be very dangerous, indeed. If this Al-bert man has knowledge into the events of our time, he could very well sway the pharaoh into believing he has the sight or some other power leading that fool to believe he has become a God. I'm afraid Ahkenaten is easily swayed when it comes to his religion. If Al-bert was in a position to give Akhenaten the power to crush those who do not believe as he does, we would all be in terrible danger."

Jessie knew it was not her place, nor was it permissible to tell Sakura how events would eventually play out. Instead, she leaned forward toward Sakura. "Before we do anything, we need to make sure the man I speak of is actually there. It is possible he relinquished his soul to the past and has receded into the background of whatever priest he once was. If that is the case, then we don't have to worry as much."

"And you are sure this Al-bert man has no powers."

Jessie nodded. "He is no priest. He is a historian…a man who digs up the past and studies it. I'm wondering if he chose to return to the soul of the priest and has not possessed the body or done anything other than find an old home for his soul." Jessie picked up a rock and tossed it into a nearby stream.

"It's just too hard to know right now."

"And we need to know." Cate shook her head. "That still makes him dangerous."

Jessie nodded. "I agree, but not as dangerous as Quinn was when he came to your time. Possession is very different than returning to a past life, and Quinn was very good at possession."

Cate nodded. "Agreed. But to answer the problems you are dealing with, Jessie, if the spirits are crying out for justice, and they want this man's soul, if we can find and send his soul back to his own time, they will take him wherever it is they have waited to go."

Sakura nodded. "That would solve your spirit problem and remove the darkness from around my queen." She parted the flames to show Akhenaten sitting on his throne and staring into space. "But we must hurry before Akhenaten starts sending his troops out to crush the likes of me. Jessie, is there any way you know of that we could lure this priest out into the open? Make him show himself?"

Jessie thought for a moment. "Albert was an accomplished archaeologist. Let me see what mystery *really* pushed his buttons and see if we can lure him out with that. If we can get him to respond to something he once loved, then we'll know his consciousness is a more active part of the priest. If that's the case, we'll know what to do."

Cate chuckled as she often did when hearing Jessie speak. "Push. His. Buttons. Another one of your strange sayings."

Jessie returned Cate's smile for a quick moment before turning back to Sakura. "Albert is a digger, and what diggers do is try to find answers to some ancient mystery or secret."

Sakura frowned. "Do you not have historians who can tell you what happened during our time?"

Jessie glanced over at Cate, who nodded for her to explain. "We do...but...well...along the way, your writings fell into disuse, and eventually, no one could translate them."

Sakura's hand went to her mouth. "That is impossible."

"Not only is it possible, it's true. Your entire history was lost for over three thousand years until someone found a stone that acted like a translator. That tablet was only discovered one hundred years ago. Since then, we've been able to decipher your language on the pyramid walls and tombs and…"

A quick intake of air made Jessie stop, and Sakura held her stomach as if in pain. "Our tombs…our pyramids…desecrated by your historians?"

Jessie shook her head. "Oh no. Tomb robbers got to them long before historians. I'm sorry, Sakura, I shouldn't have said anything."

Sakura sat up straighter, a sadness in her eyes she could not hide. "The curse of this quest is discovering the painful truths of what happens to a people. One cannot only hear the good. As hard as it is to hear, it is more important that I save my queen, so please, continue."

With a heavy heart, Jessie told Sakura as much of the story as she could. "The tombs and pyramids were vandalized by local villagers who then sold the treasures to museums and people who could afford them. Egypt was rich and mighty in your time, Sakura, but its greatness saw a gradual decline until it is now one of the poorest countries in the region."

Sakura looked past Jessie's shoulder and into the fire. It was several moments before she spoke. "And you say this Al-bert person was one who tried to solve the puzzles and riddles left by my people."

Jessie nodded. "Yes. He was fascinated by your culture. I think if we can find out what his greatest mystery was, then we might very well bring him out into the open. After that, we can put an end to his travels."

Sakura slid off the stone and stared down into the fire. "That is an excellent plan. I would want this button-pushing man caught before he brings any harm to my queen or my people. If he has ill intent then he must be disposed of." Sakura turned to Cate. "It saddens me to have to leave so soon, but my heart aches and I need to return to my time to grieve in peace. Please understand."

Cate took one of Sakura's hands in hers. "No apologies necessary, Sakura. Jessie will do everything she can to uncover the darkness you fear and remove him from your people. She is young, but she is an amazing quester who is brave and strong. I trust her completely."

Nodding, Sakura bowed to Jessie. "You are so young, still, and yet, I know you are capable of doing everything Cate believes you can. Thank you for everything." With that, Sakura disappeared.

"I told her too much, didn't I?"

"You did what you thought best. You cannot move forward, Jessie, if you question every action you take. Her grief is understandable, but it is not your fault. One cannot ask for your help and then place restrictions on how much you disclose to them. Sakura knew that when she came through. She will be fine."

Jessie sighed. "We have our work cut out for us on this one."

Cate chuckled. "We? I do not believe *I* can be of any help to you on this one, my friend. I know nothing about ancient Egypt or the people you speak of."

"But you know me and Sak—"

"Jessie, you must learn your way just as I must learn mine." Turning, Cate tossed a yellowish powder into the fire, which spit and sputtered. "Let me share some of the wisdom Maeve has imparted to me." Cate waited for Jessie to stand beside her. "We are not wholly of this world, you and I; not in it, not really outside of it. Our job is to sense the spirit in everything we see and communicate with them so we understand what is happening around us. Spirits live in all things, they move through all things, and they have the capacity to teach us in ways we cannot imagine. What you need to do is to learn how to listen. The goddess will move you in the right direction, but you need to be able to hear her better. Listen without question. Listen with the Druid and Egyptian priestesses within you. If you do this, you will receive the answers sooner than you think." Cate held her hands out, palms down, and slowed the flames down. The picture before them was of Daniel sitting in his room just staring. "Your brother is trying to hear. He acknowledges their existence, but he is not a Druid and cannot hear them. You might if you trained yourself to hear—to truly hear outside of yourself. Perhaps they would have more to say if they knew you were listening."

Jessie nodded slowly. "I understand."

"When you return to your world, I want you to practice. Go to your favorite tree and sit and listen. Your training as a priestess cannot move forward until you master this. It is time for you to devote more of your energy to your studies. It is time for you to be what you know you are."

Nodding, Jessie straightened her back. "I will, but right now, I was hoping you'd take a walk with me and tell me more about your studies, about Maeve, about your new life in Alba without Lachlan."

"You mean...just talk...like friends?"

Jessie smiled softly. "Yeah, Cate. Just like friends."

21st Century AD

When they cast away from the dock in California, Jessie caught her reflection in the calm water. She had grown so much in the three years since she'd left San Francisco. Even her face had changed. She looked...wiser, if that was possible, and she had Cate to thank for it.

She and Cate had talked for hours in the Dreamworld as they walked among the prettiest wildflowers Jessie had ever seen. Cate shared stories of her childhood, of the day she met Maeve, and what life was like now that the old ways were being replaced by this new Christian "cult."

In all of her college courses, no professor had ever referred to Christianity as a cult. She supposed that might inflame quite a few students who were now followers of a religion that had successfully supplanted ninety percent of the old religions. Cate called it *a cult of the oppressed and downtrodden*. Jessie smiled when she said it.

A cult.

Jessie sighed as she stood up. She wondered if the modern-day Christians had any idea that the religions they were now calling cults were in the slow-moving process of taking their people back—of reclaiming what was almost lost. She wondered if it knew, like you know when you're being watched, that its day of ruling the world was coming to a end.

It wasn't incomprehensible considering the corrupt nature of the church and the financial ruin it was facing as its pedophiliac priests were moved from parish to parish to hide and extend their damage. Did they not think their day of ultimate second class status would arrive? Did they really believe the Goddess was banished for eternity? Did they truly think relegating her to the status of Virgin Mary would keep her down in the shadows?

Jessie wondered.

"The Goddess will never truly vanish," Cate had said. "But it is time for *you* to find the one within you. You alone can connect to her in a way that will change you and how you see the world forever. It is time, Jessie Ferguson. Be not afraid. Trust yourself as surely as you trust me and Maeve."

Jessie wondered if it had been fear that had kept her from embracing the Goddess. Oh sure, she had accepted the existence of the portal and the possibility of soul travel. She had even delighted in the concept of past lives and the connection of *anim cara*. But something along the way had prevented her from complete investment in the Goddess; the truth of the Goddess was all about her, but her wisdom, her way, was not a path Jessie had truly accepted.

Until now.

Now, her doubts about herself had vanished, and she relished the idea of wearing the mantle of priestess. Now, her confidence was stronger and she was ready to invest one hundred percent into the Goddess's path.

When the boat finally pulled out, Jessie stood on the bow with the wind blowing in her face and through her hair like a lover's breath. Was it the Goddess's touch she was feeling even now? Had She heard her conversation with Cate and wanted her to know, to really know the path awaiting her? Closing her eyes, Jessie opened her spirit and felt the cold breeze flow through her, swirling around her as a small tornado might.

It was time.

Closing her eyes, Jessie inhaled deeply and softly whispered, *"By the blood of the womb of all things of the earth are made holy, of the earth, of the tree of Life, blood of the womb, sacred and holy, seal the vows I make this day. From me to the Goddess, from this world to the Otherworld, the link is forged, ever to stay; so might it be. My vows are sealed, never to be revoked. My mind will ever turn to the Goddess. My vows are sealed, never to be revoked. My mouth will know when to speak and when to keep silent. My vows are sealed, never to be revoked. I will create in beauty. I will create in peace and justice. My vows are sealed, never to be revoked. I will love under will. I will love honestly. My vows are sealed, never to be revoked. I will kneel to no one, yet I will honor my Goddess, and like the willow, I can bend. My vows are sealed, never to be revoked. In beauty, I will walk all the days of my life. The Goddess is in me, and my vows are sealed, never to be revoked."*

Jessie did not know how much time had passed, but when she slowly tilted her head forward and opened her eyes, she knew a new life awaited her. She was not the same person she had been a moment ago. She would never again be that woman. She was reborn now, something outside of time, something important. Something meaningful…just as Cate had said.

Jessie smiled to herself as she heard Cate's strong voice echo the words she'd just spoken. Jessie had never heard the vows of the ritual she had just uttered, yet they were as familiar to her as the *Lord's Prayer*. She had said them in another time, in another body, and she remembered.

She remembered.

Without planning, without preparation, Jessie had accepted the Goddess and given freely of herself, and for the first time in her life, she felt whole; free and whole.

"Thank you, Cate," Jessie whispered, reveling in the salt air on her face and the warmth in her soul. She was a different person now and wondered if anyone else would notice.

Turning from the railing, Jessie bumped into Ceara, whose eyes were misty and her face smiling. "Oh my dear. You did it. You really did it." Taking Jessie in her arms, Ceara hugged her tightly. "I am so proud of you."

"You…you can tell?"

Pulling away, Ceara was beaming. "Of course I can tell. I can see it in your eyes. Silly girl, if you *feel* so very different inside, don't you think it shows on the outside?"

Nodding, Jessie stood back and studied Ceara. "I don't know what happened. I closed my eyes and…well, it just felt like I knew what I was doing."

"When the Goddess calls, we must listen. She has been calling you for some time now, but you were not ready to listen. We all come to her when we are ready."

"I'm ready."

"Yes, you are, and you have been ready longer than you realize. Now, my dear, now we may begin your lessons in earnest. Be prepared. We have a great deal of work to do. Rest while you can."

As Ceara walked away, Jessie turned back to the coastline and ran her fingers through her hair. A slow smile spread across her face.

Today was the first day of the rest of her life.

14th Century BCE

"Why did she not come?" Sakura asked Tarik as he approached her beneath her favorite cedar.

Wiping the sweat off his bald head, Tarik sat next to her. "She fears Akhenaten is having everyone in the family followed."

"Why on earth would she believe that?"

"His priests have finally convinced him the traitors he seeks are nearby, skulking about, waiting for a chance to strike. He is beginning to trust no one and has put us all on alert to watch for any odd comings and goings."

"Even the queen?"

Tarik nodded. "The movement against Aten in lower Egypt grows stronger. The hold Akhenaten has over Egypt is waning and the priest has convinced him he must retaliate There are many who would kill him in order to return to our old ways. He is becoming afraid of his own shadow and seeks to destroy those he believes lives in it." Tarik reached for her hand. The night air was warm despite a small lingering cloud cover from the afternoon. "He is even beginning to believe that Mene was poisoned."

"He is losing his senses, isn't he?"

Tarik shook his head. "Not losing them, my love, giving them away. The priest's power grows stonger every day."

Sakura nodded. This did not surprise her. "Then she is bound to the palace for the time being."

"She feels that is wisest. It is not time to make him suspicious of her, so she is willing to remain where he feels she is safe." Tarik pulled her closer. "I worry for you, my love. The king is not to be trifled with and the way his mind is plaguing him, all it would take would be one word from his priests and…and… and I cannot even bear to say what might happen."

"He would make an example of me, to be sure. It is how he has always been as our king."

"As would he his queen as well. He may love her more than life, but he would give his own to make Atenism the only religion in the kingdom."

"Do not underestimate her, Tarik. She is a very strong, very wise woman, and he is deeply in love with her. He would not allow his religious fervor to bring harm to her."

"That is where you are wrong, Sakura. He is a zealot, and as long as the queen stands with him, she will be safe. Do not underestimate him or his religious zeal."

They sat in silence with their own thoughts for a long time. Finally, when Sakura spoke, she did so in a hushed tone. "I have sought help."

Tarik released her hand. "You did not—"

"I did."

He turned to fully face her. "We had an agreement, Sakura."

Sakura nodded, feeling him pull away. "Yes, we did. We said I would not go through *unless* our lives were at risk. Well, my queen's life is in danger, and by extension, so are ours. You said so yourself."

"She is *our* queen, Sakura, and you do not know this for certain. You should have spoken with me about it. We have an arrangement you violated."

"I apologize, my love, but there is an incredible darkness around her, Tarik. I'm certain you feel it as well."

"And so you thought going through would relieve her of this darkness? Without speaking to me first?"

Sakura nodded. "There was no time. I heard the call and I answered."

"And?"

"And there are others who can help. Good people...people I would trust with my life."

He turned back to her. "*People?* You saw more than one?"

Brushing her hair from her face, Sakura nodded slightly. "Yes. People. We were all together, but there is one far ahead of our time who knows...many things, and who believes she has the power to help us save the Goddess."

"One who...knows. Then she is—"

"Yes. She and I are one."

Tarik lowered his voice to a whisper. "What...what was it like?"

"It was cool and misty, like Avalon, and they sat around a firepit and watched as the worlds flickered by. They believe, my love. They believe as we do, and they understand what is happening. They...*know.*"

"They do?"

Sakura nodded. "As you saw long ago, when you went through and found Maeve. I found Cate and another one of us from the far future. Well, they are me, and I am them, and the one known as Cate is the soul spirit of Maeve."

Tarik's quick intake of breath said more than any words could.

"Yes, my love, we manage to find each other far, far into the future, as we always knew. We are together there as Cate and Maeve."

"Maeve?" Tarik shook his head. "It has been so very long since I have seen her."

"Indeed. I would have recognized your Ka anywhere. Cate is her student and she is a very powerful priestess."

"And this Cate can help us?"

Sakura shook her head. "Not as much as Jessie, a young girl from a very distant future. It is this Jessie who has answers. She is just beginning her priestess training, but the power and strength I felt from her…she has an ability she is not yet aware of."

"I do not see how this Jessie can be of so much help if she is so young. What can she do for us?"

"It is an odd and interesting tale, my love. Already, she told me a man from her time might have returned from the portal within one of Akhenaten's priests, and he could be causing problems for us if we do not quickly locate him." Sakura let this sit while Tarik thought about it.

"A priest, eh?"

"Yes. A single body has the capacity to hold multiple Ka. It is neither healthy, nor is it good, but it is possible this man named Al-bert is within a priest seeking to control it. His could be the darkness I feel."

"A priest who knows our future could do remarkable things… could get Akhenaten to believe he was capable of miracles, of magic. This is darkness, indeed, my love, and though I am not pleased you went through without discussion, it appears a very good thing that you did. No wonder Ahkenaten cannot make up his own mind. Someone in his inner circle is twisting his mind."

Sakura nodded. "Which is why I sent for Nefertiti. We need to warn her. She needs to find out who this man might be without endangering herself. It is so important we discover not only his identity but what it is he is after."

Tarik turned to Sakura. "If he already knows Nefertiti worships Aset, then he is playing a very astute game. If that is true, then time is not our ally."

Sakura nodded. "It is quite possible he does not yet know anything, but yes, if he does, she is in danger."

"Is it not recorded? If this Jessie is so far into the future, does she not already know? We have recorded so much of our history for the future to know what a great civilization we are. Surely she must know what happened."

Taking Tarik's hand, Sakura brushed her lips lightly against his knuckles. "It is a heartbreaking tale, my love, and one which I shall spare you the details. Much of our way is lost to the people of the future. The people in the future actually *lost* the ability to read our language. I believe Jessie called them higher-oh-glyphs." She felt Tarik's fingers tighten. "I know. It is a sad, sad thing, but the men of the future know even less about us than Cate and Maeve."

"How can this be?"

Sakura shrugged. "Things change, my love. Egypt...*our* Egypt, does not remain the great empire it is."

Tarik looked away and drew in a breath. "I would rather not hear more. We ought to be happy it is as great as it is and leave the future to its own fate."

"Even while our present is being threatened by it? When you left the priesthood, you did not leave your passion for our land and our people."

Looking into her face, his eyes were sad. "You are right. We must tell Nefertiti about this and then I must discover which priest might be hiding a man from the future within himself."

"Please do nothing until I hear from Jessie. She believes there is a way to bring him out of hiding...a mystery of some kind. This man...this man named Al-bert...was in love with Nefertiti and enjoyed some sort of mystery involving her or Egypt. If Jessie can find out what that is, we might be able to drive him from hiding and send him into oblivion."

Tarik nodded slowly. "Then you plan on going back?"

"No, my love. I will not go through the stones again unless we talk about it first. Jessie has agreed to come to me when she has what we need. I need you to get Nefertiti to me at once so I can explain everything to her. She will believe it coming from me."

"Will you tell her...everything?"

"No. She need not know how we know what we know. She need only know one of the priests carries within him the darkness I have been sensing and that he is a danger."

Tarik nodded. "Agreed."

Sakura pulled him to her and kissed him softly. "Forgive me, my love, for breaking our agreement, but this is just as much for Aset as it is for the queen. I do not wish to see her light grow dim beneath the rays of Aten."

Tarik ran his hands over her shoulders and pulled her to

him once more. "My soul sings knowing I never truly have to let you go. Knowing that we find each other, as we have always wished is reward enough for this life."

Snuggling into his embrace, Sakura kissed the side of his neck. "I might be able to conjure up another sort of reward for you, my love. Would you be so willing?"

Pulling her to him, Tarik leaned his forehead against hers. "More than willing."

And though his words and lips heated her skin and the very air, Sakura felt an inexplicable chill. The darkness was closing in on them.

21st Century AD

The sun was riding high as they neared the halfway point back to Oregon. Jessie was sitting in one of the deck chairs when Ceara joined her with her customary cup of hot tea.

"So tell me, my dear, what happened this morning that propelled you to the Goddess?"

Jessie replayed her conversation with Sakura and Cate and the new quest they were soon to embark upon. When she finished, Jessie put her hands behind her head and sighed. "It was just time, I suppose. It was like I needed to be told to listen. Even though I was hearing her voice in the wind and feeling her touch on my spirit, I never really *heard* her. I have no idea why I resisted, but I am done doing so."

"And you do now?"

"Oh yes. I hear her loud and clear."

"And what is she saying to you?"

"She's saying we need to help Sakura, and in helping her, we'll have our answers about Daniel's ghosts. It can be a win-win."

Ceara closed her eyes and faced the lowering sun. "You believe the evil is Albert."

Jessie nodded. "I do. It all fits, Ceara. He isn't supposed to be there, but he is. He left his family to go be with the one he loves. He was clearly messed up in the head bone. So what we have here is a crazy quester who was never permitted into the portal and could do serious damage to the ones who are there. It is my job to get him out before that happens."

"But he already knows what happened in history. He knows he can't change that."

Jessie shook her head. "If he were sane, maybe. I think he lost sight of reality. I think he lost touch, period. We can't assume old Albert is functioning rationally."

Ceara opened her eyes and stared out at the water. "How do you propose to find out?"

"Same way we got Quinn. Flush him out. Find that one thing and appeal to the archaeologist in him. There is something he can't keep his hands off; something that makes his eyes light up."

"You are making the assumption he knows who he is back then. Quinn possessed his people. Albert, as far as we know, did not."

Jessie shook her head. "As far as we know, but he could still be in there somewhere, looking outward. We have to appeal to the archaeologist who is in the priest. I think Professor Leland and the journal can help us with that."

Ceara rose and walked over to the railing. The salt air whipped her many scarves around so she looked like a colorful pinwheel. "This Sakura is powerful?"

"Very. She knew the Goddess was going to be in trouble throughout history and was trying to be proactive. Well, she and her lover, Tarik." Jessie looked over at Ceara. "How come you've never discussed the Goddess with me? I mean, we've talked about things regarding goddesses and the old ways, but you never really explained—"

"How she comes and goes? It isn't something that can *be* explained, my dear. You know that. She comes when she comes. We hear when it's our time to hear, and we come when we are called. You will experience so many different emotions in the days to come; there will be questions you have, thoughts and feelings that are new and unfamiliar. As much as you will want to turn to me or even Cate for answers, you're going to need to find them yourself."

Jessie stared out at the ocean, thinking of Spencer Morgan

and the time he beckoned her to come help him. She missed the dirty sea dog more than she'd ever admit out loud. It had been a fun, albeit, dangerous quest that gave Jessie her first inkling of what it was going to be like to have the body of a man.

She grinned. She rather enjoyed it. Now, here she was, perched on the precipice of yet another quest, only this time, putting this one to bed meant giving her brother some peace of mind, and that was really important to her.

Looking up at Tanner guiding the boat through the waves, Jessie smiled softly. There was a lot that was really important to her, and yet, the poor guy knew he never stood a chance. Day after day, he stood by her, through the renovation of the inn to her going back to school. Tanner had been her rock.

Feeling Ceara's hand on her shoulder, Jessie turned back around. "You cannot help what he feels, Jess, any more than you can catch the wind in your hand."

"But—"

"Tanner's a big boy. He knows the score. Trust that he knows what he's doing where you're concerned."

"I don't want—"

Ceara gently squeezed her arm. "It doesn't matter what you want, love. Tanner is where he wants to be, and until he decides he can't do it any more, just enjoy the time you two spend together."

Jessie nodded slowly. "I'll try. It's hard. I really care for him. I wish like hell I could give him all he deserves, but I...I can't."

"No, no you can't."

Before Jessie could say anything more, Tanner yelled from the wheel, "Whales off the starboard side! I think they're humpbacks."

Ceara and Jessie both moved to the starboard side and watched a pod of humpbacks breaching the surface as if they were posing for a photo.

"Unbelievable," Jessie murmured as one of the large mammals broke the surface face first, rising dozens of feet off the surface of the water before plunging back into it, creating a wave that knocked up against the side of the boat. The power and strength of the whales was mesmerizing.

"Incredible, aren't they?"

"Amazing."

"The power of nature is everywhere and in everything. It is not a coincidence they appeared here today, Jessie. They have come as a reminder."

"That I am part of nature as well?"

"You are a creature just like they are. They can teach you, the trees can teach you, the very wind that blows can teach you if you are willing to listen. You listened this morning and doing so will change your life."

Jessie watched as the whales disappeared beneath the surface. "I want to learn."

"That's half the battle. By listening, as you are doing now, the world will open to you like a flower. Nature may be threatened by man, but it is the Goddess's daughters who are charged with righting the scales. Believe in that, Jessie. You are the future. You and others like you can change the course of things."

Jessie shook her head. "How many times have I asked questions to the universe, but didn't slow down long enough to hear the answers?"

Ceara chuckled. "That is the way of youth, my dear. You are no longer that angry young girl who rebelled at everything. You have a path now; a path that requires you to take stock of what you know and what you don't know." Ceara leaned closer. "What do you *know*, Jessie?"

"That the Goddess is everywhere…that I need to listen… that I have a path—" Jessie paused. "And that when we get home, we have a quest to embark on."

"Exactly. Now, what is it you have in mind once we return home?"

Jessie looked back out on the horizon. "What else? We go to Egypt."

14th Century

The moon had been out hours when Queen Nefertiti and Sakura rowed quietly into the middle of the Nile. Only the gentle sound of the water lapping against the shore could be heard.

It had been three days since the queen had been restricted to the palace, and even then, it had taken Tarik and one of her trusted servants to maneuver everyone out of their way.

Once he had gotten her out of the palace, he led her to the small boat where Sakura waited. When it was clear no one was following them, Tarik shoved the boat carrying Sakura and the queen out into the water, and stood waist deep, watching them row to the middle of the Nile. Once far enough out, Sakura finally relaxed.

"It has been too long, my queen."

Nefertiti let her hand trail in the water. "There has been so much upheaval within the palace these days. I dare not risk uncovering our meetings to any one of my husband's spies. Someone has convinced him our daughter was poisoned in order to make him think Aten held displeasure with the way Akhenaten rules Egypt. My husband has become afraid and suspicious of everyone around him. He is insufferable, ranting and raving at the smallest things. Had Tarik not been so persuasive in getting me to come, I would have stayed in the palace. I care too much for you to bring you under my husband's intense scrutiny."

Sakura nodded and stopped rowing. "I appreciate your concern, as always, but it was vital I speak with you. I have reason to believe you are in terrible danger."

Nefertiti sighed, but did not appear otherwise bothered. "I have been in danger since I married him."

Sakura leaned forward. "This hurt would be far deeper, Nefertiti. This concerns the fate of the Goddess."

Nefertiti tilted her head to one side. "Continue."

"One of Aten's priests has fallen in love with you and seeks to have you as his own. I do not know what lengths he will go to achieve his ends, but I believe this priest is the dark force I was warning you about."

Nefertiti smiled. "The lust of men is not new to me, even the attractions of priests."

Sakura shook her head. "This one is different."

"How so?"

"I believe he might have the sight, or at the very least, has convinced the king he does. He has come to the palace specifically for you, which means the king is also in danger. If he intends to make a path for himself to you, then your husband could also be in danger."

"I shall simply have him banished. There is no need to worry so."

"I wish it were that simple."

"Why would it not be?" Nefertiti removed her hand from the water when she heard a crocodile slide into the water on the far bank.

"Because I do not yet know which priest it is. So far, he has managed to turn the king into a hunter; a hunter of anyone who doesn't worship Aten."

"Yet you say you do not know which priest this is? How is this possible?"

"He is crafty...evil...he is not to be trusted by anyone. This is a game he is playing where no one can possibly win."

"So, we have a potentially harmful adversary, yet he remains invisible. I know you well enough to know that you have a plan to make him visible. What is it you wish me to do?"

"First, you must show the same fervor for Aten your husband does, and then use your zeal to get closer to his priests."

"Closer? You want me to get closer to one who may be a snake?" Nefertiti smiled faintly.

Sakura nodded. When they were children, Nefertiti was far more fearless than Sakura. She would jump from the highest tree branches into the Nile, or she would swim across even though there were crocodiles on the banks. Very little frightened her, and she ran from no one. "Just get close enough so when the time comes, it is *we* who strike."

"Strike? You don't mean—"

"What I mean is this man is a threat to everything you know. Akhenaten will never know what happens to his priest once we know which one it is. He will simply vanish. You need not know the precise details, just that the deed is done."

"I do not need to tell you I do not like this."

Sakura nodded. "I know you would prefer to punish a man openly, but this is not a time for doing so. In my visions, I see a man who wraps his dark arms around you until I can no longer see you...and yet...when he opens his arms...someone else stands where you stood, all the while, the room gets colder and colder. Please, heed my warnings and allow Tarik and I to protect you."

Nefertiti reached across the boat for Sakura's hand. "Consider it done then. I will trust only Tarik within the palace walls, and though it will pain my heart, I will lift my voice up in mock support of this ridiculous new religion."

Sakura let out a pained breath. "And suspect every priest. Keep your eyes open and do not attempt to come to the temple."

"My husband suspects nothing. I will make sure it remains that way. He loves me more than life itself, and would let nothing, not even his priests, harm me. Of that, I have no doubts."

Sakura took up the oars and turned them back to shore. Unfortunately for Sakura, she had nothing *but* doubts.

21st Century AD

When they pulled into Ceara's slip, Jessie was surprised to find Daniel waiting at the pier. He waved like she had been out to sea for months instead of days, and it warmed her heart to see his smiling face.

"Ahoy, mateys!" He shouted like he used to when he was a little boy. Shielding his eyes, Daniel stood on the pier wearing baggy work jeans, black high-top tennis shoes and a blue work shirt—all telltale signs that he had been working at the inn.

"Looks like somebody missed you," Ceara said as she stood next to Jessie on the deck. Their boat ride up the coast had been aided by uncommonly good weather; a sign to Jessie that the Goddess was, indeed, with them.

"What are you going to tell him?"

"I want to tell him the truth, but—"

"He's already dealing with so much?"

Jessie nodded. "He's *changed* so much. One minute, he's

playing with GI Joes, and the next, he's discussing the military action in Afghanistan. It's frightening, really."

"Ah, my dear, think of how boring our lives would be if nothing changed. Change is such a wonderful thing."

"Change is hard."

"Is it? Do you think the trees struggle with the loss of their leaves, or that the rose hates it when buds begin to bloom? Nature embraces change. Nature *is* change. It creates it. It delights in it. Honey, mankind is the only species on this planet that doesn't accept or understand change. We fear death. We fear life. We even fear fear. Quite frankly, we're pretty weak. We have the choice of being weak or view change like Nature does: as something that is, quite simply, necessary for growth."

Jessie nodded. "I understand. Daniel's not a little boy anymore. Look at his jeans. He's already grown out of them and Reena just bought them last month."

"Your parents seem to be traveling a lot more these days. Is everything okay?"

Jessie has wondered the same thing not too long ago. It was as if, once they got the inn up and running, they'd moved on to something else. Or maybe they didn't know what to do now that she didn't need saving. "I've asked myself that question, Ceara. Maybe they just want time alone, away from the inn. They worked so hard to keep it from collapsing around us."

Ceara nodded. "I worry because they should focus in more on Daniel. He needs their support right now."

"Yeah, well, he has me, at least."

"And he trusts you. He trusts you to tell him the truth. Maybe it's time you let him know who you are."

"I wouldn't even know where to begin."

"Sure you do. The truth is always easy to tell, Jessie. It will reveal itself at the right time and give you the right words. Trust in the process, my dear."

When the boat was five feet from the dock, Jessie tossed the rope to Daniel, who caught it and pulled the houseboat closer. After tying them up and waiting for Jessie to step off the boat, Daniel hugged her tightly.

"Miss me, sport?"

"Mom and Dad have been working me to the bone. I never realized how much work you and Tanner do around that place. I'm beat."

Jessie studied his dirty clothes. She could tell by the sawdust particle that he'd been doing carpentry work. "It's nice to be appreciated." Jessie helped Ceara off the boat. "But I have a sneaky suspicion there's more to this homecoming than a simple welcome back. What's going on?"

Daniel laughed good-naturedly. "Yeah, well, I did have Ben over one night when Mom and Dad went out, and I've been dying to tell you—"

Jessie and Ceara quickly looked at each other.

"He brought over all his high-tech stuff and we actually got them on audio. He was blown away."

Jessie felt Tanner's hand slide into hers and give her a quick squeeze. "Let him continue," he whispered softly from behind her.

Jessie motioned for him to continue. "What did they say?"

"It was pretty clear really, and Ben and I agreed they're saying Towns in. I don't know what it means, but I know it agitates the hell out of them."

Heaving a relieved sigh, Jessie put her arm around Daniel and started down the pier. She had expected something far more gruesome. "Tell you what. You run ahead to Del's and have him whip up four tuna sandwiches and then we'll tell you what *Towns in* means."

Daniel's eyes bulged. "You know?"

Jessie nodded. "More than you can even imagine. Now go on. We're starving."

When Daniel was out of earshot, Jessie turned to Ceara and Tanner. "Don't tell me...the truth just smacked me in the head and demands to be known."

Ceara grinned. "The good news is that you are hearing the universe around you and you are paying attention to what you hear. It is clear what must be done, and you are obviously ready for the task at hand. Trust yourself, my dear. Trust your instincts."

"How will I be able to keep him from wanting to experiment with the portal? It's not like he won't be able to figure it out once I tell him."

"We each have to make our own way, Jessie. You don't have to tell him where it is, just that it's somewhere on the property. You'll also need him to understand that he needs to honor and respect your wishes that he stay away from it. Apart from that, there just isn't anything else you can do."

Tanner nodded and squeezed her hand again. "It's time, Jess. The longer you keep this from him, the more hurt he's going to be that you didn't trust him enough with the truth."

Jessie's shoulders felt heavy, but she knew they were right; it was time. Daniel wasn't a little boy anymore, and if her actions outside of this world were going to affect him, he needed the truth. He needed to know.

"While you deal with Daniel, Tanner and I are going to see what more we can find out about Townsend since he plays a big role in all of this. Towns in? Here we thought they wanted Albert. This is very curious."

"You think he killed them, don't you?"

When Ceara shrugged, her bracelets tinkled together like a windchime. "My dear, I don't know what to think. We best get more information before we start jumping to conclusions. Go on now. Tanner and I will see to it the boat is set and then we'll see what we can find out about Townsend."

"I have a theory," Tanner offered quietly.

Jessie released his hand and brushed his windswept bangs to one side. "Do tell."

"The men were partners, then rivals. Maybe Albert was looking for a way to foil Townsend's search for whatever *the key* was. There's something not right happening between those two. I mean, by all intents and purposes, they appear to be partners, but just about everything we read had them on different continents."

"*Keep your friends close and your enemies closer?*" Ceara murmured.

Jessie cocked her head to the side. "That's a thought."

"I think it's more than a thought, Jess. If it's true revenge is a dish best served cold, how tasty would it be for Albert to destroy Townsend's claim to fame? And I am not talking about Egypt and murder."

"I don't follow."

"I've been thinking about this the whole trip up here, and I think their last trip together to Egypt was the first domino of my theory. See, Albert had already been through the portal who knows how many times, and I'm willing to bet most of the relics they found were because he made those trips to the past and *knew* where they were. By using the portal, Albert had a bead on where certain antiquities were originally buried or hidden."

Jessie nodded. "Good. Good. Keep going."

"I think Townsend got suspicious of Big Al's newfound wisdom and artifact locator techniques, and that's when it started to get ugly. Townsend probably wanted answers Al couldn't or wouldn't give him."

"You don't think Albert told him about the portal, do you?"

Tanner shrugged. "If he did, Townsend either thought Big Al was a lunatic, or a great big liar bent on controlling their digs. My guess is he told him and wasn't believed at first, but something happened. Something that made Townsend believe it enough to come to the house, and tear it apart looking for it."

Ceara nodded. "We know the house was torn apart. We know he kept the house in public hands. It makes sense that whatever he was looking for was in the house."

Tanner started back up the boat ramp. "He wanted what Albert had or what he knew."

"You think he's our killer?"

"That, I don't *know*, but my money is on Townsend, yes. There was no reason why Albert would have killed his family. He could come and go to ancient Egypt as he pleased. Then there's his journal entry. It sounded to me as if the man was in the house when his family was being butchered."

Jessie nodded. "That's pretty good, detective Dodds. While you're investigating Mr. Townsend, see what you can find out about their last dig and what really happened to them."

Tanner and Ceara exchanged glances. "We're all over it. Don't you worry. We're going to uncover the many mysteries behind Mr. Townsend."

Jessie nodded. "I've been so focused on Albert's role, I never really gave enough thought to Townsend."

"Well, we will. You just take care of Daniel."

Ceara nodded. "Tell him everything we know."

Jessie shook her head. "Not everything. I'll tell him what we found out in San Francisco, but I am going to to have to consult with Cate before I even consider telling him everything."

Tanner planted a kiss on Jessie's cheek before whispering, "Whatever you need to do. We got your back, Jess."

Jessie turned toward Del's and started down the road. "I hope I don't need it. Besides, I have a feeling taking care of Daniel will take care of the rest."

1st Century AD

"I had another yearning for that sticky pastry you call a Cinn-a-mon roll today. That was how I knew you had come. You bring with you memories of such wondrous things sometimes." Cate was already sitting on the stones in their Dreamworld when Jessie arrived.

"I have one every day. They're the best ever." Jessie sat on her usual stone and noticed Cate staring at her.

"Do I look different?"

Cate cocked her head and looked at Jessie sideways, a slight grin playing at the corners of her mouth. "From within, yes. You feel differently to me now. The Goddess's touch does that to us. We each discover her in our own way. How did she come to you?"

"On the water. I was in a boat...and suddenly, everything just felt right. It was so amazing. It came out of nowhere and filled me completely."

"She comes when we are ready. Even goddesses do not wish to suffer rejection."

"Well, it took me long enough to figure that out."

Cate smiled softly. "All in good time."

"The thing that amazes me most is how I feel. It's like someone turned all my senses into hyperdrive, and—" Jessie paused when she saw the big smile on Cate's face. "Oh. Hyper drive is like...when a horse runs really, really fast."

"Ah, I see. So, you feel as if your senses are aflame?"

"Yes! That's the perfect description. I saw these whales and I could have sworn—" Jessie paused again. "You do know what a whale is, right?"

Cate laughed. "Of course I do, but I never thought I would have the pleasure of seeing one."

"Too cold here, I'll bet. Anyway, I saw them and I felt... connected to them."

"You will soon discover just how connected we all are to the natural world. It is a remarkable feeling, Jessie, and you'll see that you never really feel alone."

"I haven't really felt alone since I met you."

"You are terribly kind. I, too, have become fond of our visits together, even though we are never quite at peace when we meet, are we? This is what we are charged with...not to spend our lives in blissful peace as the world changes and passes us by. Our job is to be an agent of that change, and with that comes an enormous responsibility. The Goddess trusts you are ready."

"I feel more ready...certainly more than the first time." Jessie turned to fully face Cate. "Will I be doing this a lot?"

"That would depend on what *a lot* is. We are charged with something sacred, Jessie. Believe me when I say you will not always be asked to put yourself in danger, nor will you always be asked to assist us from the past. When I first called you, I had no idea I was to become as powerful a priestess as I shall be in the future. For it is in the future I learn how to better communicate with people like Spencer Morgan."

Just his name made Jessie smile. "I miss him."

"You are a strange one, Jessie Ferguson. That man is a killer and yet you find him endearing." Cate shook her head. "I am sure the Goddess shrugs her shoulders as well."

"It's not Spencer's fault he killed people for a living, Cate."

Cate bowed her head and sighed. "As I am all too painfully aware."

"Two steps forward, one step back, my grandmother always says."

This made Cate chuckle. "You have some very wise women in your life."

"That, I do. Especially you. I came here today because you're on your way to becoming a full blown priestess and I guess I need a better idea of what this gig is all about."

A slight giggle escaped Cate's lips. "I'm sorry. It is just that your speech is so foreign. By full-blown, I take it you mean no longer a novitiate?"

"Yes."

"And by *gig*, I assume you mean path."

"Yes again."

"This I can answer, but it is going to cost you."

"Cost me?"

Cate nodded. "I must know how to make those cinn-a-mon roll pastry delicacies."

Jessie laughed so hard, she almost fell off her rock. "Unfortunately, cinnamon is a spice that hasn't really been brought here yet. The Egyptians used it when mummifying, but it will be another several hundred years before it becomes a cooking spice."

"It is an herb?"

"No. It's…like a bark."

Cate's eyes lit up. "A bark? Ah. I should have known. The spice you speak of is *cinnamomum zeylanicum*. You use it to make this pastry taste better?"

Jessie nodded. "It's a wonderful spice, really. It made Venice very wealthy in the thirteenth and fourteenth centuries."

"We do not use it as such, but in Sakura's time, I believe it was put into oil. Many people used it for cleansing wounds, but no one, as of yet, would think to put it on food. I suppose I shall have to wait until then for you to come to me with a recipe for those cinn-a-mon roll pastry goodies."

"That's a deal." Jessie studied her friend a moment. "You're very different from when we first met."

Cate nodded slightly. "Tragedy will do that to us."

Reaching for Cate's hand, Jessie squeezed it. "I'm really sorry. It must have been horrible."

"Worse than horrible, but that day of the massacre when the

Romans tried to wipe us from the earth is not the only reason I am so different. You are different now, and because of it, you see me through different eyes. You are wiser today than you were when you first came across. You are no longer lost or searching or even alone." Cate sighed. "Loneliness is a slow acting poison that seeps through our soul, killing us so slowly, by the time we realize what is happening our soul has dark spots upon it. You were a lonely young girl, Jessie, but no longer. Now, you have people who love you in different parts of the world in different times. And you are loved, Jessie Ferguson."

"I feel it every day. I guess…I guess that love has really changed my life. When I open my eyes in the morning, I feel connected—to you, to Maeve, to Spencer, to all of us."

"And Sakura?"

Jessie shook her head. "Not yet, though I am fascinated by her."

Cate released Jessie's hand. "What about her fascinates you?"

"Well, the time period, that's for sure. I love ancient Egypt and all the pharaoh and Cleopatra-type history. Her deep connection with Tarik made her want to stay with him for eternity. That's the kind of love I want in this life and all others. There's so much more I want to know about her."

"This is why you came today? You believe I have some wisdom you need?"

Jessie nodded. "There's so much I want to know. I've learned all the mental aspects of time travel and reincarnation. I've read stuff. I've studied. I think I know what I need to know in my head. It's the *spiritual* side of all of this that has me sort of confused, and I can't be confused right now. I am going to need answers for my little brother."

"Ah yes…I remember. The spiritual world is the least important aspect of your culture."

Jessie nodded. "We give it a lot of lip service and self-righteous indignation, but the spirit is sadly ignored. I want to be able to reach those places you go for wisdom and inspiration. I feel like a dry sponge willing to go a hundred miles for a drop of water."

Cate nodded and pulled her hood up around her face. "Lip.

Service. I like that. It is a very interesting term, Jessie. You have accepted the calling of the Goddess in whatever form by whatever name she may be called. To be a student of the arts, you must transform yourself outside as well as in. You must be open. You must listen. You must be willing, always, to weigh your actions. Do you accept all this entails and all you must do?"

Jessie nodded.

"Close your eyes." As Jessie obeyed, Cate continued. "You must see yourself as one of us...you must believe in yourself, in the wisdom you're acquiring, in all that you know and all that you do. You cannot move forward spiritually until you accept all you've become and will become."

Jessie nodded again.

"Open your eyes and tell me what you see."

Jessie did and saw that she was wearing the light blue robe of the initiate. It was harsh against her skin, but fit perfectly. Her hood was drawn up around her face, like Cate's, signaling Druidic work in progress. When Jessie glanced up, her voice caught in her throat. They were no longer sitting on the stones of the familiar circle. Now, they were both sitting on a log twenty feet from water quietly lapping the shore. A fire blazed between them, making it nearly impossible to see beyond the water or into the forest that was their backdrop. With the water washing upon the shore, and an occasional croak of a frog, it was the calmest, most tranquil place Jessie had ever been in.

"Where are we?" Jessie whispered.

"Where all daughters go to be trained, of course."

"Avalon—" Jessie murmured breathlessly.

"You have come to me, Jessie, for training you know in your heart Ceara could not provide from the physical plane you are both bound to. I've brought us here because it is as close as you are likely to come to us for a while. It is here you will learn from me, from Maeve, from others who will have access to the inner world of the spirit." Cate lowered her hood. "It is right to be in awe of this place, Jessie. What we do is awe-inspiring. The island possesses the energy of the Goddess, of nature itself in all its fullness. Can you feel it?"

Jessie felt as though fire replaced her blood as her spirit took off.

"Jessie, you are not the only one. We, in all of our incarnations, are *the* one. It is our journey, our eternal path to keep the flames of the Goddess alive no matter what the cost. You, like the rest of us, heard the call. You felt the pull of our path, of our duty, and you responded."

Jessie cocked her head. "Do some of us not answer the call?"

"Sadly, yes. Not all of us remember. Some of us remember too late. Still, we must reach out and make sure the journey has no end. There is no destination in this quest, no final task to reach. It is never-ending, and that can be daunting to many."

Jessie licked her dry lips and folded her hands in her lap. "This is really big."

"Indeed, but it is also very fulfilling. There is so much to know, and the learning of it is a lifelong endeavor. It is, in a sense, your job. Our eternal job. It is what completes us and gives us a sense of purpose. It is also the hardest thing you will do."

Jessie nodded. "It's just...well, I can't keep jumping into you every time I have a question or need to figure something out. The portal isn't...well...we don't really know if it's stable."

"You mean safe?"

"Close enough. Jetting one's soul through space and time can't be perfect all the time. I need to be able to stand on my own two feet no matter where I go or who I am once I get there."

"You need to know how to tap into the memories and power of the spirit. That takes concentration, a belief in the powers of nature and courage."

"Courage?"

"Because of the very dangers you speak. I am quite familiar with the risks involved, which is why I appreciate what you did for us that much more. You must be both warrior and priestess, Jessie, because what you will be asked to do will require both physical as well as spiritual strength. Now, close your eyes once more."

Jessie obeyed.

"You have questions. When we question, we must pause

and listen for an answer. Do not let it linger or go unbidden. A question within us is a life all its own, and when neglected, can create many needless problems and other questions. What is the question you're dealing with right now?"

One word kept floating through her mind. Reality.

What was that, anyway? Things tangible? Things provable? Who decided, anyway, what was real and what wasn't? Who was to say whether or not ghosts were real? Maybe people were in charge of their own realities. Maybe that was why the priestesses were so powerful; they created their own realities in order to find the answers they sought. They did not allow a society to dictate what was real and what wasn't. They did not allow a society to drown hopes by throwing them into a swamp of reality. What was so great about reality anyway? If it was so wonderful, Hollywood and the book industry would have died long ago. People needed to get away from it, not define it; not always be yoked to it.

Opening her eyes, she looked at Cate. "I have to stop asking questions and start acting upon the answers I already have. I know what I need to do first."

"And what is that?"

Jessie stared into the heart of the fire. She watched as Sakura embraced Tarik. No words were spoken—none were needed. They were clearly in love, needing no words to express how they felt about each other. Jessie smiled softly as a slight breeze blew the flames, and the image flickered and was replaced by an image of Spencer standing alone on the deck of his ship. He appeared deep in thought, a longing surrounding him. Jessie knew whom he was longing for, but it was not their time.

The flames crackled and there was the woman Spencer was thinking about and longing for. She was mixing some sort of herbs for the Queen of England. Jessie wished she could have helped Spencer stay with her, but it just wasn't the right time.

The flames wavered once more, and this time, Jessie saw herself. She was wearing the familiar light blue robe and was raising her arms as if summoning something. She appeared older, maybe ten years or so, but there was a calm around her that made Jessie grin.

"You will be very powerful in time, Jessie, and not just because you have our souls. You will be powerful because you care. It is this love that will strengthen you during times of trouble. We each have gifts that fortify our power. In time, you will unwrap those gifts as you need them. What gift would you like to unwrap first?"

"The Otherworld. I still struggle with how to get there on my own."

Cate waved the fire down. "Journeying to the Otherworld in and of itself is not such a difficult task, but locating what you are seeking, then returning and using it in your own world may be more difficult. The first thing you need to understand is that your experiences in the Land of the Sidhe may seem like a dream, but they are very real. There are those who have died in the Otherworld, and when they did—"

"Their real bodies died along with them. I get that, but I'm not afraid, Cate. This is all part of my transformation. I can't let fear play any role in my life."

Cate nodded. "You are a very brave woman, Jessie, but you must approach the Otherworld with reverence and respect. You must understand what it is and how it works. One arrives and leaves only if the Sidhe allow it, and they are a temperamental group."

"I was reading a book that said you should never accept food while there. Is that true?"

Cate cocked her head to one side. "They write about the Sidhe in your time? In books?"

Jessie nodded. "They write about everything now."

"I see. It is odd to know our oral tradition changed so much." Cate heaved a deep sigh. "You must unlearn everything you thought you knew and start fresh...start with the truth of the Otherworld and not ages of interpretation of it. That might spell disaster."

"Got it."

"Excellent. Remember time is nowhere. It does not exist as we know it. You may feel like you have only been gone a few moments, and yet, when you return, you could find your family and friends gone. You must never, ever forget that the Sidhe love playing tricks, and they are masterful at them. However, if you ever get in a predicament, you can always use Maeve's name."

"I remember you saying something once about them knowing her."

Cate nodded. "Oh yes. There is still so much about Maeve I am learning, so I am unsure just how deep her connection is to them. For whatever reason, they are on very good terms."

"That's cool."

"Now, Maeve and I usually prepare an herbal tea that helps open your mind and spirit to the Otherworld." With the flick of her wrist, a recipe written in Ogham came into the fire. "This is the mixture we use."

Jessie read the Ogham as if it were English, still amazed and somewhat awed by the enormous amount of residue from Cate's soul flowing through her, enabling her to read the language.

"Jessie, I am but seven and twenty. I have many years to prepare this soul for you. It is strong by design, by plan. It is not a coincidence you feel me so keenly. Remember that." Cate flicked the recipe away. "The tea is one way, when you are *planning* to go, but the Fith Faith is another method we have used for centuries."

"Fith Faith?"

"Yes. It is a way to move your spirit from the physical bonds and time. We do this by shape shifting, following a guide you can trust or entering through a known portal."

"Our portal?"

"Yes. It could get you to the Otherworld, but I will teach you how to reach that place on your own, but you must be patient and willing to try even if failure keeps you constant company. It takes more than courage to do what it is you are wishing to do. You must be wise, willing and open to things you never thought possible." Cate took Jessie's hands in hers. "Our first meditation will take us to Tir na Mban, or Land of Women. It is a realm where you can seek wisdom from a sisterhood more powerful than any you could imagine. You will be able to move about, ask questions, seek your wisdom, in the relative safety of Tir na Mban. Explore any area you wish, seek out your grandmother if you so choose, see a vision in the great cauldron of knowledge, or you may meet your shadow-self in the darker realms of the Tir. You need not be afraid of this self. It is never good or evil. It just is."

"But this isn't the Land of the Sidhe?"

"Oh no. I would never send you there first. You must practice. You must go where you can fully explore freely without danger."

Jessie clapped her hands together. "Let's do it."

After a breathing exercise, Jessie felt every muscle melt in her spiritual body. In less time than it took her to boil water, Jessie found herself alone in the Land of Women.

21st Century AD

"Don't you look like the cat who ate the proverbial canary." Ceara pulled the teapot off the stove and poured two cups of tea.

"I went to Tir na Mban last night."

Ceara turned, still holding the teapot. "You didn't!"

Jessie nodded. "Cate showed me the way."

"That's a perfect start toward Otherworld travel."

"How did you—"

"Makes perfect sense. You can't be jumping across time without having a better understanding of all the powers that be. I would have liked to have been the one, but it's been thirty years since I've practiced my craft. There are things I can do and, surely, things I cannot do. My job is to help you along your path. My job is to support you in all you do. Remember, my dear, it is not a coincidence that I am here with you in this time. Oh, at first, I thought I had been handed a bad hand, and there were times when I wanted to cash it in here in this life. After nearly thirty years of waiting, of wondering what in Sam Hill I was doing here, you came along. You gave me a reason…a purpose. That purpose is to be supportive, to teach, to show you all I know, so do not feel guilty that you went to Cate and not to me. I can't do for you what she can."

A light pink swept across Jessie's cheeks. "Thanks, Ceara. I needed to hear that. I was feeling...you know—"

"Guilty? Don't be. You have breathed a new life into this haggard one. Now, tell me all about it. Tir na Mban is wonderful, isn't it? My goodness, it's been years since I've gone."

Jessie took Ceara's hand. "It's never too late. Come with me now."

Ceara's eyebrows rose. "What?"

Jessie nodded. "Come *with* me. It's time, don't you think? It's time for you to remember. Come on, Ceara. You went with me back to sixteenth-century England. I know you dug it. I know it crept into your veins and has been sitting there like an intense adrenaline rush waiting to explode. Well, one thing I realized more clearly when I was in the Tir is I am not in this alone. I never have been. I'm lucky enough to get to hang with a bona fide Druid priestess. It's time I helped you back to who *you* once were."

Tears filled Ceara's eyes. "I...I don't know—"

"Sure you do. Ceara, you know I'm going to be needing your help along the way. You can best help me by getting back in the game." Jessie squeezed Ceara's hands. "I need you. I need all you are and all you were. That was what I learned last night when I was cruising around in the Land of Women. I have a woman in *my* life who can greatly assist in the many quests coming my way, and I was instructed I would be a fool not to get the most out of you."

This made Ceara chuckle. "Get the most out of me, eh? That certainly sounds like something that came out of the mouth of one in the Tir."

"Because it's true. You have so much to offer. So what if you're rusty? Dust off your priestess robe, Ceara, and be my partner in this. You were right when you said it wasn't a coincidence you ended up in my time. You're here because I can't do this without you."

"You are sounding more and more like a priestess every day."

"Will you come with me?"

Ceara wiped her eyes. "I'll go. But first, I want you to take a look at the Townsend file there. Don't do anything with it until Tanner gets back."

"Back? Where did he go?"

"For supplies. You'll see." Rising, Ceara started back toward her bedroom. "If I am to go with you, I need to get myself mentally ready. While I do that, take a look at that file. It's sure to get you thinking."

Jessie opened the file. It was half an inch thick with Internet printouts, a yellow legal pad with Ceara's scribbling, and a list of phone numbers.

"They've been busy," Jessie muttered to herself, turning the first page of a catalogue of artifacts Townsend had dug out from a site in 1917. It was an extensive list of smaller scale items once belonging to the lesser queens of Ramses III. Next to each item was a number, a code, and the names of those in the excavation party.

The next few pages were journal entries from Townsend's treatise on archaeology in the twentieth century. Jessie read each one carefully and determined that Robert Townsend was arrogant in his views and pedantic in his writings. His ego jumped off the page as he likened himself to Howard Carter and Leakey. Jessie felt an immediate dislike of the man.

The next bundle of sheets were far more interesting than his jumble of esoteric words, and gave the timeline for all he had done in his thirty-odd years as an archaeologist. While the results were not overly impressive, Jessie could sense a bitterness with the fact that he had not reached the status of the aforementioned archaeologists. Still, it was evident by the map of his excavations that he was looking for something in particular. He was all over the charts, which was rare in archaeology, which didn't really work that way. Normally, you would be offered a certain area to work for a certain period of time, but that didn't appear to be the case with Townsend. He jumped from one dig to another, as if the normal rules of archaeology didn't apply to him.

The next page revealed a layout of the tombs and chambers in the Valley of the Kings, most notably, KV55, also known as the Amarna Cache. There was a marker on the tomb of Queen

Tiye of the 18th dynasty which, no surprise to Jessie, held the dates of Akhenaten's reign.

"What were you up to, Bobby?" Jessie murmured.

The entrance to KV55 was cut into the floor of the valley between a rest house and the tomb of Ramses, which was in KV6. The queen's tomb was small, as were most female tombs of the time. KV6 was an important find, as was KV9, the tomb of Ramses V and VI, and there was Townsend, once again, in the mix of it all.

Pulling out a well-drawn map of the Valley of the Kings, Jessie studied it carefully. There was a site KV62 highlighted with a tiny scrawl in Ceara's printing that said *check out.* Jessie turned to printouts regarding KV62 and caught her breath. KV62 was the infamous site of King Tut's tomb. It was discovered by Howard Carter in 1922, the same year Albert disappeared. "Oh no," Jessie said under her breath, rapidly reading the information about the tomb. She knew Tut was supposed to be around eighteen or nineteen years old when he died. Had his tomb been robbed in antiquity like the others, no one would even know his name. In the end, it was the *tomb* that was important, not the boy king. His golden death mask made him famous, but few could name one thing he had done other than die young.

"What's this?" Jessie noticed a yellow arrow pointing from the site to the bottom of the page, and another note in Ceara's hand. *KV62 was hard to get to originally because, according to Carter, the "damned excavators" of KV9 just willy-nilly dumped their debris on top of it.* Next to the quote Ceara had written *Carter and Townsend were rivals.*

Jessie was rereading the passage just as the door opened and there stood Tanner with an armload of books. "Hey."

Jessie rose and kissed him softly, taking three of the large books from him. "Hey yourself. I take it these are the supplies Ceara spoke of."

"Madame ordered a bunch from the library when we were sailing home. I think it was when you were in mid meditation. How's that working for you? You cruising around Fae Land?"

She smiled at him. "Oh, I get around."

Tanner set the books on the table and bent over to kiss her again, this time, letting his lips linger. "Of course you do. You're digging it, aren't you?"

"Dig it is not only an understatement, but a bad pun as well." Jessie read the title of one of the books *Doomed Queens: Women whose lives ended badly.* "Nefertiti, eh?"

"Ceara says you're not going anywhere until we have more info. You can't go jumping into ancient Egypt with Tut and Akhenaten, and Hat...Hat..."

"Hatshepsut."

"Yeah, her too. I don't know about you, but Egypt in the 18th dynasty sounds like a fucking scary place, Jess. You need a whole lot more data before you go flying through time. Tons of weird shit went down in Egypt. Like that Hatshepsut chick dressed up like a man in order to remain Pharaoh. How cool is that?"

Jessie set the book on the table. "Were you speed reading at the library?"

Tanner blushed. "Uh...no...not really. There was this... uh—"

Jessie playfully shoved him. "Just say it! There was that cute blonde, Bambi or Tammi or..."

"Amber."

"That's the one! You have a crush on her, don't you?"

"What are you? Twelve? Crushes are dumb." Tanner's face belied his words, as his cheeks turned bright red.

Jessie raised an eyebrow. "Then *you're* dumb. Look, I think it's cute. I told you before to ask her out. I'll bet she digs that bad boy jacket you wear."

Tanner groaned. "Jess, let me give you a tip. Guys don't like to be *cute*, especially when the girl we hang with is *okay* with us looking at another girl."

Jessie lightly traced the outline of his face. They had had this conversation a million times. She could never fully commit to Tanner knowing he wasn't the one. It wasn't that she didn't love him. He deserved better than to be the guy who kept her company while she waited.

"You'd rather be dumb?"

"I'd rather not talk about it."

The smile slowly dropped from Jessie's face. "Fine. It's still cute."

"Think what you want. Can we get back to business here?"

"Sure. Just answer me this. Did you talk to her?"

"Who, Amber? Yeah. I asked her about Nefertiti."

"Did she bat her eyes and offer to show you?"

"She offered, but there was no eye batting. Moving right along." Tanner motioned to the file on the table. "Good thing we didn't overlook Townsend. The man was scum. How far have you gotten?"

"Not far. You two have been busy."

Setting the books on the counter, Tanner grabbed a soda before lowering his lean body into the chair across from her. "Yeah, well, you know how she gets. She's got a bug up her rear on this one."

Jessie tapped her finger on the next sheet. "Did *anybody* like this guy? Seems his contemporaries were pretty critical of his methods."

"You think? You'll see at least two other Egyptologists accused him of actually stealing some of their artifacts. Can you imagine the gall?"

Jessie looked down at the file. "What a schmuck. I can't believe old Albert would have anything to do with him if he was accused of theft. That's worse than murder to an archaeologist."

"Well, we knew he wasn't a good guy. We just didn't know how bad he was."

Jessie flipped the map around and pointed to the Valley of the Kings. "He was all over the place, Tanner. I think he was looking for Tut's tomb."

Tanner reached over and pulled the top book off the pile. "The guy was fanatical to the point of scaring off the money men like Lord what's-his-name who supported Carter."

"Lord Carnovan."

"Yeah, that guy."

Jessie took the Tut book from Tanner and flipped through until she came to a page with the death mask on it. "Isn't this amazing? To think of the craftsmanship it took to create something as gorgeous and as intricate as this."

"Weird to think how advanced they were at one point and now...well...it's like they've gone backwards in time."

Jessie stared at the mask. "You think this is what Townsend was after?"

Tanner shrugged. "I think he looked and looked until he realized Big Al could get him where he needed to go. I'm not sure it was one item in particular."

"Then why didn't he?" Jessie flipped through the papers in the file. "I need a...here it is." Pulling a single sheet from the file, Jessie read it before handing it to Tanner. "Al knew where it was from his previous travels, and he had to have done something that let Townsend know he knew where to find the greatest artifact ever found."

"Think he was blackmailing him?"

Jessie shook her head. "I don't think so, Sherlock. I think Al left without giving Townsend the information he needed to get whatever it was he was searching for."

"So he buys the house so he can tear it apart looking for anything that might give him Big Al's edge."

"He wanted for free what Carter earned for himself through hard work and dedication. Townsend was a loser. His work was shoddy, and look at how many smaller pieces of his were found from the debris he hadn't even bothered to sift through. He was looking for a big score. This makes him more of an opportunist than an archaeologist. A real archaeologist sifts through the debris, sifts through the debris of the debris, and doesn't leave a site until it's been completely examined. Look at his movements. It's like he had ADHD and couldn't sit still in one place. I'm sure this did not bring him into a favorable light."

"You think he was hoping to find something huge to add to his collection?"

Jessie shook her head. "I don't think this has to do with his personal collection. Personal collections don't bring the kind of notoriety he was after."

"We need to know for sure what he was after."

"Why?"

"Because that's where we will find Albert. And when we find Albert, we get some answers about our ghosts."

"Time to go back?"

Jessie nodded. "Time to go back."

Otherworld

"This is amazing," Ceara murmured as she and Jessie walked through an oak grove stretching for miles. "We used to have these when I was in Britannia. I remember when I first came to your time and everything was made of cement, and I searched for weeks to find a forest of oak."

"Lots of forests in Oregon, but not of oaks."

"No kidding. I had to be satisfied with those." Ceara stopped and looked around. "I almost forgot how enchantingly beautiful it is." Ceara stopped and faced east. "I invoke the daughters of the sea, who fashion the threads of the sons of long life. May three deaths be taken from me! May seven waves of good fortune be dealt to me! May no evil spirits harm me on my circuit! May my fame not perish! May old age come to me, may death not come to me until I am old! I invoke Senach of the seven periods of time, whom fairy women have reared on the breasts of plenty. May my seven candles not be extinguished! I am an indestructible stronghold. I am an unshaken rock. I am a precious stone. I am the luck of the weak. May I live a hundred times a hundred years. Each hundred of them apart. I summon their boons to me. May the grace of the Holy Spirit be upon me."

Jessie could only shake her head. "That was beautiful."

"I'm surprised I remembered it. It is one you ought to memorize as well. I'll find it for you when we get back." Ceara inhaled deeply. "The air is different here."

"Everything is different here. It's cool, huh?"

Ceara looked around. "Very. So, what happened when you came here?"

Jessie grinned. "Keep walking. You'll see."

They walked for a while in silence, both deep in thought, and when they came to a waterfall that rolled loudly over a cliff and into a crystal clear pool below, Jessie stopped and took a deep breath. "When I came here I wondered what women I might encounter. Cate wanted me to learn from them, to understand that the Otherworld is not just one place, but many places. I came here not knowing what to expect. The last person I expected to meet here was her." Jessie motioned to the waterfall and the water parted, revealing a beautiful woman with long red hair. She was almost six feet tall, slender, and walked across the wet stones as easily as if she were walking across a carpet of grass. She was wearing a light yellow dress that clung to her shapely figure. "She came specifically for me and gave me very clear directions."

Ceara squinted at the woman as she walked toward them. "Oh my. Oh dear. Is that—"

Jessie smiled. "It is. Those directions were for me to bring *you*. Posthaste. Do not pass go, do not collect two hundred bucks."

Ceara's hand flew to her open mouth. "Oh. My. God. It is. It really is."

Jessie smiled broadly. "Yes, dear friend. That is your mother."

Ceara ran across the forest floor and scooped her mother up in her arms. The words flowing from her mouth were an ancient Gaelic tongue Jessie could not decipher, but she needed no translation to see the reunion of pure joy.

When Fionna had come to Jessie, she sat with her for a long time and explained why she needed to get Ceara to come back with her. Jessie had found Fionna to be one of the most remarkable women she had ever met. Once a powerful priestess herself, she currently resided in the Land of Women where she assisted female questers and young priestesses from all over the world from many different times. The power Fionna possessed was evident even as Jessie sat and chatted with her. It was no wonder Ceara had been chosen to be the first through the portal; her mother had been an incredible priestess when she was alive.

Jessie wanted to turn away from the reunion to give them some privacy, but couldn't. There was something about the two of them jabbering away that compelled her to look. Jessie's relationship with her own mother had soured long ago; Reena's staid Christian beliefs coming between them even more than Jessie's pot smoking or class cutting. She knew if she saw her mother in an afterlife like this, their reunion would not be so sweet. Oh sure, they would hug and make small talk, but there wouldn't be whatever was transpiring between these two women.

When Ceara turned from Fionna, she was no longer wearing the same wizened face from her twenty-first century life. A stunned Jessie whispered, "Ceara?"

Ceara ran back to Jessie, a woman of thirty, maybe thirty-five, with the same long red hair as Fionna, only with slightly more bronze highlights. Her face was beaming and she laughed as she made her way back across the wet stones.

"Oh, my dear, you really should have told me!"

Jessie could say nothing as she stared.

"What's wrong? You look like you didn't know this was going to happen."

Jessie took Ceara's hand and led her to a calm pool. "Look."

When Ceara peered into the pond, she brought her hand to her mouth. "Oh, my. It's…it really is me."

"What do you mean?"

Standing up straight, Ceara smiled at her. "This is how I appeared before I went through. This is who I really am!" Ceara reached out and pulled Jessie to her. "What a wonderful gift you've given me this day." Even the cadence and the way she spoke was slightly different.

"It is a wonderful gift for us all," Fionna said, gliding over to them both. She was a good six inches taller than Ceara, but the resemblance was uncanny. "I have waited a long time for this day. I never thought—" She shook her head. "I never thought you would ever be able to find your way here. When you went through—"

"I was not prepared for the way that ended. It ended poorly for me."

"It ended as it needed to end, my dear."

Jessie grinned softly. So that was where she got the *my dears* she used when talking to Jessie.

Fionna nodded. "And as painful as that may be to acknowledge, my dear, that is precisely why you went through. It was your job, your Fate, your destiny to reach Jessie." Fionna turned to Jessie. "And so far, you have filled yours admirably. It is not easy to receive the call at such a young and tender age, but so far, you have held up remarkably well. We are all very proud of you."

"How many is *all*?"

Fionna turned to Ceara. "She makes a good companion for you. You always had a quick wit and fast tongue. I don't imagine that has changed even though you now occupy the body of a humorless, depressed woman."

"She's a drunkard, *mháthair*, and I can only imagine what happened in my other lives that contributed to her addiction."

"Perhaps you will find out someday, but your past lives are not why we are here today, I'm afraid. Jessie has brought you because you are to aid her in the completion of her destiny. You must remember who and what you once were. You must purge any remnants of the woman of your time and regain all the memories of the priestess I taught you to be."

Ceara nodded. "You have no idea how much I would like that. It feels as though I am impotent when it comes to helping Jessie."

"You are not that, my dear. There is much for you both to learn from each other. That is why you are here, and who better to remind you of all you are than your *mháthair*?"

Ceara nodded. "If this will help Jessie, then I am willing to do whatever needs to be done...but first...do we have time...can we...talk?"

Fionna looked over at Jessie, and barely nodded. "I do not think a few moments together will hurt anything. Jessie, would you mind?"

"Mind? Not at all."

When they left, Jessie lay down next to the waterfall and looked up at the sky. Everything here was beautiful...the women, the environment, everything. It was a little like heaven, or how she thought heaven would be like.

She didn't know how long she had been asleep, but when she woke, she was back in Ceara's boat, lying on Ceara's bed alone, the sun long since retired. "Ceara?"

"I'm just putting some tea on, hon," she called from the galley.

"How long have you been out?"

"Only a few minutes, give or take."

Jessie slowly got up, feeling more rested than she had in months. "I guess there wasn't anything I was supposed to learn, huh?" Walking into the small kitchen, Jessie sat at the table.

"Don't be silly. I'll bet you learned more today than you have in a year. It's just a different kind of knowing...one that rises slowly to the surface when you need it most."

Jessie nodded. "I'll bet you had a great time. Was it...was it hard coming back?"

"Coming back to this old body? No, actually. It was a bit like returning to an old pair of worn shoes. It was delightful seeing my mother again...like that, but my life is here now."

"She was a beautiful woman."

"Yes. Yes, she was."

"Did she help?"

"Oh yes. And I believe everything she gave me will help us...will help *you*. She said that every day, when I take time to meditate, to go through my own private rituals, I will get a piece of me back. She...she said she was proud of me, Jessie...that she always knew I had it in me. That meant so much to me."

"I'll bet."

"She was a slave driver, that woman. She wanted perfection... no, she *demanded* it. She was the hardest taskmaster. And now... for the first time in my life, I understand why."

"Why?"

Ceara turned and smiled into Jessie's face. She looked years younger. "She was getting me ready to help you."

14ᵗʰ Century BCE

Sakura had just finished praying when she felt the familiar tingle at the base of her skull. Rising from the floor, she suddenly felt light-headed and quickly sat down on a stool leaning against the wall. She had, of course, felt this before and suspected someone from the future had come through. As far as she knew, she had never been visited by someone from the past.

Closing her eyes, she sent her Ka forth and was delighted her visitor was none other than Jessie, who was beckoning her to come to her Dreamworld. Sakura closed her eyes and went.

"You look surprised," Jessie said, lowering her hood and pushing her hair away from her face.

Sakura glanced around her. "I was not aware that you had… well—"

"Powers?" Jessie shook her head. "Not really. I've just started on the priestess path on a road toward greater wisdom. I'm barely even a novice."

Sakura walked over to the log where Jessie was standing, her movements fluid and graceful. Her presence filled the air around them, and the sheer power of her being made the trees around them stand taller. She was, in a word, a magnificent creature, and Jessie's breath caught in her throat as she studied her.

"Your gaze lingers. May I ask why?"

Jessie felt a blush creep up her cheeks. "I'm sorry…it's just… I find you a bit…intimidating."

Sakura tilted her head, seemingly amused. "In what way?"

"Look at you! You're beautiful, powerful, wise, not to mention, brave."

Sakura laughed soundlessly, her brown eyes sparkling with delight. "A priestess should be somewhat intimidating, do you not think? What we have within us is the great Goddess and all She knows and all She is. Only a fool would not be intimidated by us." Sakura looked over at the firepit and started to raise her hand, then she stopped and motioned toward Jessie. "Would you do the honors?"

Jessie looked over at the pit. There was always a fire in it whenever she arrived, but today was different. Today, she had made the call. There was no fire. "I…I don't know how."

"Of course you do. We are one with the elements, Jessie, and they are part of the natural world in which we live, no matter what era. Call upon it, and it shall dance at your fingertips. Just remember that you do not actually control it. It works with you, as one."

Jessie had seen Cate and Maeve do it a dozen times and it appeared so simple for them. It looked like all they did was communicate using hand signals. Jessie turned to the firepit and motioned like she had seen Cate do.

Nothing happened.

"Concentration is vital, Jessie. You must do more than will something to happen. Call upon the fire's spirit, call to it much like you called me."

Jessie thought about the fire as another element, as a thing of life, capable of both creating and destroying. It was powerful and...up it rose. Slowly at first, full of too much blue...like it was going to poof out, but it struggled for a moment until it finally reached half the height of Cate's usual fire.

"I did it!" Jessie said, raising her hands slowly and watching the fire rise. "That was fantastic!"

Sakura nodded. "Well done. Never doubt the power of your own mind. Faith and confidence have helped me out of many a bind." Sakura glanced about once more. "So, what's brought you into the sanctity of my spirit this day? Have you found a way to reach our elusive quarry?"

Jessie nodded. "I believe so. You already know how limited our historical perspective is in regard to your time. It will help if I could see the world through your eyes, to experience your life the way it really is. It will also help if I can leave some of my memories with you."

Sakura studied Jessie over the fire. "You are worried."

"He could be a very dangerous man to you all."

Sakura nodded. "I understand, and I appreciate you inquiring first, but you are always welcome here. Always. Now, what is it you believe will make our jackal reveal himself?"

Jessie chose her words carefully. It was difficult to remember that Sakura did not want to know what would happen to her world. How did you explain to someone that your once great civilization fell to the Romans before eventually succumbing to ruin and poverty?

"There's a tomb he has always had a passion about."

"A passion...for a tomb?"

Jessie nodded. She wondered how she would feel if someone came to her from the future and told her that the White House or the Statue of Liberty had been vandalized and looted before being destroyed. What if Mt. Rushmore were defaced because its subjects were no longer seen as great men? The thought sickened her and she decided that if she really needed to know something about her future or the future of her world, she didn't wish to know more than necessary. It would be too painful to know...to watch it as it slowly happens. To be looking for it, waiting for it. It would simply hurt.

"Jessie..." Sakura's voice gently broke through Jessie's thoughts. "It is my queen's safety I care most about, not whether or not I am saddened by the future's ignorance of my people. Already, Egypt weakens under Akhenaten's rule. We have been losing power for many moons now. My concern is and always has been to make sure that Nefertiti is safe and unharmed. I am a grown woman who sees what is happening to her country, to her people. I cannot stop that. If, however, I can prevent any harm from coming to my queen, then I will do everything I can."

Jessie felt goose bumps on her arms as she stared at Sakura. "She is more than a queen to you, isn't she?"

Sakura looked away. "I do not suppose your historians ever knew about me."

Jessie frowned. She had spent a fruitless couple of hours on the Internet looking for anything she might find on Sakura.

Sakura shook her head. "It is as it should be, for fame is not my path. My path is, and always has been, to assure the safety of my sister."

"Your..."

Sakura's grin broadened. "Yes. Nefertiti is my half sister. We discovered it inadvertently when we were children, but by then, my path had already been chosen. Our mother determined it was best if no one knew. That way, no one could use me to get to Nefertiti. You see, we were both born and raised under the power of the Goddess, and we swore to our mother we would take care of each other. When Akhenaten took her for his wife, we knew the dangers, but none of that mattered. It was understood from the beginning what was most important: to find a way to balance damage done by his religious fervor." Sakura continued. "You see, your desire to protect your little brother is in keeping with my calling to protect my sister."

"My brother?"

"Oh yes. Of all the feelings and emotional images I pick up from you, your concern about him is very clear. It is this concern that brought you here. It is your love of him I see. Tell me what is happening in your world, Jessie. Perhaps our meeting today can be mutually beneficial."

Jessie shook her head sadly. "He keeps hearing voices… and…" Jessie didn't know how much to say, so Sakura motioned to the flames, which parted to reveal Daniel's bedroom. He was not in it, but a dark, almost fuzzy haze hovered above his bed. "How do you guys do that so easily?"

"The flames can only reveal that which is connected to us by strong, emotional bonds. Do not ever be afraid of saying what is in your heart, for that is the seat of all our power."

Jessie looked up from the flames at Sakura, remembering, of all odd things, a lecture she heard in her first year at the college. Apparently, the Egyptians thought the brains were so useless, they actually pulled them out through the nose prior to mummification. "At first, I thought it was cool that he found something to be interested in, but then, I don't know…one night, I went into his room and felt this…this chill."

Sakura cocked her head to one side. "What kind of chill? Describe it."

"It was cold and dark, as if something threatening and intimidating were in the room. It went to the marrow of my bones, and that was when I knew I needed to help him. There's something not right happening where we live."

"These spirits…they are in your home?"

Jessie nodded. "And believe it or not, they have something to do with you and why I'm here."

"I see. Then it appears we are in a position to help each

other. I will do what I can to help you find the man you think must have something do to with these spirits, and you can help me keep my sister safe. To do so, you must stop worrying so about my reaction to your knowledge about my time. I would not use that information for any gain or self promotion."

"I just didn't want to hurt you."

Sakura waved the flames closed and then sat down, pulling Jessie down with her. Up close, her kohl makeup looked tattooed on her face, and her hair held a satin-like shine.

"You are a very kind soul, Jessie. You are thoughtful and kind. It is nice to know my Ka remains benevolent, but there are dangers afoot and you need not spare my feelings nor worry about my reaction to what you know to be true. You must have faith that I am as strong as I appear."

Jessie nodded. "Fair enough. By my calculations, King Tut is already alive."

Sakura's eyes grew wide. "Tutankhamen? Yes, he lives, but he is but an infant."

Jessie nodded. This, she already knew. What she did not know, what no one really knew, was the true parentage of the boy. "We know very little of him. He does not live long."

Sakura nodded. "I did not see a long life for him, but I did see greatness."

"Oh, there is, but not in anything he did while alive. His fame and history come as a result of his death. The items in his tomb were...*are* priceless. They are the pride of Egypt...I also think there was something in that tomb our guy was after...or at least wanted pretty badly."

"And this is why you want to bring him to us."

Jessie nodded. "Once we cull him from the priestly herd we can send him back through to his time." Jessie looked at Sakura. "We can do that, can't we?"

Sakura nodded. "While it is not a thing I have done, that doesn't mean I cannot. Nefertiti's life is already in jeopardy from all that is happening here. We do not need more worries from a man who does not belong and is here for his greed alone." She shook her head sadly. "Man is greed in a skin suit."

This made Jessie grin. "I don't think he would hurt her, but any man who would leave his family behind while they were being murdered in order to travel three thousand years into the past to be with a woman he thinks he's in love with should be considered a danger, don't you think?"

"Quite. We will continue to think him so, however, there is not, at this time, a tomb being prepared for the boy."

Jessie nodded and parted the flames with a wave of her hand, smiling inwardly. It was one of the coolest things she had ever done. In the flames was a tomb almost completely finished. "That's what the experts in my time say. They believe there was not enough time to build one for him, and that, perhaps, the discovered tomb was one of Akhenaten's."

"Akhenaten's? That cannot be."

"The current pharaoh's image, hieroglyphs and cartouches were destroyed after his death because of his religious heresy. Akhenaten may not be well liked during your time, but shortly after his death, he was possibly placed elsewhere." Jessie closed the flames. "Historians and Egyptologists are still unclear how it all went down."

"My sister believes Akhenaten means well, and believes his intent is more practical than spiritual. We knew he would probably alienate the people, but I do not think we ever realized to what extent. I will look into the tomb building and see what comes of it. What is it this man was looking for?"

"Perhaps the most important find in all of Egypt's history. It is a golden death mask."

"Ah yes. I know of that which you speak. Many of our kings had them made. They are beautiful, are they not?"

Jessie said reluctantly. "I've only seen one."

"Ah. Then the others would be where?"

Damn. Jessie looked away. "They may be in a private collection somewhere. There's only been one mask like that found. At least, none other were ever recorded as being found."

"Oh. I see." For the longest time, Sakura stared into the fire as the mist from the waterfall rose higher into the air. When she finally spoke, her voice was soft and low. "The Egypt I know and love seems to have suffered from its own excesses. I suppose that happens to every great civilization eventually."

Jessie nodded. "You don't know the half of it. Trust me. My country is on the exact same road to ruin. It's heartbreaking, really."

"Indeed. But I cannot worry about the future of Egypt until my sister's present is safe. I will do what I can to spread the word about the golden mask and see if he does not show his true self. Once I find out who he is, I will come to you." Rising, Sakura turned from Jessie. "I appreciate all you do for all of us, Jessie. I know it can be a burden, but you have chosen this path and anything the rest of us can do to assist you on your own personal spiritual journey, do not hesitate to lean on us."

Jessie thought she saw tears in Sakura's eyes. "I lean on you guys every day." Reaching out, Jessie hesitated as she touched Sakura's shoulder. "The truth is...I am nothing without you. I was nothing before Cate, and I've worked very hard to make something of myself. Now I'm a woman of substance. I matter."

Sakura slowly turned to Jessie. "Some day, you will come into your powers the likes of which none of us could ever dream of possessing. Some day, you will reach down inside yourself and find a strength that will frighten even you. When that day comes, you must seek out Cate."

"Cate? Why wouldn't I come to you?"

"Cate is as powerful as she is because she has gained the wisdom of those of us who have reached out from the past...and future. She has learned from all of us who have remembered, just as you do. She is the one who can point you in the right direction when times are difficult. Trust her completely. I do."

Jessie tilted her head to one side. "Do you have much contact with her?"

Sakura shook her head. "Not yet, but I will. Cate will become an incredibly strong priestess one day, in large part because of me."

"How do you know all this?"

As she started to walk toward the waterfall, Sakura said over her shoulder, "From the one person who controls this entire play."

"Maeve?"

Sakura grinned. "Of course. Now, come with me and spend the day with the real Maeve."

14th Century BCE

Their times on the Nile were some of Sakura's best memories. They would often row to the shore, make love, eat some fruit, drink some wine and lie in each other's arms for hours, just watching children play on the river's edge. These were the peaceful moments when they left their jobs on the dock and concentrated solely on each other. It was not difficult to focus on Tarik's muscular body and lean waist. He was as fit as any man Sakura had ever seen, and she loved the feel of his hard body pressed up against her.

They had been a natural fit since she could remember, and she looked forward to these peaceful times of floating down the river as if they had not a care. They would talk about the comings and goings in court, the gossip, the tales, all the things that would take them away from their somber issues they faced daily. It was Sakura's favorite time.

"I do not like you putting yourself in danger, Sakura, even if it is for your sister," Tarik said after she told him about her visit with Jessie. "Are you certain there is no other way to keep your sister from harm?"

"I shall not be in any real danger, my love. I am merely the purveyor of information that might very well bring him to us."

"I do not like the sound of that, Sakura. If the priest is, indeed, the one you seek, I shall—"

"Do nothing. We cannot risk your duplicity being discovered. We must keep you as close to Nefertiti as possible. I will not risk exposing you."

Tarik pulled her closer. "You are ever my shield, my love. I will not sacrifice her safety, but what you intend to tell him does not exist. There is no tomb being built for Tutankhamen, and it does not sound as if the learned men from the future know much about our tombs or which pharaoh is in which tomb. It does not appear men in the future know much of *anything*."

"It does not matter that the information we give him is false, only that he acts upon it."

"But I still do not understand how it can help. The man is obsessed with the queen, not the boy."

"Jessie believes his family was murdered because of his knowledge about where a golden mask is. This man...this Albert, has been coming and going through the portal for some time. In all of his journeys, he was able to gather information and use it to locate our...art-i-facts."

"Art-i-facts?"

"That is what they call the king's sacred objects looted from his tombs. Men from the future collect things stolen from our tombs and graves. Some are paid handsomely to find them, others sell them to museums."

"Our king's sacred objects end up in a museum?" Tarik bowed his head and shook it sadly. "What is to come of us if our greatest treasures are sold to the highest bidder?"

Sakura nodded. "You do not wish to know. I know, my love. It is tragic."

"It is beyond tragic, Sakura. It makes me glad I do not listen when anyone other than Maeve comes to me. It would make my spirit weep to know what happens to our people. I do not have your strength."

"Oh Tarik, you are so much braver than I could ever hope to be. I am afraid for your safety every day. At night, I pray that Aset watches over you, that she enfolds her arms around you and keeps you safe from prying eyes."

"And she does. We are quite a pair, Sakura, but I swear to you, I will do all I can to help you find this man. You say he is interested in Tutankhamen?"

"Yes. According to Jessie, Al-bert was very close to discovering his tomb and was planning on using that information to further his own ambitions. Something went terribly wrong and his family was murdered. He came through the portal and Jessie believes he never returned. She is sure he is here."

"I despise cowards. If this man left his family to come here..." Tarik shook his head again. "I could find this man by sniffing for the greatest coward."

Sakura snuggled up to his bare chest. "I believe you could."

"I do not see why I cannot simply find him and kill him."

Sakura told him about Daniel and the spirits. Tarik listened impassively, pulling Sakura closer as she spoke. When she finished, he kissed her hard. "You are such a good woman, my love. And Maeve? What of her? What does she think of all this?"

"She frightened me some. All that power, all that wisdom wrapped in one calm and poised priestess. She was almost as intimidating as you are, my love."

"She is far more intimidating than I. I should know. *I* cower in her presence."

"Do you…do you miss her?"

Tarik pulled away so he could see Sakura's face better. "Miss her? Sakura, if you only knew how often I feel that tingle right here. She comes and goes so much, I do not have time to miss her."

"Why do you not share this with me?"

"I am sharing it with you now. She is with me so much, I am just used to her being there."

"Then it is no wonder she is so intimidating. She carries so much of you with her."

"Indeed, she must."

"I can see her in your eyes sometimes."

Sakura shook her head. "She has a reverence for the portal that defies logic. Jessie, on the other hand, enjoys the quest. She is the perfect quester, for she has a thirst for it that I have not seen in anyone. She was born to it, I believe, and will serve us well."

Tarik grinned. "You like her."

"I do. She has a fire in her belly that makes me proud. She has a priestess's spirit and a warrior's heart. She has everything she needs to be very good at the quest: heart, spirit, passion—"

"And you have a passion for warriors."

Sakura rolled over on top of him. "I have a passion for *you*."

Tarik groaned playfully. "I am a mere plaything for you this life, my priestess. Do with me what you will."

"I plan on it, but first, we must agree to do this *my* way. I know you do not agree. Nefertiti can help me make this happen. Trust us, Tarik. We work quite well together. What I need you to do for me is to spread the word about the mask. It will be made of solid gold with…" Sakura paused here to access Jessie's memories. "Mosaic tiles inlaid throughout with our precious lapis. It is…it will be spectacular."

"And what will you have me do once we find this man? He is a priest, a confidante of the king. It is not for me to drag him away from court."

"I…we're…well…we're going to send him back to his own time so Jessie can put an end to the ghosts that haunt her brother."

Tarik sat up. "Do you know how?"

"Not quite."

Tarik opened his mouth, but Sakura placed her fingers lightly on his lips. "We are not sending him back into his own body. He may very well be dead. The spirits who are waiting for retribution will take care of the rest if he is. Jessie believes he is dead, but she is unsure as to how that transpired. We do this for Jessie and her brother. She does not yet realize the depth of the ominous evil clinging to her emanates from those angry spirits."

Tarik held her closer. "You have not told her this?"

"Not yet. I am afraid Jessie is going to need our help far more than we will need hers, but there is more information I need before I can tell her anything."

"They are that evil?"

Shaking her head, Sakura pressed herself closer to him. "No. They are *that* angry."

21st Century AD

After crossing eleven possibilities off her list, Jessie decided she would rather have her talk with Daniel in the place affording her the most strength; the forest behind the inn. She hadn't anticipated that telling him the truth about the house and portal would be so difficult. She was its protector; she was the guardian of that particular gate, and every time someone found out, the portal became that much more vulnerable.

It wasn't that she distrusted Daniel or thought he would want to use it. Next to Ceara and Tanner, she trusted Daniel the most. He would do the right thing once he knew. Daniel always did the right thing.

As they hiked up to the familiar little clearing where three enormous oak trees stood guard like soldiers at Buckingham Palace, Daniel peppered her with questions about where they were going and why she wanted to talk to him, and and and.

"This is about *them*, isn't it? You found something out, didn't you?"

In so many ways, he was still a little boy, and maybe that was why she was so protective of him still. Yes, there was something about his ghosts that scared her, but she hadn't been able to pin it down. She had tried several rituals, spent time alone in his bedroom and even visited the attic, but whatever was sending those chills through her eluded her. She just knew…no, she *felt* there was something sinister about their presence…something evil.

And that didn't make sense to her.

If they were, in fact, Albert's murdered family, then they were victims of a heinous crime. They were not evil, but had been the recipient of an incredible act of cruelty. They were children, after all. They were not malignant beings.

So, where *was* the evil and anger coming from? What had changed?

Suddenly, Jessie stopped walking. Of course! *They* hadn't changed. *She* had. She was now an initiate, learning about her powers and how to control them. She had stepped into her powers and was able to pick things up she hadn't been able to before. Accepting the Goddess wasn't just lip service. It turned on switches Jessie didn't know existed within her. She hadn't felt the intensity of the evil before accepting the Goddess, but she did now. Another switch had been flicked on.

When they came to the clearing, Jessie stopped. Silently, she requested the spirits of the Nemeton allow her entrance to this, her sacred place; a place she had found months ago while collecting a certain fern for one of her rituals. It had called her to it, beckoning her, urging her to see it for its sacredness. The

Druids revered the number three, and here stood three oaks in a triangle with their leaves touching high above the clearing. She had come here occasionally, and attempted to make contact with the faerie folk…the beings who occupy the space between worlds who can slip easily from one world to the next. She had hoped to learn something from them, but also knew they did not trust humankind because of the way humans were destroying the natural world that was their home.

She had also read that the right people with the right attitude and spiritual awareness could call upon them and experience their realm. This clearing, with its three trees of wisdom and a stream running behind it, was the perfect setting for faerie folk, and Jessie knew that someday when she had enough wisdom and power, she would come here and make contact with them.

Someday.

Right now, however, she needed the strength of this sacred place in order to share a part of her world so very few people believed in. She needed the wisdom of the Goddess to be able to tell Daniel a secret that had irrevocably changed her.

"What are we doing?" Daniel whispered, as if sensing the sacred nature of the clearing.

She hadn't wanted to share this, her most important secret in a coffee shop, so she opted for here, her favorite spot in the world.

"This is a sacred place, and I am asking for permission before entering it. It is the respectful thing to do."

Daniel nodded as if understanding. "Okay."

Jessie turned to him. "We can go in. Have a seat over there on that log."

Daniel walked past the firepit Jessie had built the last time she'd come. It looked much like the one in the Dreamworld. "Cool place. You must come here a lot."

"Why do you say that?"

He nodded to the firepit with his chin. "You've built a firepit, arranged the logs and you knew right where to come." He shrugged. "Elementary, really."

"You have *got* to stop reading so much Sherlock Holmes." Jessie chuckled.

"It's still cool."

"Yes, it is. I love it here. It's peaceful, quiet and look at all the different colors of green."

Daniel looked around. "Oregon sure has turned you into a nature lover."

"Or something."

"These oak trees are huge."

"They're special." Jessie waited for him to give her his full attention before continuing. "So am I."

She had expected him to crack a joke or make some smart-aleck remark, but instead, he nodded.

"I brought you up here because there's something really important I need to talk to you about."

"The ghosts?"

"Sort of. Actually, this is about me."

Daniel's face dropped. "You're not—"

"No, no, I'm not using again. It's nothing like that." Jessie paused and sent up a silent prayer. "Well, after you hear what I have to say, you may think I'm on drugs, but I'm not. I've never been better in my life."

Daniel nodded slowly. "Good. Things have been so much better since you started college and stopped being such a jerk."

She smiled. "Yes, they have...and there's a reason for that. That's what I want to talk to you about. I know you're going to have a lot of questions, but let me get through this first, okay?"

Daniel's face registered fear of the unknown, fear of losing the one person he truly counted on in his young life. "You're not sick or anything, right?"

"This is a good thing, sport. There's nothing to be afraid of. It's just...well...let's just say it will explain *a lot* of things you may or may not have noticed about me since we moved here."

"Okay. Good. I was getting sorta scared."

"Well, don't be. There's nothing to be afraid of. It's rather exciting."

"Is it you and Tanner?" His eyes grew wide. "Are you guys getting married or something?"

"God, no. It's...not like that. Now hush, and let me get through this." Jessie moved over and sat next to him on the log, suddenly feeling a calm wash over her. She had no doubt it was the Goddess. "The first thing I want you to know is that I've found out a few things about your ghosts."

"I knew you'd find something."

She nodded. "We did. They were murdered."

He leaned back and blinked. "Murdered? Someone murdered them?" Daniel quickly covered his mouth.

"That's okay. Look, this is all going to sound way out there, so save your questions, okay?"

"Sorry."

Leaning forward, Jessie put her elbows on her knees. "The ghosts were people from a family who were murdered in the inn. The inn used to be where our old house is back in San Francisco." She waited for Daniel to say something, but he maintained more self-control than she expected. "The husband and dad, his name is Albert, left them when they were being killed and they want his soul back."

Daniel's mouth opened and then shut again.

"You can ask."

"Where did he go?"

Jessie blew out a breath. "Now, this is where you're really going to have to listen with an open mind and hear me out, okay?"

Daniel nodded. "Okay."

Jessie nodded. "Mom and Dad have always raised us to believe that souls go to heaven, right?"

Daniel nodded.

"And you know not everyone believes that's true, right?"

"I know I don't."

"Do you want to know why I don't believe it?"

"Because you're not a Christian?"

"No. I don't believe it because…well…because I know better. And I know because I have the ability to go back in time." She paused again, and to her surprise, he said nothing.

"I've traveled into the past and have met the people who used to have my soul, so I know, firsthand, that souls transmigrate. They do not go to heaven or someplace with rainbows and sunbeams." She waited while Daniel digested this in silence. He said nothing, so she continued. "Because of who I am and what I can do, I know what your ghosts want and how to give it to them." Jessie tilted her head to one side. "You're awfully quiet. Are you trying to decide if I've lost my mind?"

"No. I can't decide what question to ask."

Jessie nodded. "I'm sure. Now, I know how crazy that must sound, but you have to remember one thing, sport. I have never lied to you. Ever."

"I know."

"And I'm not lying to you now. I'm not speaking metaphorically or in riddles. I'm not high. I'm not joking. I am not doing anything but sharing the most important thing in my life. Do you understand?"

He nodded. "Your telling me you can travel back in time."

"Right. See, there is this thing called a portal and it allows people's souls to travel back and forth in time. It's like a seam in time that my soul slips through."

"Just your soul?"

Jessie nodded. "Just my soul. The rest of me stays behind when I enter the portal. The portal is located in our inn. I found it, I thought, by accident, but there are no accidents in the Goddess's universe. I was chosen by those who came before me...who *were* me."

"Whoa. You really aren't kidding, are you?"

"No, Daniel, I am not. The portal is an amazing thing, but it isn't something just anyone can use. This man, Albert, the head of the family who was murdered, somehow found the portal and used it to get back and forth to ancient Egypt."

"Why Egypt?"

"He was an archaeologist. You can imagine what an advantage it would be to know where all of those relics were buried."

"Oh hell yeah. Wait. He used the portal when he wasn't supposed to?"

"Right. That was his first mistake, but more about him later. This is about me and why I said I am special. I don't just have the ability to *use* the portal, I am the Guardian of the Gate. I am now and have been for many lives. It's been my job throughout the centuries, in all sorts of different incarnations, to make sure the portals are not used for any evil design or personal gain. You see, I come from a long line of very powerful priestesses who honor the Goddess and are in charge of keeping her alive in the hearts of as many people as we can. In order to do what I need to accomplish in my lifetime, I have become an initiate into the priesthood of Druidry." Jessie stopped here and realized that anyone listening to this would probably have her locked up.

"You're a Druid." It was not a question.

Jessie shook her head. "Not yet, but I am on that path. I am being educated in the ways of the Goddess and the inner workings of Nature." She leaned across and laid her hand on his. "I know this is a lot to take in right now, but—"

Daniel's eyes lit up. "By Ceara? She's the one teaching you, huh?"

Jessie nodded. "And others. Others who are far wiser than the likes of me, but who live thousands of years from now." Jessie rose and walked over to the firepit. She had only raised the fire in the pit once in real life, and that had taken just about every ounce of energy she possessed, but when she had done it the other day with Sakura, it felt so natural.

"I was meant to find the portal, meant to travel across time, meant to—"

"Where did you go?"

Jessie turned from the firepit. "The first time, I went to the first century AD. Cate, that's the Druid priestess I once was, called me to come. She...well, it's a long story, but she needed my help."

Daniel nodded, but Jessie couldn't tell if he was believing any of this or just pacifying her until he could call the men in the white jackets.

"Anyway, the changes you've seen in me are a result of everything that has happened to me because of the portal and my travels and the people I've met." Jessie knew she would have to show him. Turning back to the firepit, she drew in a breath, said a quick prayer, and exhaled slowly. This had to work or she'd lose his faith in her forever. "I want you to watch this fire, okay? Don't take your eyes from it." She knew everything was energy...if she could summon enough energy...

"So, my ghosts are somehow connected to this portal in the inn."

Jessie nodded, her back to Daniel as she studied the firepit, feeling the energy build inside her. "Yes. Albert left them and they want his soul back. I've been…well…let's just say I'm in the process of trying to make that happen."

"In the first century?" Daniel joined her at the pit.

Jessie shook her head. "No. I'm afraid I stepped into the wayback machine for this one. He went to ancient Egypt. You know, pharaohs and pyramids and all that."

"Sweet."

Jessie looked at him out of the corner of her eye. "You *believe* me."

Daniel nodded. "Jess, when I first came to you about the voices, you didn't laugh or blow me off or anything. You were really cool about it. You could have called me crazy or told Mom and Dad you thought I was losing my mind, but you didn't. You didn't make fun of me or anything. What kind of brother would I be if I turned around and did that to you? I've got ghosts. You've got…well…cooler shit than I do."

The energy continued to mount, and Jessie felt the initial spark of it in her fingertips. "It was easy to believe you after what I've seen."

"So, what have you seen?"

"It might be more believable for me to *show* you what I've learned. Stand back a little. I'm not yet proficient enough to keep from making mistakes." Jessie turned to the firepit and put her hands out over the dry sticks as if she was warming them. At first, nothing happened, but then, as she put forth more concentration, the dry grass under the sticks began to smoke.

Daniel moved closer to the smoke. "No way."

Jessie did not respond. It took everything in her will to focus the energy to do what she wanted it to do. As she lowered her hands closer to the sticks, the smoke turned into a spark and the dry grass caught fire. Lowering her hands, Jessie felt a bead of sweat on her brow.

"That is totally awesome! How did you do that?"

Jessie sent a prayer of thanks to the Goddess before wiping

her forehead with the back of her hand. "I'm in training. It's not a magic trick or anything. We use the flames like a...well...like a crystal ball of sorts."

Daniel stared at the fully grown fire and murmured, "Seriously cool." Looking over at Jessie, he said, "If I didn't believe you before, I sure do now. My sister the priestess. Can you tell me how you did that?"

"I could. But then I'd have to sacrifice you to the Goddess."

Daniel's eyes started to bug out when he realized she was kidding. Sitting back down on the log, he motioned for her to join him. "Tell me everything. Oh my god, this is so cool. One minute, you're a druggie pissing Mom and Dad off, and the next minute, you're in college and hanging out with the local bad boy and the town crazy lady. It's all starting to make sense now."

"You know Ceara's not crazy, right?"

"Oh, I know, but come on, Jess. Everyone who knows you has seen the change in you. Ever since you got back from..." His eyebrows shot up. "Something happened when you went to Wales, didn't it?"

"A lot of things happened to me. That's the point of this little chat. I'm—"

"Special. Yeah, I get that. Loud and clear. Should I bow or something?" Daniel laughed and Jessie punched him playfully in the arm.

"I have responsibilities now; things not of this time that are sacred and important. The portal allows me to get to where I'm needed most. Right now, that's ancient Egypt, and I need to find the man who let his family die. Once I do that, I think we might be able to rid the inn of your spirits."

"Ancient Egypt. How cool is that? What's it like?"

"Well, the truth is, I only have remnants of memories of Sakura, that's who I was back then. I seldom experience it as if I were truly there. It happened once, though, and totally freaked me out."

"Can you tell me about it?"

Jessie stared at the fire, proud of herself. "You remember a couple of months ago when we were tide pooling and we saw that booze cruise?"

"Yeah."

"Well, not long after that, I was..." Jessie hesitated. Saying it aloud sounded far sillier than she thought it would.

"You were what?"

The thought of Spencer Morgan made her smile. "I was a pirate in the sixteenth century."

"No way! There were female pirates back then?"

"Well, yeah, there were, but I wasn't one of them." She hesitated a moment before laying it all out to him. "I was a pirate by the name of Captain Spencer Morgan."

Daniel hit his forehead with the heel of his hand. "Aw, man, you get all the fun. You were a *guy* pirate?"

"Like you read about. It was so incredible, too There I was, sword in hand, fighting for my life and the lives of my crew. It was...well...it was one of the coolest things I've ever done."

"How come you remember that one?"

"Long story for another time. Suffice it to say, I normally experience a few moments of their lives and then our souls become one and I am more of a passenger than the driver. If you think about it, aren't there times when you wonder how it is you know something? Or have you ever gone someplace and felt like you'd been there before?"

"Like *déjà vu*?"

"Sort of. The term *déjà vu* literally means already seen. It's pretty much our bullshit explanation for that which I do, which is remember. Since our scientists can't explain it in scientific terms, they write it off as wish fulfillment or fantasy. What it really is is the residual memory of who you used to be. Does that make sense?"

"So this is all about reincarnation."

Jessie nodded. "Yeah. That's not to say heaven doesn't exist for some souls, because I tell you what, after all I've seen and experienced, I don't cast aspersions on *anything*, not heaven, not hell, not ghosts or faeries or pirates or gnomes or elves or even unicorns. *Anything* is possible. You remember that when the time comes for you to believe something your brain tells you is impossible. *Nothing* is impossible. *Nothing* is an accident. Do you think it's a coincidence that the inn used to be where we lived in San Francisco and now we live in it here in Oregon? The odds of that happening are three hundred million to one. We thought we moved to Oregon because I was a fuck-up, but even *that* wasn't an accident. I fucked up. We came to Oregon and ended up in the house we were meant to live in."

"Whoa."

Jessie nodded. "Yeah, and it's pretty whoa-ing at times."

"So we sorta followed the house here." Daniel held his head in his hands. "That's amazing."

"Me and the portal were meant to be, and here we are. Once I knew what my purpose was in this life, I got my shit together as fast as I could."

"Does Tanner go with you?"

"No. And that's what I really need you to hear. The portal isn't a toy. It isn't a means of taking a vacation from our reality. The portal exists for a purpose, and that purpose has to do with protecting the natural world. The only reason I've been using it to get to Egypt is because those ghosts are tied directly to the woman who may have started this whole time slipping adventure, and it's my job to get an evil man out of there and back where he belongs before he can do any more harm."

"So that's what you meant by Guardian of the Gate."

"Yeah. It's my job now, and when someone from the past needs me, I go back."

"Is it dangerous?"

The fire crackled and sputtered as if in answer. "It can be. If something happens to my body here in this time, then there is no place for my soul to return. It will remain in whatever time I sent it to as part of the person living with it."

"Do you control where you go? I mean, it's not like HG Wells' *Time Machine*, is it?"

"It's not. I try to control it by thinking of the past me I want to reach, but that's not always completely accurate. That's why I can't just cruise into any time period and take the passenger seat."

"So you've seen two of your past selves?"

"Three. Two priestesses and the pirate."

"The *guy* pirate."

Jessie smiled. "The soul has no gender. We are what we are when we need to be. It took some getting used to being a man, but like I said, it's not like my consciousness is running the show. It pretty much melds with the one in charge."

"Then how do you know when it's time to leave? How do you get back?"

"Well, the person you're in knows you're there. At some point, they release you. If they go to sleep or lose consciousness, there you are, in the driver's seat. That's how I ended up in a sword fight. I entered Spencer just as he had his clock cleaned and was about to get killed."

"Oh hell no, you were in a *sword* fight?"

"Yeah, but let me tell you, I sucked and was scared shitless."

Daniel frowned. "Yeah. I bet you were. What if he would have been killed?"

"Then I would die."

"So it *is* dangerous? Really dangerous."

"It can be."

"But does that mean you can change history?"

"That's exactly what I wanted to know when I first started, and the answer is no. I can't go back to when Lincoln was shot and prevent him from getting shot, but I *can* tell someone who shot him and where Boothe was hiding. You see, you have to remember one funny thing about history; we only know one half of a percent of what *really* happened. For instance, when I went to this one queen and told her where she needed to move her troops, that conversation doesn't show up in the history books, but her actions, her about-face with her army did." Jessie grinned.

"You got to talk with *a queen*? Man, you're sure lucky."

"Daniel, you must swear to me you will *never* breathe a word of this to anyone and that you will not, under *any* circumstances, try to find it and use it yourself."

"Aw, Jess…but it sounds like so much fun."

"Well, it's not. I mean…it is in a way, but not like that. I told you, it's *not* a toy. I have to have your word that you will honor everything I've just told you and never tell another living person."

Jessie reached in between one of the stones and withdrew an athame. It had the head of an eagle at the end of the black hilt and a very sharp point about six inches long. "This is an athame. It is used for many of the sacred rituals. It is seldom used to cut anyone or anything, as it is more symbolic in nature. Today, however, I'm changing that. Today, little brother, I need you to swear a blood oath that you will *never* speak of, write about, use, or in any way reveal what you know about the portal."

Daniel looked at the knife and then up at his sister. "You're not kidding."

Jessie sat on the log and set the knife in her lap. "No, I'm not. I struggled a long time with whether or not I should divulge this, my greatest secret to you, and in the end, I decided I could tell you as long as I knew you were bound to secrecy, as long as you swore to protect it, like I do, with your life."

"And if I break the oath?"

Jessie exhaled loudly and stared hard into his eyes. "Then by the powers the Goddess has vested in me, I will have to find a way to silence you forever."

Daniel's jaw dropped open. "You don't really mean—"

"I am the Guardian of the Gate, Daniel, and I have come to love and cherish those on the other side of it. If you or anyone else jeopardizes those I care for or make the portal vulnerable in any way, then I am bound by the Goddess to do what I must to ensure it never happens again. It is my responsibility now, and it is with the greatest faith I have in you that I've shared this."

Daniel blinked slowly and then stared at the knife. "Is that what you'd use?"

Jessie picked the knife up. "No. This is for the blood oath you're going to take right now." She took Daniel by the wrist and turned it over so his palm was facing up. "Close your eyes. This will only hurt for a second."

Daniel jerked his hand away. "You're really going to cut me?"

"Just a little. Trust me." Jessie held her hand out and waited for Daniel to place his in it. "It has to be done, Daniel. We can't leave here until I know you're bound by a sacred oath."

"Can't I just swear to stick a needle in my eye?"

Jessie grinned. "You could if you were five. Come on. Trust me."

Daniel lay his hand, palm up, in Jessie's. "Think maybe you're taking this Goddess thing a little too far?"

Jessie abruptly turned to the fire and with one hand waved so the flames spit and parted.

"Oh crap."

Turning back to him, her eyes narrowed. "The blood oath will make me rest easier. I have a job to do, and even though you're my family, I have a greater obligation."

Daniel couldn't take his eyes off the flame, so Jessie used the moment to draw the blade across his palm. "Shit! That hurt!"

"I told you it would. Now, come here." Jessie pulled Daniel to the fire and closed his hand to a fist so that some blood dripped out of the bottom and into the flame, sizzling as it landed.

"Okay, now repeat after me."

"*By the Mother of All Things; By the Tree, the Well, and the Fire; By the Nature Spirits, the Mighty Dead, and the Shining Ones; By the wisdom which echoes in the forests and in my heart; I swear this Oath! I am Your True Worshipper. In Your service I will keep Your ways.*

In Your service I will give respect to all things.

In Your service I will strive to be true to myself. Make me Your Adopted One, Accept me as Your Foster Child,

And gift me as I gift you. O Shining Ones!

I give You my love, my honor, and my worship—Asking in turn for Your love, Your wisdom, and Your power.

Hear my Holy Oath, And if I break my Oath,

May the Sky fall upon me—May the Sea engulf me—May the Earth open beneath me—May this Fire consume me

So do I swear!"

As Daniel repeated, Jessie squeezed his fist so more blood sizzled into the fire making the flames leap and twist around each other as if eager for more. When he finished, she took a handkerchief from her pocket and pressed it into his palm. "I have a salve back in my room that will heal that right up."

"Salve?" Daniel pressed the handkerchief into his palm.

"Part of the Druidic tradition is knowing how to heal, how to use what nature gives us to heal things like cuts."

"I swear, Jess, I'll never tell a soul. Even if I was being tortured, I'll never tell."

Jessie mussed up his hair. "I know you won't. I wouldn't have told you if I didn't think I could trust you. And I do." Jessie held her hands out and lowered the flame until it sputtered twice before going out.

"Jess, that is so damn cool. What else can you do?"

"You'll see when you put that salve on your hand." Jessie picked up a stick and pushed the embers around, making sure that there was no hazard of an ember blowing out. "The rest is top secret."

Daniel stood and watched as she poked at the embers. "So, now what? What happens to you and your real life?"

"I live my real life. It's important I don't neglect this life. It's easy to do when you're slipping across time." When Jessie leaned over the fire, her ankh fell out of her blouse and swayed back and forth.

"Did you get that from your travels?"

She tucked the ankh back in her shirt. "Nothing tangible can come through the portal, but yes, I got this from my travels. I got it in Wales, from one of my former selves. It's another long story."

"You have a lot of those."

"Yes, I do."

"You're pretty cool, Jess."

She smiled and sheathed the athame. "Thanks. It took me long enough. Now, I want you to stay in one of the guest rooms until I can get this thing sorted out. There's something about our ghosts that's really beginning to bug me and I'd rather you not give them an audience."

"They can't hurt me, can they?"

Jessie started back down the hill. "Remember what I said about anything being possible. I'd rather not take the chance."

"Okay. I'll stay out of my room on one condition: you tell me everything you know about one of your past lives."

"You want to know about Spencer Morgan, don't you?"

Daniel nodded. "I want to hear everything."

Jessie laughed, and for the next hour, she regaled Daniel with stories about pirates, secret chests and Queen Elizabeth's court.

14th Century BCE

By the time Tarik finished explaining to Nefertiti what Sakura's plan entailed, they had completed two full rounds of the courtyard.

"It is as dangerous as that?"

"My queen, this priest is obsessed with you, and though he has not made a move to hurt you or molest you in any way, he is still very dangerous. We must bring him out of hiding so your sister can return him to his own time."

Nefertiti nodded. "I do not like Sakura endangering herself, but there is none other who can do as you suggest. No one in either upper or lower Egypt possesses the power my sister does."

Suddenly, Akhenaten appeared in the garden. "Tarik, are you chief of my guards or are you chief of guarding my beautiful wife?"

Tarik bowed. "I am the former, your grace, though it would be an honor to be the latter as well."

Akhenaten laughed a little like a woman might. "Ah, Tarik, your wit does, as usual have a bite to it." Gliding down the stairs leading to the garden, Akhenaten took Nefertiti in his arms and kissed her. "You are such a beauty, my love, that these flowers hang their heads in shame."

"You always exaggerate so eloquently, my king."

"As much as I would love to stroll around our garden with you, I did come in search of my Chief of Guards. You may stay and listen if you wish, and then perhaps, we will have time to take our own stroll around the courtyard."

Nefertiti bowed her head ever so slightly. "As you wish, my husband. I shall stay."

Akhenaten strode over to Tarik. "I have word from one of

my loyal men there is a temple to Aset hidden among the rock ruins east of the city walls. People have seen a priestess coming and going in an area where there should be no activity."

"I shall check that as soon as—"

"No need. I have put Hakim on that minor detail. If it is a temple, it cannot have many followers. The people are afraid of another rock slide in that area. It is worrisome that the heretics are so bold as to have a temple just outside my walls. We must make an example of this brazen priestess and her followers."

Tarik felt his stomach lurch and he could sense Nefertiti's fear from behind. "You have done much to wipe out the old ways, my king. Surely this is just a rumor from a subject who wants to be in your favor."

Akhenaten rubbed his chin. "I had not considered that possibility, although now that you mention it, it does seem a bit arrogant that anyone would be so flagrant to have a temple so close to my palace." Akhenaten reached for Nefertiti. "What think you, my wife. Have we accomplished our goal for a new religion, or are there heretics knocking on our very door?"

Nefertiti sighed. "There will always be insurgents, my king, for that is the way of the weak."

Akhenaten laughed. "Well put. Fine. Tarik, my loyal man is Bakari, the wine merchant. You may check out his story and see if he isn't merely trying to get into my inner circle."

"And what of Musa?" Tarik knew Musa coveted his position and was always trying to make a name for himself. He could handle Bakari, but Musa would not be as easy.

"Worry not about Musa. He has his duties and he tends to me well. He has greatly helped with the transition to the new way. You take care of Bakari and let your king worry about the rest."

"I will do my best."

Akhenaten patted Tarik on the back. "Of course you will. Now, tell me about a mask made of gold? Is someone making a gift for their king?"

Tarik's stomach seized. "You have eyes and ears everywhere, my king. You would know better than I."

"You toy with me, Tarik. I know you have heard these

rumors. You know everything that goes on in my court. Is this a gift for me? Should I not know, or at least pretend not to know?"

Tarik glanced over at Nefertiti, who stepped up to her husband. "Shh. It was to be my gift to you, my husband. I had threatened the artisans to keep silent, but you know how we love gossip. Please, speak no more of it, lest you spoil the whole surprise."

Akhenaten's face lit up. "There is more?"

Nefertiti nodded. "From our daughters. We have planned an elaborate celebration for you, but it will ruin it for them if they know you know."

"Then I shall render my lips useless on the subject, my wife, so as to not ruin their joy at surprising their father. A celebration? How delightful."

"Indeed." As Nefertiti hugged her husband, her eyes bored into Tarik, who took his leave.

Tarik immediately left the courtyard and headed to the corner of town where Bakari often sold his wine.

"Bakari!" Tarik said, dropping coin into the merchant's palm. "The king has sent me to tell you to escape from the palace to Lower Egypt as quickly as possible."

The fat little wine merchant wiped the crumbs from his beard. "Escape? How? Why?"

"We have received word that the heretics plan on killing you for revealing one of their temples. The pharaoh is concerned for your safety and requests you leave this instant. I am to escort you as far as Izrack, and then you must be careful to travel only at night and sleep during the day, staying clear from anyone until we send word."

The wine merchant quickly began packing his wares, his face white with fear. "I do not understand. If the pharaoh fears for my safety, would I not be safer within the palace walls?"

Tarik shook his head. "There are spies even within the palace walls, I'm afraid. He treasures you as a loyal subject and wants to know you are safely away from any danger. Now, if you would like to present your doubts to the king himself—"

"No...no, I understand."

Tarik stepped up to him, his broad chest in Bakari's nose. "And he wishes to know where you got your information about the temple."

Bakari averted his eyes. "By my own eyes, of course. I am a merchant, after all, and I—"

Tarik placed his hand on the hilt of his sword. "Do not displease me, merchant. I have come to help you and you lie right to my face? Should I cut your tongue out before we start our trip so I do not have to worry about being lied to again?"

"The priest," Bakari said, his eyes fixed on Tarik's sword. The priest told me. He said I would receive great rewards if I gave him the information he was seeking."

"Which priest was this? What was his name?"

"He...he did not say."

"Tall? Short? Light? Dark?"

"He came at dusk, his face shrouded in darkness. I could only tell you that he had a limp of sorts. No, not a limp, a strange gait."

Tarik released the hilt of his sword. "Gather your goods then. We will be off momentarily."

Bakari nodded. "I understand."

"You will be duly repaid for your services, Bakari. Let's be off now, and pray to the great Aten that our journey is swift and goes unnoticed by prying eyes."

As they rolled out of sight, Tarik pulled his sword from its sheath and set it upon his lap. Once he got rid of Bakari, he would have to see to Musa. Musa was not a man to take lightly, and if he could win a name for himself by dragging Sakura from her temple and parading her through the streets, he would stop at nothing to see it happen.

What Musa didn't know was that Tarik would also stop at nothing to ensure that never happened.

21st Century AD

"I told you to have faith in him," Ceara said as she filled her watering can. "Your brother is nobody's fool."

Jessie sat at the small table in the boathouse and opened up her laptop. "I was so proud of him. He was really brave."

Ceara looked out over the top of her glasses. "Do you really think the blood oath was necessary? I didn't even know you knew how to do one."

Jessie looked up from the laptop. "Yes, I do. I can't choose to follow the Goddess and the rituals when it suits me and ignore Her when it doesn't. I've watched my parents do that with their religion my whole life and I won't be like them. I can't afford to be."

Ceara continued filling up the can. "Then the Goddess has chosen wisely in you. Tell me more."

"Well...I finally did it."

Ceara turned the water off. "The fire?"

Nodding, Jessie didn't find what she was looking for and closed the laptop. "It was incredible. That feeling, the raw energy...was indescribable."

"Well, indescribable is pretty descriptive. I am so proud of you. I remember when I started my first sacred fire. It filled me with a sensation that I could do anything."

"It was harder than I thought. I've been practicing for weeks, but I guess it wasn't going to happen until I stepped on the path. Cate and Sakura make it look so easy, but I got to tell you, my brain was working overtime to get that spark going."

Ceara started watering the plants that adorned the edges of her deck. "It takes faith and the wisdom that everything is made of energy. The manipulation of energy is what true magic is all about. It is what the Druids and the Pagans before them understood. It is what, I'm sure, the ancient Egyptians understood as well."

"You know, when I was little, my mom had a refrigerator magnet that said faith is action based on belief. I always pooh-poohed it because it came from one of her Christian magazines; but now, I get it. It applies to any kind of faith."

"The Christians have not cornered the market on faith, my dear. Times are changing and you are in the eye of that change. You are the beginning of a spiritual revolution that is going to change the face of the world. Even as the Muslims rise against those who are different, even as the Christians and the Mormons send their missionaries out into the world to change and corrupt entire cultures, you are on the brink of a return of ancient religions and a spiritual path that could be the only thing that saves this planet." Ceara faced Jessie. "When Cate said you were the one, Jessie, she didn't just mean you were the one to help her out of their bind. She meant that you are the one who has the potential to help save the world."

Jessie was too stunned to say anything, so she just stood there with her mouth open.

Ceara shrugged. "What do you think?"

"It makes total sense. One of us from my future had to have seen what the world was going to end up like and...and..." The reality was almost too great for her to utter.

"And so he or she went into the past?"

Jessie nodded. "You knew, didn't you?"

"I had my suspicions, but it is not my journey to puzzle out. It is for you to come to know when you are ready."

Jessie shook her head. "If I am supposed to do something big it's because every one of us has done something big. Cate saved Maeve and the Druids on Anglesey. Sakura is going to do something around Nefertiti, and Spencer saved the world from economic ruin. It's what we do, isn't it?"

"Except what you do could be far more significant than economics or spiritual enlightenment, my dear. If you from the future were searching for a way to save the planet from the hands of mankind, she would have surely had to go to the past to start there."

"But if that's true, why is the planet in such bad shape?"

"Compared to what? Remember, my dear, that time is not linear. The you of the future exists right now, just as the you of the past does. We do not even know if the future you contacted Cate or Sakura first. There are so many possibilities of whom she originally approached."

"But you're sure it started from me in the future?"

Ceara shook her head. "Jessie, have you ever wondered how it was Cate came to you? Why *you*? Why not someone further into the future? Why not someone in the Middle Ages? Why you?"

"She knew because someone told her."

Ceara grinned. "Good girl. Now you're starting to see how this works. For Cate to have made the leap to you, she had to already know you existed. There is only one way she could have known that...someone *told* her about you. Someone who knew you would be needed." Ceara tossed her deadheads into the trash. "The next time you get a flash of something futuristic, it won't be something you saw in a movie. It will be the remnants of your memories from that time." Ceara put her clippers back in the watering can. "This whole element of time boggles your mind, doesn't it. Your future you knows about them because *you* tell her." Ceara waited for this to sink in before continuing. "I don't know what you do or how you do it, but somehow, someday, you manage to tell yourself. You manage to reach her and you tell her something about all of this, and when you do, and she goes as far back as she can to see if she can't right the wrongs before it's too late."

"And how do you know this?"

Ceara snipped off another flower. "Because it's what I would do. Way down the road, when you become very powerful and understand all you are to be, you will seek your future self. It is she who is powerful enough to go back and gather the information needed for you. I've put a lot of thought into this, and I have come to the conclusion that Sakura didn't make the first trip across time. She *couldn't* have. We can't make the jump without having already established contact. Someone *had* to have made contact with her first...someone who *knew* she existed. Someone who knew about the portals and how they work. The only way someone could know that Sakura and Cate existed—"

"Was if I told them."

"Bingo."

"It makes my head spin."

"Because you keep wanting to see time on a string, and it isn't. Some version of you from the future remembered. We don't know what or how much or even whom but someone besides Cate or Sakura got this ball rolling. You see, my dear, you must become so good at what you do and so powerful, that your future souls remember much more easily. In doing so, they are able to better handle the tasks ahead of them."

Jessie pinched the bridge of her nose. "You're right. I keep thinking of those damn timelines we did in high school, and time isn't fixed."

"Not even remotely. Right now, the future yous live, just as Cate and Sakura live. We exist in parallel universes which are far from linear. Someone ahead of you reached back and started this in motion, and Cate chose to come to you."

"Why didn't she tell me?"

"She may not know. Remember, we have access to some of their memories, but not all of them. We cannot know what Cate knows or remembers about any of the other yous who have joined with her. As you and she grow stronger, so do your residue memories of her for future times."

"And Cate and I are becoming closer."

"Exactly. The bond you are creating won't be able to be suppressed or ignored by your future souls once she dials in. When she does that, she will know of not only you, but Sakura and Spencer as well. When she does go back, we can't know when she makes contact with Cate. Perhaps it is when Cate is a young girl or an old woman. It is impossible to know."

"So she might have contacted Cate when Cate was too young to do anything or even know anything about this path."

"But the memories of you would still be there, and she could not act upon them until she became older and wiser. Then she comes to you when the time is right."

Jessie shook her head. "Just when I thought I was getting the hang of it." Picking up the watering can, Jessie took the clippers out and watered the hanging plants. "So Maeve didn't start all of this?"

Ceara smiled. "I never said that. You and she are connected in a way that is stronger than anything I could ever conceive of. Her role in the shaping of your destiny cannot be overlooked."

Jessie nodded. "My destiny...I've been thinking about that a lot, Ceara, and I've been wondering if maybe going back to school next term isn't a big, fat waste of my time."

"Why is that?"

Jessie followed her as she moved to the next flower box. "Because I am studying a discipline that is flawed. I'm studying subjects that so-called experts profess are facts, when the truth is, they couldn't find their ass with both hands. I'm living a history the history books know nothing about and are wrong when they do think they know something."

"Welcome to the real world."

"What does that mean?"

"What you've just described applies to nearly everything modern man touches. Remember when eggs were bad for you for about five years? Then someone said, wait, no, we were wrong. Eggs are good for you. Then they said aspirin is bad for you. No, wait, aspirin is good for your heart. Over and over again since I've been in this pathetic excuse for a body, some "expert" has spent his career drilling some non-fact into our heads as fact. The world used to be flat, remember? The sun used to orbit the earth. These things stayed true until someone proved them false. So, what's the moral of this repetitious story? Accept nobody's facts except your own." Ceara reached over and clipped a half foot of ivy strand. "Is this dead?"

Jessie nodded.

"How do you know?"

"Because it isn't alive once you cut it from its source."

"No? Is that a fact or is it your fact?"

"Uh...just a fact, I guess."

Ceara walked down to the tiny kitchen and put the flower in a glass of water and said, "Well, *my* facts tell me this ivy has excellent regenerative powers, but I'm going to do more than tell you. I'm going to show you. Then, it will become your fact." Ceara placed the ivy in the glass of water and headed back out to the deck. "It's not your professors' faults they can't show you, but you, my dear, have the power to put their ivy to the test. Don't squander those tests simply because you wish to be told facts. True wisdom comes from finding those facts out for yourself."

Jessie nodded. "You sure you're not a professor?"

Ceara chuckled. "I profess nothing, but I am a student of life whose job it is to teach you how to navigate waters you think you see through clearly, but do not. The truth, Jessie, always lies somewhere in between fact and fiction. It's your job to sort out where it is and come to terms with it in your own life." Ceara picked her clippers up. "No one is going to feed you the truth, my dear, and if they do, you need to spit it out until you can figure out just what it was they put in your mouth."

"Ouch."

"It is my job to get you ready. So, you're going to stay in school and get what you can from it so you can go out into the big bad world and get a job you love. Whatever happened to being a professor?"

"I would feel like such a hypocrite."

"Then you've given up before you even started. You can always teach from a different perspective than your professors. Wouldn't that be a breath of fresh air for college students everywhere?"

"I suppose."

Ceara chuckled and said something under her breath. "It took twenty years for a Druid to master her craft, Jessie. What you're going to master is more than just Druidry. You're going to need to be very patient. Are you ready to begin?"

Jessie nodded.

"Good." Ceara started down the plank and Jessie watched her as she stopped to chat with the houseboat neighbor next to her. Jessie couldn't imagine life without her and wondered how much time they had left. The body she'd been living in was the body of an old, decrepit alcoholic who hadn't taken very good care of herself. And although Ceara had done her best to clean her up, some of the damage was irreparable.

When Ceara finished chatting, she turned and waved for Jessie to follow. "Come. There's work to be done."

14th Century BCE

When Tarik arrived outside the hidden temple of Aset, he realized he was too late. Musa was prodding Sakura forward about fifty feet from the opening. Tarik's immediate reaction was to reach for his sword so he could cut Musa's head from his neck. He hated Musa, but he couldn't afford to kill him right now.

Releasing the hilt, Tarik inhaled deeply and tried to rein in his emotions. It was difficult watching a man like Musa be so near her, let alone touching her. He had to swallow his anger back and it was bitter to swallow. He would get them out of this alive, but only if he took every step carefully and without anger. Musa was no fool. Surely, he had men stationed around the area, so killing him would not be wise. Not now.

"Is this the heretic our king sent you to retrieve?" Tarik asked as he stepped out from where he'd been hiding.

"Why do you want to know?" Musa stopped and snarled at Tarik.

"It is not I who wants to know, but our king. He has sent me to discover the truth of the rumor." Tarik forced himself not to look at Sakura, knowing his eyes would betray him. He had always looked at her with such love, even a donkey like Musa would see it.

"It is no rumor, Tarik Gbish. This woman did not deny the charge."

Tarik willed his heart to slow. "And what charge is that?"

Musa was still sneering, as he always did when called to task by his superiors. "She is a heretic worshipping Aset."

The fact that Sakura did not deny her calling did not surprise Tarik at all, but his heart was heavy knowing what her fate would be if Musa had his way.

"Have you found her temple?"

Musa shook his head. "I grabbed her out here, among the rocks. She refuses to show me the temple, so I was going to force her by cleaving off one finger at a time until she chose otherwise."

Tarik shuddered. "I do not believe the king ordered torture, Musa, and it would be ill-advised to proceed."

"Maybe he did. You think the king tells you everything, Tarik Gbish?"

Tarik stepped up to him now and towered over the man. Musa reminded Tarik of a plump rat protecting a tiny nut. "I *know* he did not. Dismembering a priestess is not what the king desires, nor is it what *I* will allow you to do." Placing his hand on the hilt, Tarik's nostrils flared. "I will remove your head from your shoulders should you even remove your knife from your belt."

"You cannot stop me, Tarik Gbish. It is not your duty to—"

Tarik towered over him now, a long, thick shadow across Musa's face. "It is my *duty* to protect our citizens from unlawful acts against their person. You were not given the powers of judge and executioner, Musa. Your job was simply to find the heretics. You did so, now let her be."

Musa glowered at Tarik now, even as he took a step away from the massive guard. "Don't be a fool."

Tarik bridged the gap once more. "Choose your next words wisely, Musa. You are speaking to the Chief of the Guards and I am not to be trifled with."

Musa sent a look over at Sakura before licking his lips and returning his glare at Tarik. "I will take her to the king and let *him* decide what to do with her. Does that suit you?"

"What would *suit* me is for you to find the temple as you were told to do and not overstep your bounds, priest."

"Look around you, Tarik Gbish. There is no place a temple could be hidden among these rocks. You can see that as well as I can."

"Yet you were going to torture her to find a temple you are unsure exists?"

"She knows something."

"That is not your place. You have done your job. Now, I will take her to Akhenaten and let him decide her fate." There was nothing he could do, short of killing Musa, to save her, and doing that would only cause suspicion and perhaps place him in a position where he could no longer protect his love.

No, he had to let this play out for as long as he could until he could find a way to save her. Tarik wondered if he still had the power. Could he call upon the very Goddess powers he had turned away from when Akhenaten came to power? Could he go where he needed to go and do what he needed to do before anything happened to Sakura?

Musa turned to Sakura and grabbed her roughly by the arm. "*I'll* take her to him then. She is *my* find."

Tarik stepped in front of Musa. "She may be a heretic, Musa, but she is still a priestess and deserving of your respect. Since I do not trust you to act accordingly, I will escort both of you to the pharaoh's chambers. Then, I will bring my men back here and we will find the temple you cannot locate."

"Be my guest, Tarik Gbish. You can look all you want." As Musa pushed Sakura ahead of him, Tarik prayed to Aset to help him save his lover.

21st Century AD

Jessie was just finishing cleaning the Rose Room in the inn when she felt the familiar tingle at the base of her spine.

Closing and locking the door to her room, Jessie lay on the bed and began the deep breathing exercises Ceara had shown her. There was a certain breathing, a certain pace of the heart that was a catalyst to propel her to the Otherworld. It was the breathing, the meditation and the ankh that enabled her to go where few human beings ever got to go.

The Otherworld.

What an incredible place it was. It was scary and fun all in the same breath, and she wondered what the Druid priestess standing in the middle of a field of orange poppies wanted.

"Poppies?"

Cate grinned and nodded. This wasn't their Dreamworld, where they usually met. This was the Land of the Sidhe, where anything could go wrong and you trusted very little of what you heard and saw. Had Cate summoned her here?

Cate nodded. "It's a faerie favorite." She waited for Jessie to hug her before continuing. "Thank you for coming so quickly. You must really be learning."

"Ceara's a good teacher."

"And you, a good student. I've called you because what I was afraid of happening has happened. Sakura needs our help. She is in trouble."

Jessie's breath caught. "The priest?"

Cate shook her head. "The pharaoh. He has imprisoned her as a heretic. She does not know what he has planned for her, but she believes he may kill her before she can help you with your quest and save Nefertiti."

Jessie watched as the poppies all blew in the same direction. "What were you doing there?"

Cate smoothed out her robe. "I, too, am a student. I was attempting to access Sakura's memories about the ankh you're wearing when something happened—something dark and disturbing that frightened me. I jumped out as quickly as I could in case something terrible was happening in her life."

"You mean...like...death?" The thought of Cate dying was like a frozen ice pick to Jessie's heart.

"Yes. When I came here and she did not heed my call, I called for you."

"What can I do that you couldn't do?"

Cate took Jessie's hands as she always did when what she had to say was important. "It is more a matter of what *we* can do. If the two of us can call her to come, if we are strong enough so she cannot ignore us, then maybe we can see what is happening in her world and if there is anything we can do to help."

"And if she does not come?"

"Then we must assume she no longer lives."

Jessie blinked quickly. "Maybe she could be unconscious or hurt or something."

"That something is not a risk I wish for either of us to take. It is too dangerous, and that feeling...it was too dark...evil. No, we will wait here and see if she comes through to us. If not—"

Jessie felt this intense sadness wash over her at the thought of Sakura being dead. "Isn't there something we can do besides try to get her to come here?"

Cate watched the poppies blowing in the breeze. "Maeve. Maeve could find her for us."

Jessie nodded.

"Tarik might, but it has been so long since he has practiced the craft. Maeve said he is more warrior than priest."

Jessie swallowed back her fear. "Look, I'll wait here in case

Sakura shows up…or in case she is…still alive. You see if Maeve can't at least tell us what is happening with her."

Cate let go of Jessie's hands. "It is difficult not to care, isn't it?"

Before Jessie could answer, someone answered for her. "Sometimes, Catie, one can care too much."

Turning around, both Cate and Jessie stood immobile as Maeve walked into the poppy-filled clearing. She wore her priestess robe, her arms tucked inside. Her hood was down, revealing a kind face and warm gray eyes. She seemed both of this place and not of this place.

"I was doing a bit of healing for Lachlan's people when I felt you leave me, Catie. I wish you would tell me before you go…traveling."

Cate met Maeve halfway. "I'm sorry, Maeve, I didn't realize—"

"You must *start* realizing, Catie. When you leave our world, it disrupts everything in mine, and I know your soul is no longer with me, where it belongs. I do not know if something has happened to you or if you are on another one of your travels, but it is disconcerting." Maeve reached out and caressed Cate's cheek with the back of her hand.

"I'm sorry. It won't happen again."

Maeve's face softened. "I am just pleased to have found you here. I do not know what I would do…" She looked up and saw Jessie as if for the first time. "Jessie."

"Maeve."

"So, which of you is going to tell me what is going on here? Why have the two of you come here, of all places? Why are you not meeting in your Dreamworld?"

"I summoned Jessie here because Sakura is in trouble."

Maeve's left eyebrow twitched. "And what did you think Jessie could do that you could not?"

Cate shrugged. "I could not reach Sakura. I tried to get to her, but there was this evil surrounding her. I thought maybe Jessie's history might direct us, or maybe she might know something I do not."

"And does she?"

Jessie stepped next to Cate. She had never seen Maeve be so stern toward Cate and it was a little scary. "I can try."

"I see. So the two of you decided to try to help Sakura from this dark place."

They nodded in unison.

"She needs us, Maeve. If something happens to Sakura, we will never be able to help Jessie rid her home of the spirits who are plaguing her brother, or stop that man from using the portal whenever he wants."

Maeve sighed. "You two worry me."

Cate glanced over at Jessie. "It is not our intent."

"Oh, I *know* what your intent is, Catie, my love. You intend to ask me to go across time and back into poor Tarik in order to get the answers you seek."

Jessie tilted her head to one side. "Why is he *poor* Tarik?"

"Because my powers make him yearn for that which he gave up. He could have been a very powerful priest, but he walked away."

"For *her*."

"For life."

Jessie shrugged. "Same thing."

"Perhaps. Tarik made his decision long ago, even though it cost our spirit greatly. That price pains him every time I am with him, for he tastes the sweetness that is no longer available to him."

Cate nodded sadly. "That is the way of the warrior."

"Quite. Am I correct in assuming you want me to go to Tarik and see whether Sakura lives?"

Cate and Jessie looked at each before nodding in unison.

"I see." Maeve walked beyond them, her back to them. For a long time she did not speak, and Cate and Jessie did not move. When, at last, she turned around, her gaze locked onto Cate's. "I will do as you ask, but both of you need to understand what dangers you are facing each and every time you slip through, even when you go across time to each other." Turning to Jessie, Maeve did not soften her voice. "You know something of history, Jessie. People in our time do not live long. We die early from many maladies and much violence. You have seen, firsthand, the violence toward our kind. Every time you come to Catie, you risk your life." Turning back to Cate, she continued. "And you know naught of her world and whatever dangers lie therein. I am not pleased with you both stealing around in the past where dangers you know nothing of lurk around every corner. Sakura could very well be dead for all you know. And what then? We die. It is part of the cycle. You cannot race around time trying to save each other."

Cate and Jessie both bowed their heads.

"While I understand and appreciate your concern for one another, neither of you is strong enough or wise enough to handle all of the unseen dangers time travel entail, and I will not proceed with this until both of you swear to me you will never go off again without telling me."

Jessie nodded. "I swear."

"Catie?"

"Must I tell you when I go across to Jessie?"

Maeve looked back and forth between them. "I suspect the two of you will find more adventures together than you will separately, so yes, Catie, my sweet, I cannot have your soul whisking away, forward and backward without knowing why and where you are going."

Cate bowed her head. "Then I swear as well."

Maeve cupped Cate's chin and lifted her face. "I sound angry, but I am not. You do not know the emptiness and loneliness my spirit feels whenever you go. It takes my breath away like jumping into freezing water. I cannot heal when that comes over me. I can barely concentrate, but heal? Impossible."

"I'm sorry."

"I just wanted you to understand what happens to me when that experience washes over me. It is very unpleasant."

"From now on, I shall let you know...I didn't realize—"

Maeve placed her fingertips gently on Cate's lips. "A priestess *must* realize, Catie. She must think every action through and weigh the consequences of her actions. She must consider every outcome, think about every potential repercussion. We must be mindful of both positive and negative outcomes. Let this be the greater lesson for the two of you; whether in this world or another, you are always accountable for your actions."

Cate and Jessie both nodded.

"Good. Now that you both have sworn, I will do as you ask and see if Tarik's soul is bereft of his lover's soul. You two wait here. I shall not be gone long. Do not wander around here or follow any of the Sidhe should they come talk with you. Just remain here and with the Goddess' help I will return with what you need to know." Maeve turned to go, then stopped and looked over her shoulder. "And what, pray tell, will the two of you do if she still lives?"

Cate deferred to Jessie, who answered, "I'll see what's happening and help if I can."

"And why you?"

Jessie looked at Cate before answering. "Because I don't have a Maeve yet. If anything should go wrong, I'm more expendable than Cate."

"No," Cate said, firmly.

Jessie smiled at Cate, and continued. "Didn't you hear what Maeve said about how she feels when you leave? No one feels that way when I go. There isn't an *anam cara* in my time yet, so I should be the one to take any risks that need to be taken. It's only right."

Maeve smiled softly and returned to Jessie, lightly kissing her on the forehead. "You are such a brave little thing. Your capacity for love is surpassed only by the strength of your loyalty, both of which come from that tiny woman standing next to you as well as the Egyptian woman, Sakura. Among others. Just remember what I said about accountability. You cannot change the past—but you can most certainly become a part of it." With that, Maeve turned away and disappeared into the forest.

"She constantly amazes me," Jessie whispered.

"I know. I feel that way daily." Cate stood next to Jessie watching the spot where Maeve had left. "She is the most incredible being I have ever encountered." Slipping her hand into Jessie's, Cate made no move to leave. "Do not worry, Jessie. She is out there and she will find you. She always has. And when that happens, it will be the best thing that has ever happened to you."

Jessie turned and faced Cate. "Actually, the best thing that has ever happened to me, is you."

Cate looked up and shielded her eyes from the sun. "That is so sweet, Jessie."

"Cate, are we friends? I mean…can two people who share the same soul be friends?"

"I consider you a very good friend, Jessie, and if we lived in the same time, I would want you to be my friend. Why do you ask?"

"I get awfully lonely some days."

Cate squeezed Jessie's hand. "I know that feeling. Until Maeve found me, in a tree, of all places, I was adrift like a leaf on the water. And when she finally reached me, my life fell into place. She will come, Jessie. I swear she will. She always has."

Jessie nodded. "I do know she is out there. I just hope it doesn't take too long for me to find her. Or him."

"As long as you stay on your path, Jessie, you will eventually find her, or she, you." Cate gently touched Jessie's shoulder. "And until then, you will always be my friend, Jessie. Always. You must just remember that being your friend is second to being a priestess. The priestess I am becoming cannot always warn you or tell you things that you must learn on your own. There will be times when I will wish to tell you, but cannot. There will also be those moments when I will not want to tell you, but must. Regardless of which scenario it is, you must know in your heart that I care and I always will."

"And that would be why I love my Catie so much." Maeve came out of nowhere and wrapped her arms around both of them. "She lives," she said, as all three women touched foreheads. "Though Tarik is unsure how much longer. She is in terrible danger, Catie. You were right to leave when you did."

Cate pulled away. "I want to help her, Maeve. *We* want to help."

Maeve stepped back and shook her head, "No. This is not for you."

"But—"

"I said no. If you wish to help her, then Jessie is going to have to go through. She knows more about this evil man who does not belong there than you do."

"I think I can help," Jessie said softly.

Maeve nodded. "I believe you can, but you must be exceptionally careful. Tarik is very afraid. This is not going well and he fears for her safety. He fears a great deal. That makes me fear for you, Jessie. I will not have you sacrifice yourself no matter what you wish to do."

"I know."

"No, I do not believe you do. You and Catie have inexplicably become friends. Your souls in the times in which you live recognize each other as separate entities; different beings even though you share the same soul. The loss of you could pierce Catie's heart and send her soul reeling. This, I cannot abide. Her well-being is now directly tied to yours, thus, I must admonish you as I would her."

Jessie nodded slowly, her eyes filling with tears. "I understand."

"It will require more than an understanding, Jessie. You may have traveled across time a dozen or so times, but that does not mean you are any closer to understanding how the portals work than the first time you went. There is still so much for you to learn, so much for you to know."

"Then teach me, Maeve. I'm ready. I want to know more. I *need* to know more. You said it yourself, this is my path. I'm a Guardian, I'm..."

"You are not *a* Guardian, Jessie. You are *the* Guardian." Maeve sighed and pulled her hood up. "I suppose it is time I taught you both what it means to be a Guardian and how to protect us."

Cate stood on tiptoe and kissed Maeve's cheek. "What better way to spend an afternoon than being taught by you?"

Maeve forced a frown. "I don't know which of you I ought to whack with a stick first."

Jessie's smile grew. "Pick me."

Reaching down for a branch, Maeve did just that. "Now that I have your attention, here is what you must do if you're going to help Sakura stay alive."

14th Century BCE

The catacombs beneath the palace were cool and damp and Sakura heard dripping from one corner and a skittering animal from another. Her "room" was a corner of the cavern filled with flickering lamps and a single stone bench. Two guards stood erect like the many statues in the city, never responding to any of her questions. They did not even speak to each other, and Sakura wondered if perhaps they weren't mute.

Closing her eyes, Sakura inhaled slowly and deeply, trying not to panic or let her mind go to those dark places minds go when fear sets in. She needed to believe Nefertiti or Tarik would come. They would not let any harm come to her. What she needed to do was slow her heart down and become calmer so she could think—so she could reach that special place.

It was clear Akhenaten's men had some idea of where her temple was. Musa had said he couldn't find it, which meant he suspected, but that was it. That was good. The temple was at the end of a labyrinth of stones and boulders buried deep within the rocks surrounding the palace. There were many, many avenues one could take that would lead to empty caverns and dead ends. A few of those dead ends contained the skeletal remains of those who could not find their way out. Musa obviously did not have an exact location of the temple and was clearly too afraid to go looking for it himself. The only reason *she* knew where it was was because Tarik had shown it to her the day after he had first encountered Maeve and the crevasse that had once propelled him to another time. Once there, Sakura thought it would be the perfect place for a temple. Perhaps it could still be. If they couldn't find the temple, perhaps Akhenaten would be satisfied with one heretic he could use as yet another example of what happened if the people didn't fall under his spiritual guidance.

She didn't want to be that example, but she had refused to lie about the most important thing to her. She refused to bow under the weight of his religious changes, no matter what the consequences. Of course, now, here she sat in a dimly lit cavern waiting to see if she would share the similar fate of the rest of the caught anti-Atenist priests and priestesses before her. Akhenaten was not known for his mercy to the rebels. Depending on his whim, he could have them disappear, be publicly tortured or executed. Nefertiti would not allow the latter two, of course, but at what cost to her? She had appealed twice to his mercy and convinced him to stay their execution. Sakura could not rely on his mercy or Nefertiti's pleas this time. She would have to find a way out or risk placing Tarik and her sister both in danger of being discovered. She wasn't at all sure how she was going to do that, but she'd find a way.

Hearing heavy footsteps coming down the stairs, Sakura rose and peered around the corner. Coming to the bottom was Tarik, who first addressed the guards before approaching her.

"Come with me," Tarik said gruffly, grabbing her arm and shoving her ahead of him. "You, get her something to drink, and you, get her a real seat. There is no need to treat her like a barbarian."

The guards looked at each other before scurrying up the stairwell.

Tarik gently nudged Sakura ahead, and pointed to a second set of stone steps that led down to a darker pit. When Tarik yanked a torch off the wall, he motioned for her to go down the stairs and into a large chamber that had obviously been used to torture other priestesses before her. "Down."

Sakura carefully made her way down the stone steps and into the chamber. The smell of old blood assaulted her nostrils, as she turned back toward Tarik, who placed the torch in an empty holder in the wall. The shadows on the wall jumped back and forth.

"Do not speak," Tarik whispered, placing his fingers on her lips. Wrapping his arms around her, he held her tightly to his chest. "Forgive me, my love, but I must keep up pretenses. Your capture has put your sister and me in an awkward position. We must be cautious."

"Does she know of my capture?"

"She does. It took everything I had to keep her from coming down here." Tarik stepped back and studied her. "Musa did not harm you?"

Sakura shook her head. "He seemed to want to get as far away from me as possible once he brought me in."

"Good. Now, Nefertiti will be coming down shortly, but only after I make sure Akhenaten is kept busy. Do not let her stay long. She is worried and it shows, so you must convince her to comport herself better. If she is not careful, she could put us all in danger."

"Who was it? Who did this?"

"My men tell me it was a priest."

"Do you know which he is? Was it that blackhearted Musa?"

Tarik shook his head. "I do not know. Bakari admitted he received his information from one of the priests, but he could not identify which one. Since Akhenaten had them all shave their heads, it has been nearly impossibly to tell one from another." Tarik paused and listened, his muscles tensing. When he heard nothing, he continued. "He believes the priest had an awkward walk, but that is not important to us at the moment. We have to find a way to get you safely away from here. Musa is acting suspicious, and the king is agitated and in a hurry to see who would dare serve Aset right under his nose. Sakura, my love, I am at a loss as to what to do. We could leave now, just the two of us, and by nightfall we could be—"

"Always on the run. No, Tarik, we are not running. There is much more at stake here than my life. I do not wish to endanger either you or my sister, and running would only mean we could never return. This is our home and we have responsibilities here, Tarik."

"But your safety—"

"Is secondary, my love. This is about Nefertiti." Taking Tarik's face in her hands, Sakura kissed his mouth. "We must find the right priest. Tell the priests in the palace I have information one of them has been searching for. We must bring them out into the open. Keep Akhenaten away from me for as long as you can. If we are lucky, the right priest will show himself."

Tarik kissed her tenderly. "I will not allow anything to happen to you, my love, regardless of how much you want to save our queen, so tell me what good it will do you if we find out who the priest is now?"

Sakura smiled softly and lovingly ran her hand across his bald head. "He is the reason we are in this, is he not?"

Tarik nodded. "Part of the reason, yes."

"If he has chosen to be a player in our time, then he must move when it is his turn. It is now his turn."

"When it is *my* turn, I shall kill him for exposing you."

Sakura laid her palm against his cheek. "No, my love, you will not. His death here will help no one, especially Jessie, and I intend to help her even from the confines of this hideous place."

"He did not reveal himself when we laid our treasure before him. Why do you believe he will do so now?"

Sakura cringed as a rat scurried across the floor. "Because this time, I am going to offer him something he truly wants."

"And what would that be?"

"Nefertiti."

When Tarik finished his tale, Nefertiti stood by the queen's chair while Akhenaten had his back to her on the balcony. He was too far away to hear Nefertiti whisper, "He knows...not about me...he knows the priestess held below is my sister."

Tarik's eyes grew wide, and he had to step away from her before Akhenaten turned around.

When Akhenaten turned from the balcony, Tarik and Nefertiti were both surprised to see tears on his face. "What am I to do with her now, my love? The sister of my wife...a heretic priestess? My heart breaks. I have never been in such a position. Have you known?"

Tarik bowed his head, but Nefertiti strode across the floor and took him buy the chin to hold Akhenaten's gaze. "Of course I did not know, my love. I have not seen Sakura in many, many moons. I assumed she ran off with that fur merchant she was smitten with. I had no idea she was a priestess of Aset. My heart is cleaved in half as well."

Akhenaten's bare chest heaved as he stifled a sob. "Musa

said he could not locate her evil temple, though he spent much time looking. Perhaps if she gave her temple up, I could... permit her to live." Akhenaten paced across the floor, his loin cloth shimmering in the sun as it moved. "My wife begs for mercy, my priests want to see her tortured and condemned, and...and..."Akhenaten wheeled toward Tarik. "And what do *you* think I ought to do with my heretic priestess?"

Tarik backed away as if slapped. "You might...you might consider sending her away, my liege. She need not be the embarrassment you fear her to be. You need not have to hurt her in any way."

Nefertiti nodded. "We could fake her death while allowing her to live out the rest of her days in the south."

Akhenaten shook his head. "My detractors will shout from the mountaintops that even my own family worships outside of Aten."

Nefertiti glanced over at Tarik. "I beg you, my love, listen to Tarik. We can find a way to show your persecution of heretics while allowing my sister to live. Surely you would not sacrifice my beloved sister."

Tarik saw a glimmer of hope in Akhenaten's eyes. As much as Akhenaten wanted a grand display of his power, he did not wish to bring sadness to his beloved wife. "It can be done, my king. You can appear to be relentless in your pursuit of heretics while allowing the beloved sister of your wife a chance to start a new life elsewhere."

"Musa knows of the priestess, but he knows not her relation to my queen. Perhaps...perhaps this is the way to do what you advise, Tarik." Akhenaten paced more, a sheen of sweat appearing on his oiled chest. "But what of her temple and her followers? It must be destroyed and they hunted down and killed. I cannot appear lenient. I cannot appear weak."

Tarik nodded. "There appears to be quite a labyrinth beneath the rock and stone. It will take some time and a good number of men to locate the temple within. I can take a group of men at dawn and comb every inch of those rocks until we find the temple or her subjects."

Akhenaten rubbed his temples. "I will have to think more

on it and ask Aten for guidance." To Nefertiti he said, "I would rather cut off my arm than hurt you or bring sadness to your beautiful eyes. You must know that, my love."

Nefertiti nodded. "I do."

"But I cannot allow such heresy in my kingdom. I cannot let the populace believe I have allowed her an ounce of compassion or a slice of mercy. It would make me appear weak, and that cannot be. Her actions have put me and her sister in a terrible position; one that could have dire consequences. I must do the right thing by Aten. Aten will show me the way."

Nefertiti swallowed hard. "I understand, my king, and I would never ask you to do anything that would bring displeasure to the throne."

Akhenaten shook his head sadly. "She is your sister. How could she betray you so? How could she betray Egypt?"

"I wish I knew. Perhaps if I could speak with her, I might—"

"No. You must distance yourself from her. There are enemies everywhere, and if they discover her betrayal, if they find out who she truly is, it may open doors we might not ever be able to close. No, my love, you must cut all ties with her until I decide what must be done."

"I understand."

Tarik suddenly cleared his throat. "She is safe out of the light, and no danger to you or your power. I suggest keeping her alive until she agrees to show me the way to her temple and her followers."

"That is a brilliant idea, Tarik. I ought to keep your counsel more often and stop listening to the prolonged prattling of my priests. They make my head hurt. Do not go far from the palace, Tarik, for I will need you to assist in moving her once she has shown you to her evil lair."

"And what of Musa? Shall I take him with me to the temple?"

"Musa left complaining of stomach ills and went in search of herbal remedies. I shall send word he should join you. Do not attempt to silence him, Tarik. That would be ill-advised."

Tarik nodded and began backing out of the room. Nefertiti held her hand up to stop him and turned to mouth the word *garden* to him. He nodded once and backed out the door. He wasn't ten steps out the door when he ran into the head priest, Efru.

"Watch where you're going, you oaf."

Tarik stopped and glared at him. "Mind your tongue, priest. I am not one of your prattling priests," Tarik growled.

Efru started to reply, when Akhenaten beckoned him in.

"Ah, Efru, good of you to come so swiftly. I have some questions for you—" Akhenaten's voice floated through the door until it closed, leaving Tarik to ponder the priest's role in all of this. Something did not seem right about that priest, but he did not have time to discover what that was. Just how quickly he could get Sakura away from the palace was the only thing he could focus on.

Deep in his heart, he feared it might not be quickly enough.

21st Century AD

Tanner had been sitting on Daniel's bed for the better part of an hour. When he finally got up and walked into the hall, his hands were clammy and he was paler than usual.

"Are you all right?" Jessie asked, pulling him into a guest room and into one of the high-back Victorian chairs. Jessie and Ceara had agreed to wait outside while Tanner took a read of the room using his empathic skills. Whatever he read had scared him. That much was obvious.

"What is it? What did you feel?"

Tanner ran his hands through his hair and shook his head slowly. "That was awful. Those spirits aren't just pissed. They are bat-shit crazy...and...I know this will sound nuts, but it seemed like they *knew* I was an empath and did everything they could to make me feel all sorts of gross stuff. Those spirits are sons of bitches," he said, shaking his head again. "Fucking creepy."

"What do they want? I mean, besides Albert's soul, what is it they're after? Why have they suddenly gotten so agitated? What's going on with us?"

Tanner held his hand up. "There's something bothering them about time. There's some sort of time element involved here; some issue revolving around the timeliness of getting Old Al's spirit back in the bottle. That's what's got them pissed off."

"I don't understand."

"We never noticed. The clocks in Daniel's room aren't working, Jess. Neither is my watch. They've been trying to tell him time is of the essence."

Jessie walked out into the hall and peered in Daniel's room. Sure enough, neither his wall clock nor his alarm clock had the right time. When she returned, Ceara had gotten Tanner a glass of water. "Is Daniel in danger?"

Tanner took the glass and shrugged. "He'll be fine until the timer runs out."

"What happens then?"

Tanner sipped the water and leaned back in the chair. "I have no idea, but they're willing to hang around until the time runs out."

"What do you mean?"

"Jess, the inn has had so many people trying to make this place work, and one after another, people failed. Until you guys got here. Suddenly, these ghosts appear. Well, it's not a coincidence. They know you're the one. They *know*."

Ceara clicked her teeth together as she flipped open the file she'd brought with her. "Ghosts are particularly sensitive to anniversary dates and things of that nature." She rummaged through a stack of papers until she found the one she was looking for. Pointing to the article they'd found while in San Francisco, she shook her head. "I can't believe we almost missed this."

"What?" Jessie and Tanner put their heads together to look at the paper.

"Her death. Albert's wife was killed August 22, 1922. Today is the nineteenth. I'll bet if we looked we'd see that almost everyone who tried to live in this house was driven out on or around that date."

"Three days from now? That doesn't give us much time."

Ceara shook her head. "Time is their issue, not ours. Our unanswered question is why Daniel? Why did they choose to haunt Daniel when it's Jessie who can travel across time?"

"That's why Daniel is staying the week at a friend's house. I had to get him out of here."

"That's only added to their pissed off mood too, Jess," Tanner said. "They feel like you're fucking with them."

"Well, fuck 'em! Whatever it is they want from my little brother is going to have to wait." Jessie stormed out of the guest room and walked into Daniel's room, her neck and cheeks holding a blush.

"All right, listen up, you fucking poltergeist rat bastards! I'm doing everything I can as fast as I can to bring Albert's soul back to you, so…Back. The. Fuck. Off! I'm not your goddamned gopher or medium or girl Friday, so cool your jets. Whatever it is you want from Daniel, you are not, I repeat, *not* going to get by acting up, so chill out. You think *you're* pissed off? Well trust me, boys and girls, you don't want to see me pissed off!" Jessie was glaring up at the ceiling, hands on her hips, daring them to come after her.

To her surprise, they did.

A glass of water next to Daniel's bed fell off his nightstand and broke, sending water all over the hardwood floors.

"Now see? That seriously pisses me off! You want my help, then get a damned grip."

Tanner was standing at the door. "Umm…Jess?"

"Stay out of this, Tanner. I'm sick of this shit. I'm a goddamned Druid priestess, you know? What kind of priestess am I if I let the damn spirit world torment my brother and run my life?" To the ceiling she yelled, "You hear that? This is *my* game now, and if you want *anything* to happen in your favor, you'll simmer the hell down and let me get some work done." Jessie cocked her head and listened before looking at Tanner. "Feel anything?"

Tanner tentatively stepped into the room. "Uh…actually, yeah. It's…calmer."

Jessie returned her glare to the ceiling. "Good. Keep it that way. You've played your card. Give me a fucking day or two to play mine!" With that, she wheeled past Tanner and down the stairs.

"That was insane," Tanner said, following closely behind her. "Do you have any idea what could have happened?"

Stopping two steps before the end, she wheeled around. "No, I don't, but I can imagine what will happen if we don't get his ass back here in three days."

"Three days? Ticktock, man, ticktock."

14th Century BCE

"Time is not our ally." Sakura sat next to Jessie on the log on the coast of Avalon and kicked a pebble into the water. The ripples were several different colors of blue.

"No, it's not, and I'm really sorry, Sakura, but we don't have the luxury of waiting for things to happen naturally. We have to move them along by our own power. We have to regain some control over this."

Sakura nodded. "I understand that, Jessie, and I'm doing everything I can to get to this priest, but so far, he has not shown himself. Are you certain he is in my time?"

"I am. It's time for your sister to put it out there…to make a move on one of them. Something. I'm desperate." Jessie took Sakura's hand. "And what about you? We don't have time to let you sit around waiting for the nut job Akhenaten decide your fate."

Sakura nodded. "I see. Yes, he is, and no we don't. Do not worry about me, Jessie. My sister will not let anything happen to me, and neither will Tarik."

"Look, we're getting you out of this today. I'm staying with you until you are safe."

Sakura looked at Jessie and smiled softly. "It is no wonder Cate loves you so much. There is a courage deep within you that bespeaks of the warrior living within you."

"Cate does love me, doesn't she?"

"You are very important to her. It is evident every time I see her and every time she speaks your name. It is a pleasant surprise to her. She had no idea she would feel so strongly about you or care so deeply. You do not understand that the depth of her emotions for you often gets in the way of her doing what needs to be done. She was not supposed to bond so with you."

"Yeah, I don't think Maeve is too happy about it."

Sakura nodded. "Their bond is unlike anything I have ever witnessed."

"Maeve would take on all the gods and goddesses if they threatened Cate."

"So would Tarik. It is just their way."

Sighing, Jessie stared out at the beauty of Avalon. "Anyway, I feel the same way about her. It's like she's one of my best friends. She's very special." Jessie turned to her. "So are you." Jessie held the ankh out for Sakura to see. "This has made it all the way to me and carries with it the power for me to reach these places. You have opened so many doors for me, Sakura, and right now, I intend to do the same for you." Standing, Jessie held her hand out. "Come on. Let's end this once and for all and put your life on the right path. I'm not going to let anything happen to you."

As Sakura reached for Jessie's hand and took control of her own being, Jessie watched from the passenger seat as Sakura returned to the dank, wet, catacombs beneath the palace and straight into the grasp of the priest.

"Another heretic priestess brought down by your own demon Goddess, eh witch?"

Sakura fought off the haze from her visit with Jessie as he approached her. It was Efru, head priest of the palace who was once a kindhearted man who did not relish titles or power. Once Akhenaten changed the religion over, thereby handing his own priests more power and more control than any had previously experienced, Efru had changed dramatically. Even his own priests steered clear of him, afraid he would find disfavor with them for some slight transgression. Lately, he had pushed the pharaoh into ordering more executions, more tortures, more death and destruction of the old ways. If rumors were to be believed, he had such a network of spies that his power in Upper Egypt was second only to that of the pharaoh.

"She is no demon, priest, and there is no rebellion," Sakura said softly. "Rebellion suggests wrongdoing and the only wrongdoing is what you and your bloodthirsty priests do to the citizens of this great country."

Efru, who was much shorter than Sakura, stepped up to her, his breath smelled of garlic and rotten teeth. "You believe that drivel, witch? Do not make me laugh."

Sakura did not back away. She had never liked this man, but the smell assaulting her nostrils felt more like it was coming from his soul than his mouth. Appraising him carefully, she realized he was better looking than she first estimated, despite his crooked nose and thin lips. His eyes were clear and dark, filled with hate and venom as he glared at her. This was no pious individual who cared about the Ka or the afterlife or anything else of the spiritual realm. This was a man hungry for power, for control, for all of the things a true priest disdains.

"Your bitch Goddess won't be causing any more problems for us, now will she?"

His language caught her slightly off-guard. "If worshipping freely is a problem, then yes, she will continue to be a problem to you and those like you."

Efru turned as if to walk away, then whirled around and abruptly backhanded her. "Do not trifle with me. I am far more powerful than you could even imagine and could destroy you in the blink of an eye."

Sakura righted herself and licked the blood from her lip. Everything about him was wrong. Everything. He was not as he appeared, and she knew. She *knew*. "You are a complete nut job, Efru," she said, throwing Jessie's terminology out. When she did, his pupils dilated as the word registered within him. He knew what she meant. He understood exactly what she had called him.

His second backhand was proof. "How dare you?"

Sakura wiped her lip with the back of her hand, her hands forming fists. Towering over him, she stepped into his space, causing him to move back a step. "I dare because I am a true priestess of Aset and you...*you* are false, Efru, and do not belong here."

Efru tilted his head to one side. "And *you* do, I suppose?"

"More so than you. You see, I *know* of your evil designs and of your feelings toward Nefertiti. I *know* who you are and what you seek."

Efru's grin surprised her. "If you knew who I truly am, you would not be so foolish as to speak to me that way. You would know I could crush you like that." He snapped his fingers.

Sakura stepped up to him, driving him back a step. "You do not frighten me little man."

"Then you are a fool. Do you not see I hold the power of life and death in my hands? *Your* life and death? One word from me and the king will destroy you in a most unpleasant manner. One word, Sakura, is all that need pass through my lips."

Sakura wiped more blood from her lower lip. "You are very arrogant for a man whose game has just been outplayed. You see, I *do* know who you are, and yet, I am unafraid of you. You are nothing but a tiny little maggot. I have the Goddess with me always and she will crush you and your plan beneath her unrelenting heel."

"She will never truly make a comeback. Akhenaten has changed the course of Egypt's religion forever. Your goddess, though once proud and powerful, will remain secondary to the one God. You are wasting precious time and energy hanging onto a spirituality that is lost and gone forever."

"If that is so, then why are my people and I such a threat to you? What have you to gain by destroying us?"

Efru appeared puzzled. "Destroy you? Oh silly woman, you better double-check your *powers*. I did not bring you here to destroy you."

Sakura tried to keep her expression passive. "What do you mean?"

Efru grinned. "Do you truly think that idiot Musa would ever have noticed the comings and goings of a single woman among the rocks and ruins? The man is a self-serving peon looking to raise his station anyway he can. The lowest of life forms, really. He does my bidding, and my bidding only."

"More so than the king's?"

Efru laughed. "If you know as much as you say you do, which I highly doubt, then it is in your best interest to cooperate with me and give me that which I seek."

Sakura felt sick to her stomach as she looked into a pair of eyes that held no compassion or gentleness. He was evil and it rose off him like heat from the desert. "You seek the love of one who is already married, who loves her husband, who will never, ever return your affection. She cannot be so easily manipulated."

Efru shook his head. "Manipulated? Who needs to manipulate her? Hasn't she done a fine job of putting herself in this position?" He stepped closer, standing on tiptoe to reach Sakura's ear. "She worships at Aset's tit, does she not? What do you think her beloved husband will think when he finds out?"

Sakura stood her ground. "That is impossible."

"Nothing is impossible, as you know. I have been following Nefertiti for months now, trying to figure out where she goes, what she's doing, what her secret is. I could not locate the temple. You've managed to hide that deep within the rocks, I'm sure, but I did manage to see you coming out of them. When I saw the two of you the other day...I knew I had you...*and* her. And I make it a habit to get what I want."

Sakura swallowed hard, but did not budge.

"I see you are beginning to understand the straits you and your queen find yourselves in; a predicament, mind you, that you *can* help her out of."

When Sakura found her voice at last, she managed only one syllable. "Me?"

"Yes, you."

"I would rather die than betray Nefertiti." Sakura breathed in deeply, and did everything in her power to allow Jessie to see through her eyes, to feel her fear, to know what was happening to them. She needed Jessie's wisdom now, and could only hope...

"Isn't it ironic to discover if you do not betray her, she will die."

Sakura shook her head. "Now, you bluff. If you love her as you profess, you would not be threatening her."

"Are you willing to risk both of your lives to prove it? Do you really believe I need to bluff? I hold all of the cards. This is *my* play, *my* drama to act out any way I see fit. Akhenaten is so busy with his transformation of the religion, he sees little else. I am his eyes and ears in his court now. I am the one who knows what is really happening. I have the power to make him do and think whatever I wish. He is a man obsessed, and obsessed men are blinded by their obsessions. The king is blinded by two things...his obsession with Aten and his love of his wife. It is the latter I am going to exploit."

Sakura shook her head, trying to give Jessie a clearer picture. She was feeling faint, sick to her stomach, weak in her knees. He was mad. "What makes you think I won't just tell the king about your plans?"

"Who would listen to you? You're a heretic. Are you willing to risk both your lives to prove it?"

"What is it you want from me?"

"From you? I want nothing *from* you. What I want from *Nefertiti* is for her to betray her husband. She needs to show him the truth about the woman who goes down in history as a staunch supporter of Atenism."

"You lie."

"Do I? If you think you know who I am...if you have *any* idea of what I am capable of, then you know what I say is true. The fate of your queen is in my hands and mine alone. You can save her life by letting Akhenaten know she has followed you into the darkness of Aset. Then she can go away with me."

"Save her life? To what end? What purpose will it serve to anger Akhenaten so?"

Efru stepped closer to Sakura, causing her to press herself deeper into the wall. "Akhenaten is an idiot, Sakura. He is one of the greatest fools in history, with his lame attempt at establishing a religion nobody wants but him. He does not deserve his queen any more than he deserves to be known as a great leader. Do you want to know what happens to him upon his death?"

Sakura shook her head, but she knew the gesture was meaningless; he was wrapped up in his own power and knowledge.

"This whole, stupid city falls to ruin, and the rebels he's so damn afraid of do everything in their power to remove his name from every obelisk, cartouche, hieroglyph and statue." He made motions with his hands. "Wipe them clear, as if they were embarrassed he had been their ruler." Efru stepped closer, his breath hot on her face. "He loses, Sakura, because he is a loser. If Nefertiti truly is your friend, if you truly care about her the way you say you do, you will help distance her from the pharaoh who goes down in history as a complete moron. He has nothing to offer her any longer. Like his name on the obelisks, she disappears from history. She gets barely a glance. Whether he kills her or she leaves with...well...under less murderous circumstances is entirely up to you."

"He would never kill her. He adores her."

"Maybe *he* isn't the one who kills her, but trust me, they have plenty of enemies even among their own court. I can tell you this for certain...she disappears. Forever." His smile reminded her of curdled milk. "Are we beginning to understand each other?"

Sakura went inside, deep, trying to draw as many of Jessie's memories from her as she could. They were there. She was sure of it. She just needed to access them. She needed to know what Jessie knew. "Why would she go anywhere with you?"

"With me, she can worship her Goddess freely wherever we go. She will be free from this charade she plays with her idiot husband and the whole of Egypt. Think about it. She can take her daughters and train them in the way of the Goddess as well. She might find her happiness with a man who loves only her. There will be no more Kiyas or concubines, no more children born not of her loins. I will shower my love upon her every minute of every day. It would be the kind of life she deserves, away from all of this."

Sakura blinked several times. Flashes of Jessie's history flew through her mind. While she couldn't catch it all, and it was blurry and vague, she knew in her heart what Efru was saying was true. Just because she didn't want it to be true didn't mean it wasn't. Her sister was in danger as long as she stayed in the palace.

Efru backed off. "You *do* recognize the truth of my words, don't you? Be a smart girl then and convince your queen to abandon her life at the court and leave with me. I may be the only one who can save her."

Sakura could see no way out. If Nefertiti died, chances were the Goddess would follow shortly. "I do not want her to leave in disgrace. I will help you relieve her of her duties, but not under the shadow of betrayal and disloyalty; not with disgrace."

"You are in no position to make deals."

Sakura stepped away from the wall and towered over him. "Is this how you would show her your love and adoration? By making her leave the palace in disgrace?"

Efru licked his lips, but did not step away. "How else would she be willing to leave?"

"If Akhenaten felt her life was in danger he would insist she leave for Lower Egypt right away. He would never allow her to stay if the threat was so close because *he* is a man who knows how to love a woman."

Efru raised his hand to Sakura, but this time, she blocked him. "Take care, priest. You'll not lay another hand on me if you wish to have her by your side." When Efru backed down a bit, Sakura stepped closer.

"And if what you say is so, why has he not sent her away already? Why would he leave her in danger?"

"Because he loves her. He needs her. He believes he can protect her."

"But you and I both know he cannot."

Sakura shook her head. "If you can convince him that he cannot, he might be inclined to send her away. You can tell him, and I can explain it all to her, and maybe we can get her out of the city without bringing disgrace to her name. I'll not do this in a shadow."

Efru thought about it. "If I could get Tarik Gbish to agree with me...to help me...perhaps we can do as you wish."

"I can."

"How?"

"Tarik and I were once...lovers. I believe he still loves me. I can get him to help you."

"He would save the queen's life at all cost?"

"He will if he believes doing so will save mine. He is a very protective man where the queen is concerned...and me as well."

Efru laughed. "There will be no saving yours, I'm afraid. The only thing *you* can do is leave this life knowing you have spared the queen hers." The smile left Efru's face. "Are you not at all interested in knowing how it is I *know* the fate of all these people? How I know what happens?"

Sakura stood erect. "I am assuming you have the sight, Efru. I've heard the stories that you are a very powerful priest. Apparently, the rumors of your powers have not been exaggerated."

He puffed up his chest. "Indeed, they are not. It is too bad it took you so long to understand the power of the man before you. I could have used a priestess such as yourself." Turning away, Efru stopped at the door and slowly turned. "You are more than meets the eye yourself, and the only possible danger to me. It will not hurt my feelings to know you will soon be dead."

When Efru left, Sakura sat back down on the floor, closed her eyes, and practically screamed for help.

"I won't let you sacrifice yourself, Sakura," Jessie said, as she pushed through the mist.

"Now, we know who Albert is. All we have to do is get to him there; separate him from his base, and—"

"And then what? I am in no position to send him back to his own time. I am not even sure I know how to do that. I do know I cannot do it unless we are near the portal, and even then—" Sakura shook her head. "I do not see any way out of this except by giving Efru what he most desires."

Jessie shook her head. "Don't do anything yet. I have a few tricks left up my sleeve. Leave it to me." As Jessie left, a plan began to unfold before her. "You just stay alive, Sakura, you hear me? Without you, both Nefertiti and Daniel will be in serious danger."

"Where are you going?"

"Where I always go when I need help...Cate and Maeve."

Sakura stopped following Jessie and watched her as she made her way to the forest's edge. "There are two souls more connected than the moon and the sun, than the earth and the sky, than bees and flowers. Those two souls are going to get us out of this, I swear."

"How can you be so certain?"

Jessie turned and waved. "Because they've never let me down. Just hang tight. You'll see."

When Jessie disappeared and Sakura reentered her own consciousness, she sighed heavily. "Hang tight," she mused, shaking her head. Her life hung by a thread and the person hanging on to one end of it was a very young, very inexperienced priestess with the strangest vocabulary Sakura had ever heard.

When Tarik entered the cavern, Sakura was instantly on her feet.

"What is your condition?" Tarik asked stiffly as he moved away from the prying eyes of the guards.

"I managed a few moments of rest, wherein I can go back to Jessie and—"

Tarik pushed her around the corner and stepped up to her. "Keep your voice down," he ordered.

"Tarik, are you well?" Sakura tried reading his eyes, but he would not look directly at her. "Tarik?"

Tarik whispered. "I am...I am not quite sure how *he* is, but *I* am terribly warm in here. This country of yours is dreadfully hot." Tarik's eyes finally met Sakura's, and held a light she had never seen. For a long time, they stared into each other's faces until Sakura ever so quietly whispered, "Maeve."

Tarik nodded. "I am here to create a plan that will save you both."

Sakura's eyes sparkled. "Both?"

"Yes. You and your sister as well."

Sakura nodded. "Jessie said she would...throw out a trick from her sleeve. You must be the trick."

Maeve smiled. "It is what we do for each other. There is a great deal at stake here besides whether or not Nefertiti remains at the palace. The priest needs to be dealt with and we *must* return his soul to his own time in less than two days' time. To do that, we must get him to the temple and into the portal. I can help you get his soul into the portal and back to his own time. That is why I am here. Once we have the soul of the priest in the portal, we will have to poison his body so he cannot ever return to this time."

Sakura's eyes were wide. "I...I cannot condone the killing of a priest, Maeve."

Maeve nodded and laid a hand on Sakura's shoulder. "Neither can I, but do not worry. The priest and his intentions are darkness and evil, Sakura. You need not concern yourself with his welfare. We will take care of the soul. We need you to remove the vessel he uses."

Sakura sat heavily on the stone bench. "If there is a safe way for me to get Efru to the temple without arousing suspicion, I do not know what that is."

Maeve took a few steps toward her before kneeling in front of her and taking her hands. "That is because you are not a Druid. We Druids know the secret of getting people to do exactly as we wish."

Sakura cocked her head to one side. "Oh? Is that the trick?"

"I do not know what trick Jessie spoke of. Her language is often...confusing. Perhaps she meant something else. It is no trick nor is it magic."

"Then how do you *Druids* manage that feat?"

Smiling, Maeve kissed the back of Sakura's hands. "With the truth."

"The truth?"

Maeve nodded. "The truth."

Nefertiti sat at her table shaking her head as Tarik, with Maeve still at the helm, stood by.

"I am...sorry, Tarik, if I am not taking this as a queen might, but I am ill-equipped to fully understand how the priest has the consciousness of man living three thousand years in the future. It is...a bit much even for me to believe."

Tarik moved closer. "The Goddess is powerful, Nefertiti,

but this man, this one being named Al-bert, could do incredible damage not only to you and your sister, but Aset as well, and that is only in our life."

"I thought you said you were going to get my sister out of the palace. That is all that matters to me."

"I will...*we* will...but we must first get the priest out of our way. Time is running out. If we do not find a way to remove him from the palace, you will lose more than your life."

Nefertiti walked over to Tarik and grabbed him by the chin. "Look at me."

Maeve leveled her gaze, feeling the powerful shoulders draw back. His body was massive, and she was not at all comfortable in it.

"There is something...different about you. What is it? What is wrong with you?"

Tarik shrugged. "I am just trying to save my love and her stubborn sister. We cannot allow Efru to carry on with his plan to make you leave with him."

"Not that I ever would."

"You would if it meant saving Sakura's life. Fortunately, we will not have to wait and see how that plan works out. We must move forward with our own and crush this little man before any harm comes to any of you."

"He has no power. All I need to do is tell my husband—"

"You will tell him nothing. We cannot allow the king to kill this priest. We need him alive, Nefertiti. *Alive.* He has but one objective, and that is to have you. You are the key to this whole situation, so we are going to use you to get him to the temple." Maeve took a deep breath, and wondered how these people lived in this accursed heat. "We can kill Efru once we get him to the portal, but not before."

"I still do not see the reason we must waste our time with his Ka. Who is he to you? Why should we care one fig about what happens to him or his spirit?"

Maeve leaned closer. "Hear me, Nefertiti. He is a dangerous man who poses a danger to someone I love, and I will not allow that to happen. If I can get all of us out of this without the loss of any life but his, so be it, but he must die."

Nefertiti shook her head. "My sister will not allow the killing of a priest in her temple. Of that, I am sure."

"Your sister may have no choice. There are times, Nefertiti, when we must all make sacrifices that change our souls. If your sister will not dispose of the priest, then I will."

Nefertiti abruptly grabbed Tarik's face and peered into his eyes again. For a long time, she just stared into his eyes. "You are not Tarik, are you?"

Maeve shook her head. "I am not. The body is his. I am merely…borrowing it so I can help your sister and you get out of this alive. Do not be afraid."

For several drawn-out moments, Nefertiti moved her head from side-to-side, all the while gazing into Tarik's face. "I am not afraid of you, Tarik. I could never be afraid of you, but I knew there was something not right. It was the manner in which you continued to refer to me by my name, as if we were equals, as if you were a woman. There is a female lurking in that hulking body, is there not?"

Maeve nodded. "Indeed, there is. I came through the portal to help. You must now trust in both the Goddess as well as me."

Nefertiti stood back. "The Goddess is, indeed, still alive and all powerful to be able to accomplish this. Where is Tarik's Ka?"

"He is here, only deeper inside, watching to make sure the women he loves are not harmed by your priest."

"*Women?*"

"Sakura and you. He loves you, Nefertiti, as his queen, as the sister of his lover, as the woman who refused to let the Goddess die. He knows what your death would mean to Sakura and has allowed me in so I may help. I am here to prevent that."

"Why? Who *are* you?"

Maeve stepped back and bowed. "I am Maeve, Druid priestess from far into the future, and I am here because your sister's soul is the soul of *my* soul mate, of my beloved, and though her death in this time may not seem like it would be of any interest to me in mine, that assumption would be incorrect. It is *her* soul I travel thousands of miles into the past to save, and so now I ask you one more time, will you take Efru to the temple so that I can send his soul far away from you and my beloved?"

Nefertiti blinked several times before nodding. "I will do what I can. Is Efru a madman?"

"To leave his family to be slaughtered so he could come here and weave a plot to gain your affections are not the acts of a lucid creature. He *is* mad, and that is precisely why he is so dangerous."

"And you do this to serve the Goddess?"

"I may serve the Goddess, Nefertiti, but I also serve those who own my heart, and I'll let nothing happen to them or their loved ones if I can help it."

Nefertiti smiled softly. "What an incredible woman you must be to love so deeply and for so long."

"The incredible thing is to be loved back just as deeply. I am here to protect Tarik's love, my soul mate, as well as Jessie and you, of course."

"Jessie? Who is *she*?"

Maeve smiled and looked into the distance. "Jessie...she is... well...that is a story for another time. Jessie is a Guardian who guards the portal. She is the...friend of my love, the heart of my heart. She asked me to help save your sister, and I ...well...I have agreed. What say you?"

Nefertiti nodded sagely. "I can do no less than assist you in the saving of my sister and your loved ones, but you must permit me my indulgence regarding your...being here. It is a rare event one sees the Goddess's handiwork."

Maeve smiled softly. "Things are as your people believe them to be, only the mummification process need not be so elaborate or even done at all. The soul, or Ka as you call it, does, indeed, go on. Sometimes, it remembers bits and pieces of its past, others, it remembers nothing except the lessons learned."

"But it does go on."

"Yes."

"When are you alive?"

"I am over a thousand years into the future."

"That far? Oh my. And what of Aten? Is he—"

Maeve shook her head. "He is no more, and that is all I wish to tell you, except you need to know your sister is a very powerful priestess who has much to accomplish in this life."

"Yet, she never said anything to me about this...this...ability of hers."

"It is not our way, nor would the Goddess approve. Not everyone can use the portal successfully, Nefertiti, which is one reason why Efru is so mad. The portal calls to you, invites you, cares for you, takes you where you need to go, not the other way around. He is not where he is supposed to be and it upsets the balance of time. As Guardians, we are duty bound to keep that balance. It is up to us to set it back right, and we must make haste to do so."

Nefertiti nodded and drew herself up to her full height. Suddenly, she appeared every bit the regal queen legends made her out to be. "What, exactly, is it you need me to do?"

Maeve inched closer. "Call for your priest and tell him you are willing to go with him, but not before you make your last offering to Aset. Tell him you must go today and you will leave with him from there."

"And what of my sister? How do we keep her safe?"

Maeve stepped up to Nefertiti. Lowering her lips to her ear, she whispered, "Here is what you're going to have to do."

Having finished with Nefertiti, Maeve made her way back to Akhenaten's chamber, where the pharaoh was taking a bath.

"What news, Tarik? More spies? More heresy? More rebels?"

"Worse, my king."

Akhenaten held his hand up to stop the bathers, and with the flick of a wrist sent them away. "What could be worse than imprisoning my beloved wife's sister?"

Watching as Akhenaten rose and slipped a robe around his shoulders, Maeve wondered at the expense of running such a palace. Perhaps the Egyptians' lack of future power lay in the financial ruin at the base of the pyramids and tombs, elaborate temples and palaces. She'd never seen anything like it. Gold and jewels everywhere and servants? Servants were everywhere.

"My men have come to me with news of a plot to assassinate Nefertiti and your daughters."

Akhenaten's face went slack, but he immediately recovered, his voice booming. "Who? Who would *dare*?"

"There is the thought that if enough harm comes to your loved ones, you will rescind your closing of all other temples and revert back to the old ways."

"That is ridiculous. I can easily protect my wife and children. Do they not realize who they are dealing with? I am king!"

Maeve bit her tongue. She had been spared men like him in her life and time. Men did not parade around half-naked, beating their chests and declaring themselves almighty and all powerful. This king had lost control of his kingdom long before Albert showed up.

"They are well aware of who you are, as well as what you represent. They care not about who you believe you are."

"Do not be insolent, Tarik. Remember your place."

"My place, your majesty, is saving your wife and sister. My queen's life is in danger and I will stop at nothing to ensure her safety. I apologize if I have over—"

Akhenaten held his hand up to silence Tarik. "I do not believe you have ever spoken so many words at one time."

"I am sorry. I did not mean to overstep my bounds, but there is not much time."

"No, no, that is quite all right. I assume you have some idea of what I ought to do? Shall I call Efru and have a counsel of war?"

Maeve shook her head and wondered how this man was fit to reign *anything*. Did all of his people make decisions for him? "I believe it would be wise to move your wife and daughters from the palace under nightfall. Efru and I can take them to Lower Egypt until things settle down and you have the chance to seek out the remaining heretics. It is the best thing you can do."

"And Sakura? What of her? You know I cannot let her live. As much as it will hurt me to do so, I must make an example of her."

"I'll take her with us. Your family can be safe, my king,

but not as long as there are spies and heretics inside the palace walls. I swear to you I will not let anything happen to any of them, but you must trust me."

"Take her with you? I would appear weak if I were to let her live. No. I cannot allow that. I am sorry, but my wife's sister knew the consequences of her decisions. She chose to follow the wrong deity."

"Who is to know? Let them think what they wish. Do you not have a body somewhere in this palace you can burn and call hers? No one need know you allowed her to flee."

"But she *must* pay, Tarik. I cannot allow what she has done go unpunished. Aten knows the truth. I cannot hide that from him."

"Then let me take care of her. We will let the queen believe you have allowed her sister to live, but when we get to our destination, I will see to it that Sakura is killed in an accident. This will appease your people and keep your wife from blaming you for her sister's death."

Akhenaten rubbed his chin in thought. "I suppose…I suppose that would appease Aten."

"Appease Aten and keep your wife from hating you for killing her sister. That is a grievous outcome you might never recover from."

Akhenaten nodded. "Fine. See to it she does not suffer. Aten need not be so appeased." The pharaoh strode over to the balcony and stared down at the garden. It was several moments before he spoke again. "They are cowards. Every last one of them."

Maeve said nothing.

"Cowards who would attack women and girls have no place in my court."

"They are a weakness your enemies intend to exploit. Take that weakness away and they will be forced to deal with you. Just you."

The pharaoh turned, his face solemn. "I want to meet each and every one of them face-to-face, Tarik. I want to see the faces of those who would threaten my wife." Slamming his fist in his hand, he growled. "I will kill them all."

"Shall I tell the queen to prepare for the journey then?"

"I will tell her myself."

"Good enough. Then, if you have no further need of me—"

"Thank you, Tarik. When will you leave?"

"Nightfall. It is safest then." Turning, Maeve strode toward the door.

"And Tarik...I trust no one, and I mean *no one* else is to know of this. If anyone asks where you have gone, I will tell them I sent you to quell an uprising in the south."

"Understood."

When Maeve got back down to the chamber where Sakura awaited, she removed herself from Tarik after sharing the plan with Sakura.

At last, they were ready.

"It is for the best," were Akhenaten's final words to Nefertiti when she and her daughters were packed and ready to go. As she paced the floor, her robe flowed about her, making slight swishing noises. She had left her husband with those final words echoing in her mind, wondering if they were doing the right thing.

"You called for me?" Efru now asked, standing at the outer chamber door. It took everything she had not to fly at him and wrap her long fingers around his skinny neck. He disgusted her. She hated everything about him, and though she was clear this man was not the priest she had known, it mattered not. She despised him and wished him dead.

"Goddess protect me," she murmured before beckoning him to enter.

Efru entered, bowed, and started to rise, when Nefertiti said, "I did not give you leave to rise." Her words came from her like a frozen rope.

Efru sank back to one knee and remained there. "Forgive me, my queen."

Nefertiti walked around him. "Your queen. Your queen. That is an interesting choice of words. Rise and take not your eyes from my face."

Efru said nothing as he rose.

Glaring at him, she growled between gritted teeth, "Have you spoken to my husband?"

"Yes, my queen. He has—"

She held a hand up. "That will suffice. Do not answer more than I ask. Are you aware we shall be leaving this night, never to return, no matter what the king says?"

"Yes."

"Go on. What more do you know?"

"Tarik and I are to escort you to the south. Once there, he will return, but you and I will continue on, never to return to Egypt."

Nefertiti stepped up to him and stared down at him for quite some time. Her disdain oozed from her. "You have traveled a great distance to be with your queen, haven't you?" She held a hand up. "Do not answer. Many men have desired me, priest, and many more have secretly loved me, but none, save you, have traveled nearly as far to be with me." She looked down at his eyes and watched as his pupils dilated. "You see, priest, I know more than you realize."

"How is that possible?"

"All things are possible with Aset. My goddess is far more powerful than ever your Aten was. She has kept me abreast, informed, and allowed me to see beyond the body you wear. I know *precisely* who you are."

Efru waved this away. "Impossible."

Nefertiti raised an eyebrow. "Oh? Would it be *impossible* for me to know that your real name is Al-bert?"

Efru went white and he took an intake of air that made him squeak. For several seconds, he merely blinked, as if doing so would make the truth vanish.

"You need not say anything one way or the other. The goddess has equipped me with the means by which to detect the truth, and believe me when I tell you I know the truth." Nefertiti walked over to her chair and sat down. "A part of me is flattered you would leave your time in order to bask in my presence, but that part is nothing but a woman's vanity. It is that vanity that wishes to know, Al-bert, is history kind to me?"

Efru swallowed so hard, the sound echoed through the chamber. "Your face is one of the most recognized faces in the world."

Nefertiti sighed. "Ah then, so it is my beauty which makes me memorable. How very shallow."

"Oh no, my queen, you are known for much more than that. It is just that your beauty is so uncommon throughout the ages that it steals men's souls."

"And apparently, from where you stand, that is no exaggeration."

"I would like the opportunity to explain."

With the flick of her wrist, Nefertiti silenced him. "You are here, and that says a great deal. There is one thing you can do for me that *might* gain you that which you have coveted enough to come so far for." Nefertiti motioned for Efru to step closer. "Allow me to pray one last time in the temple before we leave. It will not take very long, but I need to pay my final respects before we go."

"I see no harm in that. Can you find your way in the dark? It will be dark by the time we get there."

Nefertiti nodded. "I can. I am surprised you cannot."

"The priest was not near the opening when I came through. I have sought it many times, which was how I discovered Sakura used it for her temple. It was just a matter of time before I followed you and discovered where the mouth of the temple is. Still, it is deep within that giant maze, and I did not come all this way to die in a labyrinth."

"Then I will show you to the temple, though I do not know where this opening is you speak of."

"It is no consequence to us now. If it pleases you, I will return shortly so you may say your goodbyes. I am not a hardhearted man."

Nefertiti ground her teeth. "I have already said them." Nefertiti rose. "I am prepared to leave this instant."

Efru squinted at her. "Why have you so easily agreed to leave the palace and all that you love?"

"I'll not lie to you, Efru. I love my husband very much, but my heart and spirit belong to the Goddess. Akhenaten's obsession with Aten as sole deity has caused nothing but sorrow and division in Egypt; a sorrow now jeopardizing myself as well as my daughters. So, although I love my husband dearly, I cannot allow that love to bring harm to the women who love me. I am, after all, one of her chosen ones, and I will return to rule Egypt one day with or without Akhenaten at my side."

"As long as this is no trick. I have my own means of taking care of those things close to you."

"Careful how you speak to me. I have spoken truly and freely with you, Efru, and now, I must ask you do the same."

Efru nodded again. In all the time he had been within the priest, she had never spoken directly to him. Had he known beforehand she was truly a believer in the goddess, he would have found a way to switch sides and be more supportive of her, but everything he'd read said she *assisted* Akhenaten in the changeover of religions.

"I...I have loved you for many years before I discovered this magic room enabling me to gain access to your time. I came time and time again into this body, whose spirit was weak and afraid. He felt he was going mad from seeing all the images and memories from my futuristic world. I tried to forget you, to leave this world alone, but I could not. Every time I was in my world, I yearned to be near you."

"You have never given me cause to make me believe your intentions toward me were dishonorable."

"Because they never were. That's why I gave you no outward sign of my feelings for you. You are, first and foremost, my queen, and I will always honor my queen."

"Yet, you force my hand, you who captured my sister, you threaten us. Is this how you show your love and devotion? Is this the man you want to be? The man you want me to love?"

Efru sighed loudly. "It was Musa's doing. He has been wanting to get closer to the king, and he thought bringing in the witch would give us better leverage. He did not know, of course, that she is your sister. Do not worry for her safety. Tarik has arranged that she come with us."

"And what of my husband? What becomes of him?"

"Well, he is such a fanatic his death will become cause for celebration. Your life will be much better off if you leave him to deal with the rebels and heretics. He will have nothing but problems with it from here on out and will bring nothing but misery to the populace. Trust me...you will be better off without him and the problems that will rain down on him."

Nefertiti felt an enormous weight settle on her shoulders. It saddened her to think of what he had done to their people. "I shall meet you at the front gate, and then we can go to the temple."

Efru bowed and began to back out. "You are making the right decision, my queen. His reign will end in disgrace, his priests killed, his name erased. I swear to you, I will take good care of you."

When Efru was gone, Nefertiti waited for Tarik to come out from behind the dressing partition.

"Well done, Nefertiti."

"I hope so. My sister's life, all of our lives are in your hands, Druid priestess. Care for us as they were your own."

Sakura felt Jessie and immediately responded, leaving the dankness to go to a warmer, cleaner place. Anywhere was better than this dark cavern filled with vermin and stale air. She welcomed the quiet shores of a place called Avalon and welcomed more so, the young woman named Jessie waiting for her there.

"Time is running out for all of us, Sakura," Jessie said, poking the fire with a stick. "What's going on there?"

"Maeve has come to help and I believe she is going to send him back this evening. If she cannot send him back, then no one can. She is our only hope."

Jessie nodded. "True. She's the one, that's for sure. She rocks, but we don't have much time."

Sakura nodded, as if understanding. "There are many people counting on her."

"There always are. Sometimes, I wonder how she does it."

Sakura cut her eyes over to Jessie. "You are in love with her."

Jessie blinked. "Maybe I am. I've never really thought about it that way. I always thought of myself as Cate's friend."

"You ought to think about it. It is so clear you are in love with Maeve, and I could not blame you for feeling so. She is a most impressive woman."

"She isn't the only one. We take care of our own, Sakura. I've been in danger before and I'm not afraid. We're not going to let anything happen to you."

Jessie motioned for the flames to part. Together they watched as Tarik walked down the stone steps, stopping to say a word or two to men along the way. Sakura knew by the way he held himself that Maeve was controlling him. She had a grace, an eloquence of royalty, and a poise that were unlike Tarik's. As much as she was glad their lives were in Maeve's hands, she wanted her lover back.

"You'll get him back," Jessie said softly, "but right now, all of us are in danger. You do what she tells you to and we'll all be fine. Be strong. Be brave, and know that you have more wisdom within you than you could ever imagine."

Rising, Sakura took Jessie's hand. "Have you ever had a great love?"

Jessie shook her head. "No, Sakura, I haven't."

"Well, when you do, you will understand what you're willing to do in order to keep that person from harm. There isn't anything I won't do to help Tarik or my sister, including trusting your Maeve." She turned and patted Jessie's shoulder. "Go home, Jessie. We will get the priest to the portal and send his evil energy away from our time. I just hope you know what you're doing in taking it back."

Jessie put the flame out and nodded. "Take care of yourself, Sakura, and thank you for all you've done."

"I haven't done anything yet, but when I do, I hope it will do you proud. Thank you…for everything. I will never forget this." Sakura returned to her self just as Tarik entered the chamber.

"Is my sister well?"

Tarik knelt before Sakura and stared deep into her face. Then his lips betrayed a slight grin Sakura knew was not truly his.

"Maeve."

"Yes. I know you would wish to have Tarik back, and you

will. Everything has been planned to ensure your sister and the priest have one last prayer in the temple. She is preparing now to leave with him, and I need to take you to see Akhenaten before we join them."

Sakura nodded. "Then all is in order? We are really leaving this night?"

Maeve appeared grim. "I do not trust this priest, and feel his duplicity now more than ever. I do not know what trickery he is up to, but you must be on constant guard. I feel he is threatened by you. Do not trust anything he says or does, and do not turn your back on him."

Sakura's eyes began to water. "I wish him dead already."

"I am so sorry that it has to be like this. If it is any consolation, it is a life I have lived more than once. In order to keep the earthly religion alive, I had to leave my country as well. As long as we face persecution, as long as there are those who try to dictate what it is we should believe in, we are never safe and cannot stay long in one place. It is how it has always been."

"Is it this way in Jessie's time? Do we ever succeed?"

Maeve shrugged. "This I do not know. What I do know is that tonight, we must send the soul in the priest's body back to his own time, and until that happens, you must be ever alert for some trick of his. Once we send him back, your sister will be free to go and do as she pleases. Is that not what you wish?"

Sakura sighed. "It is. My heart is heavy with having to leave her, but as long as you and I are together...Tarik and I...then I shall be happy. Perhaps...when Akhenaten dies, I can return here to live out my days."

Maeve smiled softly. "Perhaps."

"Maeve, are you certain you can do what need be done to Efru's soul?"

She nodded. "It is not I who will do anything, Sakura. As usual, I have help in these matters. All will go according to plan. You shall see. Now, please, let me take you to see Akhenaten and then we shall meet Efru and Nefertiti at the front gate." Maeve rose and Sakura reached for her wrist.

"Thank you, Maeve. Thank you for all you've done for us."

Maeve stepped up and caressed Sakura's cheek. "Your fate today is tied with Jessie's of tomorrow. It was time for Albert's soul to be expunged and time for Nefertiti to leave court. It is all tied together the way the Goddess meant it to be. Do not worry. We shall set everything right this night and you will have the chance to live out your days honoring Aset."

Sakura felt a single tear run down her cheek. "I would like that very much."

"Good. Then it will be so."

21st Century AD

When Jessie entered Daniel's room, it looked like a thief had been in there and turned everything upside down.

"Damn you," she muttered, bending over to pick up some of the books strewn all over the floor. "What do you want from me? I'm giving it everything I have here!"

As Jessie cleaned up, she paused to listen. There was a tapping sound coming from the ceiling. The ceiling was the floor to the attic room Daniel had discovered when they first arrived. Jessie hadn't been up there in over a year.

"The attic," Jessie murmured, scooping up piles of paper. "You want me to go look in the attic?" She listened, the tapping grew stronger. They were getting stronger now, able to affect objects and manipulate items. This was not a good sign.

Again, there came tapping.

"Fine. You want me to see the attic? I've been there. There's nothing there but trunks of old clothes." Kicking some of the debris under Daniel's bed, Jessie headed up there.

The attic was like any attic of the Victorian era; you could stand up in it because of the pitch of the roof, and there was a small window looking out to the forest in the back of the house. Along the wall were a few old trunks she and Daniel had already gone through when he first discovered the attic. It had been easy to miss in all the construction they'd started upon arrival. The stairs to the attic were the kind that pulled down from the ceiling, and no one had really noticed it was there.

Standing in the dusty room, Jessie looked at herself in the stand-up mirror occupying one corner of the room. She looked tired...and angry. This whole thing was really beginning to piss her off. It was bad enough she had had to leave Sakura to face whatever it was her future held, but to be practically bullied by a bunch of ghosts was more than she could stand.

"It's bad enough I had to move Daniel to a friend's house for the week, but now you start messing with his stuff and then bossing me around? I don't get you. You're going to get Albert back, so what's your problem?" Jessie waited to hear something and then realized the futility of it.

Sighing, she pulled over an old three-legged milking stool and sat down. It had really bothered her to have to leave Sakura, but Cate had come to her last night in their Dreamworld expressing concerns Maeve had over believing Efru. Maeve did not feel the priest was dealing honestly with them in regard to Sakura, and felt Sakura was still very much in danger.

Jessie had already been inside one body that was in a bloody swordfight. What did she have to fear from a priest, for Pete's sake?

Smiling at the thought of Spencer, Jessie leaned on her elbows and looked at the chest. Ever since her adventure in sixteenth century England, she'd become fascinated by chests and wooden boxes. The one they sought back then was a wooden box with carvings all over it. It had been completely handmade by Lachlan.

As Jessie sat there, she began thinking about the chests before her. Why were they still here? There were so many people who had tried to make the inn a success, yet, no one had ever taken these out of the attic? That seemed odd.

Rising, she walked over to the first chest and opened it up. Yep, there lay the same old clothes and hats she and Daniel had discovered the first time. Pawing through them, she found nothing of interest. Closing the lid, she decided to try moving it. It wouldn't budge. "That's weird." She removed everything from the chest. There were only seven garments and five hats.

Jessie put her shoulder to the side and tried pushing it against the wall. Still, it did not move.

"Okay, now you have my attention. It's an empty wooden chest. I'm a relatively healthy young woman and I can't get it to move an inch. What's up with that?" Jessie looked under it to see if it was nailed down. "Nothing."

Pulling the milk stool over, Jessie sat in front of the chest, elbows on her knees. It was time to call on her powers and see if she couldn't figure out what in the hell was going on.

Closing her eyes, she breathed deeply, sending herself to a meditative state that allowed her to access her past memories and see things she did not know, remember images long past and gain wisdom from her other souls.

She had a flash of Spencer on a Spanish galleon. He was in the belly of the boat, looking at his plunder, flipping lids of chests open, and pawing through nets and baskets filled with goods.

And then he came upon a chest similar to the one in front of Jessie. Opening it, he began throwing its contents to the floor, until the whole thing was empty. He stood and stared at it a long time, before going to his knees and feeling underneath the chest. He felt around for some time before a smile curled his lips and he did something to the chest that made him laugh.

The vision disappeared and when Jessie opened her eyes, she remembered what it was Spencer had done.

Getting on her hands and knees, Jessie felt under the chest just like Spencer had done. As her hand made its way through cobwebs, Jessie's fingers searched for what did not belong on the bottom of a chest. When her fingers hit the slender metal piece, she grinned and sent a silent thank you to Spencer. Flipping the metal piece around, Jessie watched in amazement as the bottom of the chest slowly rose on one side, like a trap door. "What have we here?" Jessie whispered, watching as the bottom rose.

What Spencer had been looking for in his chest was a chest with a false bottom. That was exactly what this chest had, and whatever was in the secret compartment weighed enough to keep Jessie from being able to budge it.

When the trap door finally stopped its incline, Jessie peered into the chest and saw a black velvet cloth lying across the top. With a trembling hand, she pulled the cloth back to reveal a leather journal. Underneath the leather journal, she saw another black velvet cloth lying across something rectangular. Taking one corner of the cloth, Jessie started to draw it back when she saw gold.

"Oh. My. God," she uttered, pulling the cloth completely back to reveal four bars of gold. "Holy shit." Running her hand over the cool, smooth bars, she looked guiltily around her. "What were you *doing*, Albert?" Jessie tried to reach in and pick up one of the bars, but it was so heavy she had to use two hands, and even then, it was a struggle to get it out of the chest. "Jesus, how much do these things weigh?" Setting the gold bar on her lap, Jessie estimated its weight at thirty or forty pounds.

Putting it back next to its sisters, Jessie opened the journal and was surprised to see it was Carolyn Gibson's journal, Albert's wife. "What do you have to say to me, Carolyn?" Jessie said, flipping through the journal. "And what is your journal doing in here with this gold?"

Jessie skimmed through Carolyn's journal, reading about the typical boring day of a housewife in 1922. At first it was filled with what the neighbors were doing with their house, family gossip and feelings of sexual frustration with her absentee archaeologist husband. Then, as the weeks continued, Jessie could feel a change in her attitude about life.

June 2, 1922

I should not be surprised. I am more surprised at my reaction. Robert has professed his love for me, and I admitted to him I returned his affections. He is a wonderful man, caring, loving, intelligent. Unlike Al, he talks to me about their Egypt digs, his goals and dreams. He is a remarkable storyteller, full of life and vibrancy when he speaks. His eyes light up when he tells of this pyramid or that temple.

Al always makes me feel so small and stupid, as if I am not intelligent enough to understand what he is saying. But not Robert. When Albert spent that month in New York at some archeological conference, Robert and I became closer. At first, he just came for dinner or took us all out for dinner. The kids really loved that. Al never takes us anywhere. Then, he started coming over when the kids were in school...and now, here we are...in a predicament I am not the least bit sorry to be in.

I only wish I knew what to do beyond this moment.

Jessie paused and looked over at the gold. "I have a good idea what you did, Mrs. Gibson, and I'm pretty sure it cost you your life." Turning the pages, Jessie read about their affair, about how often Robert came over or would take her on a picnic to Golden Gate Park. She was in love with him, and the longer Albert was off doing his job, the deeper she fell in love with Robert Townsend. And she minced no words about being in love with him. They were already planning on taking the kids and moving to Egypt as soon as she could arrange a divorce. And then...in August things started to change.

August 1, 1922
Robert believes Al has become suspicious of him. I have tried to assuage his feelings of paranoia, but with all we are doing, with all the duplicitous activities surrounding us, it is no wonder. Al continues to act strangely and speaks of Egypt in the present tense. Robert thinks he is delusional and is worried he might snap. A few months ago, I would have disagreed with him, but no longer. There is something wrong with Al, but I am afraid of backing him into a corner. He has become so volatile these last few months, I don't want to face his anger. The other day, he barked at Kristine in a manner that was not necessary for not picking up her shoes. The children appear afraid of him and we all look forward to his next visit to Egypt. When he goes, I will go to the lawyer Robert has suggested and file for divorce.

August 2, 1922
Robert and I cannot imagine being apart much longer. The children adore him, and he is more a father to little Leland than ever Al was. He is a wonderful man and I look forward to being his wife even if it is in the far away and exotic land of Egypt. I have been reading a great many books on the country, and though it is a very poor country, it is filled with beautiful people, wonderful food and, of course, all that history. It will make Robert so happy to live there.

Tonight, he came over, and after we made love, he told me he ran into someone who had just returned from New York. When he asked about the conference, the man said Al had not shown up. Could he be having his own affair? I feel the emotions of guilt lift from my shoulders. When Robert asked the man about it, he said that there were rumors that Al was losing his mind. Robert and I had been wondering that for months, but now, if the archaeological community was talking about it...it could be true. Robert believes this is my way out. If there are those who are willing to say that Al has been acting strangely, I should be able to procure a divorce.

The way he has been acting toward the children is a little scary as well. He continues to refer to "the way children used to be." I don't know what to think any longer. He can't seem to coexist with us in the present. Maybe all that sun has made him go mad. Maybe he lost touch with reality. Whatever the case, Robert says I need to see the attorney. I want to, but in truth, I am afraid of Al's reaction. He is no longer the man I married and I am afraid of him.

August 4, 1922

Al is on his way home from some conference or meeting in New Mexico. He said he was seeing someone about one of his artifacts. He thinks I don't know what that means, but I do. When I told Robert that Al was going to New Mexico, his face got red and he swore. He hardly ever swears, but this time, whatever Al is up to incensed Robert. He left the room and started making phone calls. He left shortly after I told him, saying we would discuss it tomorrow.

August 6, 1922

I write with a shaky hand, stunned by what Robert discovered. Apparently, Al has been selling off many of the artifacts he brings home to private collectors for a tidy profit. It is illegal and Robert has no idea how much he has sold, but he is furious at Al and has threatened to bring him up on charges. I tried calming him down but he was livid. The man Al went to see in New Mexico was some sort of buyer of antiquities, and Robert said the man pays handsomely. I told him I hadn't seen any money or any new purchases by Al. It could be in a new bank account. I don't know. The truth is, I no longer care. I want out, and when Al comes home, I am telling him I want a divorce.

What made me mad today was Robert has been pressuring me all along to get a divorce, but suddenly, he wants me to wait until we can find out where Al is putting his money. Robert said he needed to go through his catalogue and see what Al was selling. He left in a huff. I

*am quickly tiring of the men in my life huffing and puffing around. If
Al has money hidden somewhere, I will find it. I will find it.*

Jessie peered over the journal at the gold bars. "Looks like
you found it," she said, returning her attention to the journal
once more.

August 12, 1922

*Al has returned and is acting stranger than usual. No sooner
did he get home than he went upstairs to take a nap, asking not to be
disturbed. After an hour, I went to check on him and he was not in
any of the bedrooms. I saw him go upstairs, so I know he was up there,
but I could find him nowhere. It was very odd. When he did come
back downstairs several hours later, his mood was greatly improved.
He was almost merry. I worry for his mental state. He was whistling,
cheerful, and even offered to play with little Leland. I watched him
carefully, wondering at the change, and then I asked him if we had
any extra money for me to get a new dress for one of his upcoming
dinners. He said we had plenty and to get whatever I wanted.*

*Al is never that generous where clothes are concerned. I wonder
how much money he is making selling his artifacts. I also wonder
where he went when he said he was taking a nap. Perhaps next time I
ought to follow him. Does he have a secret lair? What in the world is
going on with him?*

"If only you knew, Carolyn, it would have really blown your
mind." Jessie stood and stretched before sitting back down on
the milk stool.

August 17, 1922

*Something is definitely going on, but I do not know what it is.
Al has been leaving the house at odd times, he says he is taking naps
and then nobody can find him, and his moods go from being joyful
one minute to yelling at all of us the next. He won't talk to me about
anything he has been doing. Actually, he doesn't really talk to me any
more. I think it is time I tell him I want a divorce. I've decided to tell
him tomorrow after one of his happy naps. That's what Leland calls
his naps. Happy naps. Even the babies see how different he is when he
comes down from his naps. Yes...I will tell him tomorrow. I must do
something to make this life more bearable. He is insufferable, Robert*

is becoming disillusioned with me that I will ever leave Al. It is time. It will be the best thing for all of us.

August 19, 1922

I told Al, and he flew at me in anger, ranting that he would never give me a divorce. He was inconsolable, almost to the point of tears. I stayed calm and told him I thought it was best and that I could not remain married to a man who held as many secrets as he was holding. He threw a pot across the room demanding to know what I knew. And then...then he realized that much of what I knew had come from Robert. I overplayed my hand and he started questioning me about how often I saw Robert and whether or not we were lovers. He threatened to ask the children about Robert, but I begged him to leave them out of it. I begged him and he laughed. He laughed like a madman. The conversation ended with Al making threats against me, against Robert, against some unknown person named Erdu or Erfoo or some such blather. He has lost his mind. Of this, I am certain. I must take the children and go this weekend, when Al leaves for one of his "conferences." I swear, the man must think I am an idiot. If I didn't know better, I would think he was seeing another woman. But he is not. He is obsessed with Egypt and only Egypt. She is his true mistress.

August 21, 1922

I did it. I asked Al for a divorce. Well...I didn't ask. I told him. At first, he seemed to think it over, and then, he laughed. He laughed and told me I was a foolish woman and that no court would ever grant me a divorce. His laughter rings in my ears even now as that of a madman, a lunatic. He said he knew all about my affair with Robert...that the two of us deserved each other. He said hideously foul things too low for me to even write here.

This may be my last journal entry for awhile. I have decided to leave him. I already have the children packed and Robert has secured a place for us to stay. I do not know how long it will take to get a divorce from him, but any judge who spends five minutes interviewing him will see that he is not sane. When he speaks of his precious Egypt, it is still in the present tense, as if he actually goes there. He seems obsessed with Nefertiti's reign, and Robert has joked he is in love with the queen. Al's obsession is nothing to joke about, however. It is a sickness now that pervades everything, and if I don't get out—

"And apparently, you didn't." Jessie flipped through the remaining pages, but all empty. She spent the next hour combing through the pages of the journal looking for something, anything, that would help her figure this out. None of what she thought she knew made any sense now. If Robert was in love with her, why would he have come in and killed her and the children? What would he have to gain? The gold? Obviously, he never found it.

It wasn't until she closed the journal that she got her answer. On the back of the leather journal was a stain. It was a very old stain, but it was pretty clear what the stain was.

There were three bloody fingerprints on the back and one on the spine of the journal. The pieces began falling into place for Jessie now. Closing the lid to the trap door of the chest, Jessie heard it click into place. Then, she placed the old clothes back in the trunk and closed it before tucking the journal under her arm and heading to Ceara's boat.

They'd been wrong all along.

When Ceara finished reading the journal, she turned it over as Jessie instructed. After studying the stains, she pushed it across the table. "Well, my dear, it would appear we've been pointing our finger at the wrong man."

Jessie nodded. "Townsend was in love with Carolyn. He wanted to take her and her kids to Egypt with him. He wouldn't have killed her."

"He didn't kill her."

Jessie shook her head sadly. "I don't think so. When we read Al's journal, we assumed he had only *heard* their screams. We didn't realize he was a reason for them."

"The man killed his entire family." Ceara held the leather journal on her lap and gently placed both hands on it. "So, the gold bars you found are Albert's."

Jessie nodded. "He was dealing in illegal antiquities at a time when payments were made in all sorts of ways. He sold whatever artifacts he could and someone paid him in gold bars."

"Gold bars that, strangely enough, he kept. Doesn't that strike you as a bit odd?"

"In a lot of ways. Which odd way were you thinking?"

"It doesn't appear he meant to be gone in Egypt, does it?" Ceara paced the floor. "A man who was done with this world wouldn't have cared about the divorce, the gold or selling artifacts, but a man who had planned on coming back for it... well, that's another man entirely."

Jessie rubbed the back of her neck. It had stiffened while she sat reading in the attic. "You think Albert's stay in Egypt was an accident?"

"Let's say, for the sake of argument, he killed his family and tore the house apart to make it look like someone had killed them...someone who had been having an affair with his wife."

"You think he was setting Townsend up."

"Let's assume, shall we, that Albert killed his family and then whisked himself off to ancient Egypt. If he hid the gold well enough, he could come back, get them, and start a whole new life."

"But something happened."

Ceara nodded. "Yes. Something big happened. Carolyn was right about overplaying her hand. If she had kept her nose out of the artifact selling, he might have let her get the divorce."

"But she became a threat because her knowing meant Townsend suspected as well, and together, they could destroy what was left of his reputation, and without that reputation—"

"Selling off his artifacts would have been much more difficult. So he kills his family, and then hides her journal along with the gold, probably thinking to use it to blackmail Townsend upon his return."

Jessie nodded. "But Albert never made it back to use any of it. He must have somehow gotten stuck back in time."

"Agreed. Or else he would have come back for all that gold." Ceara pushed her glasses up the bridge of her nose. "Unless... unless he figured out what the portal could really do."

Jessie's eyes grew wide. When she had chased Quinn down, it was for the same reason: using the portal to be richer in his other lives. "We've seen that before, but if that's true, why did Townsend buy and move the house?"

Ceara paced more before answering. "Somewhere along the way, Mr. Townsend must have discovered how much Albert had been paid. I don't imagine the antiquities market was a very large community."

"So Townsend bought the house to look for the money Albert was making, but it probably never dawned on him it would be in gold bars."

"So he never looked in the right places."

Jessie shook her head sadly. "And he figured Albert would eventually come back for it."

"Exactly. Remember, this was 1922. People either put the money in the bank or stuffed it in their mattress. My guess is Mr. Townsend was looking for the proverbial mattress."

"And when Albert didn't come back, Townsend had the building moved rather than have it destroyed so he could continue searching."

"But the trunks weren't even moved. My guess is they've been sitting in their same position all these years, too heavy to move."

"He didn't have the good fortune of having a Spencer."

Sighing, Jessie shook her head. "But this is all just conjecture."

"What *isn't* conjecture, my dear, is the fact that *you* know something he doesn't: you know how the portal works. Albert may know nothing except how to go back and forth. We can't assume the gold was for another life, just that he clearly was coming back for it at some point."

Jessie slowly turned to Ceara, who looked how she felt. "Are you thinking what I'm thinking?"

"If Albert didn't know how to use the portal—"

Jessie's hand went to her mouth. "Then Efru had to have come through first."

"And found a man balancing his sanity on a wire. Oh my…if Efru knows how to use the portal—"

"Then he has to die after we send Albert through."

They stood in silence just looking at each other.

"If Efru came through first, what happened that he lost control when Albert went back? Somewhere along the line,

Albert took control of the priest, so he's not an amateur at this anymore, Jessie. He is a threat to the integrity of the portal—a threat you must deal with once and for all."

Jessie frowned. "I can't go back there and ask Albert if he murdered his family. What would be the point?"

"Albert *knows* he can't go back to his own time, or he would have, but is he willing to cast his soul across time because he may be done playing priest to a spoiled rotten ruler who has nearly brought his beloved Egypt to its knees?"

"It's possible."

"Think about it, my dear. Think long and hard about what that man is capable of. Clearly, he must have walked in on his poor wife while she was writing in her journal. Something in him must have snapped, because the next thing we know, everyone is dead and he is missing. He meant to come back. He meant to start a whole new life somewhere else. If he believes Sakura can get him to the portal—"

Jessie was suddenly on her feet. "He's been playing us all along. He doesn't want Nefertiti. He *wants* to go to the temple!"

Ceara nodded. "If he casts himself into the portal, you will never be able to get his soul back to 1922, and it could be lost forever to you. The damage he could do—"

"Unless he *intends* to come back to our present. He knows the portal exists. He may believe the gold is still there as well."

Ceara stared at her. "Oh my. That would put us all in danger."

"I'll bet that's why the spirits are so pissed off. They know."

"They want the soul of the man who murdered them, Jessie. They want him to get what he deserves, not the chance to start anew."

Jessie grabbed her things and started for the door. "I have to get to Sakura. I have to let her know."

Ceara grabbed Jessie's wrist. "Maeve told you to stay away from her. She could still be in grave danger."

"I have to go, Ceara. I have to make sure he is sent to the right place. Who knows what he'll do to everyone once he gets to the portal. The man is a murderer, Ceara. He killed his own kids for Christ's sake! I have to go back!" Tearing her wrist from Ceara's grasp, Jessie started out the door.

"Jessie, wait."

"I *have* to go."

"I know you do, but do one thing for me. When you get there, do exactly what Maeve tells you to do. She knows what she's doing."

Nodding, Jessie started back to the inn. She only hoped she wasn't too late.

14th Century BCE

As Sakura led Nefertiti, Tarik and Efru through the labyrinth, she felt the tingle on the back of her neck. "Not now," she uttered under her breath.

"What did you say?" Efru asked.

"Not a thing."

Efru stopped. "No, I heard you say something. Who were you talking to?"

Sakura looked over at Tarik, who, though lumbering like he always did through the rock maze, was clearly not the man she was in love with. She didn't know if this made her more comfortable or less knowing that Maeve controlled him. "I was praying, if you want to know."

"To Aset? Sakura, you are a fool. Prayer to any of these gods is of no use. Men make their own way in this world. If you knew what I knew, you would see it too. Gods come and go, Sakura, and your Goddess is no exception. It's what men *do* that changes the world."

Sakura backed away from him. "You are not a priest at all, are you?" The familiar knocking at the gateway to her soul was louder and more insistent.

"Just get us to your temple, witch, and all will be forgiven."

Nefertiti looked at Sakura, but Sakura could do nothing except wait for Maeve to say something or do something to get them out of this. But something did not feel right. Suddenly, this man, this traveler from the future was becoming agitated and nervous.

As if hearing Sakura's doubt, Maeve stepped up to the little man. "I strongly suggest you refrain from your petty comments, priest."

"Oh do you, Tarik? And I suggest we get a move on so the queen can say her prayers. We need to leave before night ends."

Tarik nodded and motioned for Sakura to keep walking, but she refused. "I'm...I'm not feeling very well. It must be from being in that cold cavern." Sakura sat down, her eyes locked onto Tarik's. If Maeve was as strong a priestess as she thought, she would know something was wrong.

"Sit, Sakura," Tarik said, kneeling in front of her and taking her hands.

"There is no time to stop," Efru said. "We must be almost there. Time is of—"

"Enough!" Maeve commanded. "We will wait until she feels better. So sit down and be silent, priest. Do not forget your place."

Efru laughed. "Yeah, it's all about place and who looks at whom, and who is the boss of all the little people. Don't you ever get tired of it, Nefertiti?"

Nefertiti stared at him. "What I tire of is insolent priests who think they may call me by my given name. Sit down, Efru, until Sakura feels better." Nefertiti gathered herself up to her full six feet and jammed her hands on her hips. "And that would be *Queen* Nefertiti to you."

As Nefertiti and Efru engaged in more verbal combat, Maeve took Sakura's face in her hands and looked deep into her eyes. "Look at me, Sakura. Look at me and listen. *Analnathrak uthvas bethood, dochial dienvay.*" She said this three times and on the third time, Sakura's body went slack for just a moment, and then, as if coming out of a daze, she stared into Maeve's face, her eyes holding a different sort of wisdom.

"Is it you, Jessie?" Maeve whispered.

"It's me, Maeve," Jessie said from within Sakura.

Maeve nodded. "The spell of making I cast has allowed you to take over. And though I wish you were not here, I must assume you have come for a reason." Maeve helped Jessie to her feet. "Something has happened. What brings you here?"

Jessie nodded and tried to get over the nausea that comes when possessing a body. It was a feeling unlike anything she could put into words. "He *wants* to go to the temple so he can access the portal. He's been misleading us all this time. He doesn't want Nefertiti. He wants to slip through time."

Maeve nodded, her jaw setting. "Indeed."

Jessie looked over at Nefertiti, who shoved Efru away. Lowering her voice, she whispered, "He is attempting to get out of here any way he can. You cannot let him near the portal. If he gets close enough, he'll—"

"I understand. I see now, what must be done. He will not do so. Now, go back, Jessie. It is too dangerous for you to be here."

"I must be allowed to speak to him before you take his soul."

Maeve looked over and saw Nefertiti and Efru had stopped arguing. "But you must do it here. Now. I will protect you from the priest, but then you must remove yourself from Sakura.."

Nodding, Jessie walked over to Efru. She knew by Sakura's memories that the portal was just around the next bend. She had gotten here just in time.

"Albert Gibson," Jessie said, turning toward the priest.

Efru turned his attention to Jessie. "Who *are* you? How could you know who I am?"

"Oh, I know far more about you, Albert Gibson, and most of it isn't very pleasant."

Efru started toward her, but Maeve bridged the gap in Tarik's large and powerful body, staying between Jessie and Efru. "Careful, little man from the future. You have no power here."

Efru's eyes looked panicked. "Look, I don't know who you are or how you know about me, but—"

"I know you murdered your family for a few bars of gold."

Efru's mouth hung open, the color draining from his face.

"Yeah, I wouldn't have much to say about that, either, if I were you. You make me sick."

"You're not Sakura. What do you want?"

"Did you really think you're the only one who knows how to use the portal?"

"You found my gold? So Townsend didn't get it after all? Excellent!"

Jessie shook her head. "No, he didn't. Robert may have looked for it, but he never found it, you soulless excuse of a man."

"It's my gold! Mine! I worked day and night assuring myself of a better future. If I can just get back—"

"There is no *back*, Albert. How ironic you ended up in the past you once loved. I would have thought being with your beloved Nefertiti would take some of that pain away."

Efru looked confused. "Nefertiti? She may be a beautiful woman, but I have no designs on her. I have merely used her to get here."

Now it was Jessie's turn to look baffled. "What? But I thought—"

"That I was in love with Nefertiti? Yeah, you probably got that out of my wife's journal. I left that with the gold. She never did really pay much attention when I talked to her. It isn't Nefertiti who has my heart. It's Nefertari."

Jessie looked at Nefertiti and Maeve. "Who in the hell is Nefertari?"

Efru sneered. "Don't know as much as you thought, now did you? Nefertari is the woman I married when I was in Egypt last year trying to find some way to get that idiot Lord Carnovan to fire that other idiot, Howard Carter, so I can be the one to find the tomb of Tutankhamen. I know exactly where it is, but I couldn't get Carnovan to listen to me. He said the best he could do was issue an ultimatum to Carter that if he didn't find the tomb soon, it would be his last season. So I did everything I could to raise enough money to buy the rights to dig at that site."

"And that's why you sold off the relics."

"Yes. I finally have enough money to convince Carnovan to let me excavate instead of that imbecile Carter, and then this happened." He waved his arms about.

Jessie stepped closer. "What do you think *this* is?"

"Isn't it obvious? Somewhere along the road, my house

became some sort of time machine like in HG Wells' book. I can transport here whenever I want just by going in some room, but I haven't been able to return."

"Do you know why not?"

"I'm not sure. There were…well…things happened."

Jessie sneered at him, knowing what things he spoke of. "Things? So you came here and then what?"

"What else? I located as many of the undiscovered artifacts as I could. We'd catalogue a good number of them, but then, I started hearing rumblings that Carter was after this unknown pharaoh's tomb in the Valley of the Kings. When I realized where he was digging in relation to the tomb they were building for Akhenaten, I knew I could be the most famous Egyptologist in the world if I could get my hands on that tomb."

"And to raise money, you brought home artifacts and sold them to private collectors."

He nodded. "I did. Made a fortune off of them, but Townsend started getting suspicious. Started taking second and third looks at the catalogues…started watching me more carefully during our digs. I started to despise the man and his limited vision. There was Carter with the Metropolitan Museum in his back pocket and Carnovan, who had more money than God, but only *I* knew where the tomb of Tut is. I only hope it is not too late for my return—that no one has discovered where the tomb is."

"And what is it you think you'll do when you return to your own time?"

"I'll take my gold and return to Cairo, where my wife and child are waiting."

Jessie's eyes grew wide. "Your…you have a *kid* in Egypt?"

He nodded. "I have a future waiting for me if I can just get out of this past. I have been trapped here for longer than I cared to."

Maeve looked at Jessie and shook her head.

"A *future*? Albert, it brings me great pleasure to tell you that you're *dead*. The gold is sitting in the attic in *my* time, which, I hate to tell you, is the year 2012."

He turned whiter. "What? That…that can't be. You lie!"

"It's true. Your body is dead. That's why you can't get back. There's no place for your soul to go."

He could only blink in disbelief.

"You went through in 1922. It took that long for someone else to find both the portal and the gold. I imagine it's because no one could move the chest, so everyone just left it alone. Everyone except me."

"And who *are* you?"

Jessie looked over at Maeve one more time, and this time, she nodded. "I am the Guardian of the Gate. It's my job to make sure no one upsets the balance of time by coming and going when they aren't supposed to. You were not supposed to be here, Albert, let alone *stay* here."

"I am aware of that. I don't wish to remain here one moment longer. Why do you think I was stalking you all this time? When I entered this sickening little body, I was just outside of these ruins. I have sent three young priests to their death looking for the time machine that will take me back home, but this maze of rocks is impossible to get through. Well, I got lucky one day and saw you and the queen coming from it, so I devised a plan to get you to take me here so I can go home."

Jessie shook her head. "So, you intended to go back through the portal."

"Portal...is that what it's called?" Albert rubbed his chin. "Yes, that is exactly what I was going to do, but now you tell me that my life is over? That I am dead? If that is so, then I want to leave this pathetic little body filled with seizures and whatnot, and return to another time, any other time."

Jessie nodded. "As the Guardian, I am here to help you. We are here to help you."

Albert looked at Tarik and Nefertiti. "I just want out of this accursed place. Nefertiti, you can still save yourself, you need to leave the palace and never return, or your husband will slowly kill you."

Nefertiti remained silent.

"I can't believe this is happening this way. My plan was to return once everything had died down...you know...once the children's bodies were gone. I was simply going to return to the house, get my gold and mail my wife's journal to the chief of police with a note suggesting they check out Robert Townsend as a possible suspect."

"You were going to frame him?"

Albert reeled back. "*Frame* him? There was no framing necessary, Sakura. He killed them. He killed them all. I made it back through just when that murderer found me."

Jessie shook her head. "What do you mean?"

"Townsend found me just as I was coming out of the time machine room. We struggled, and I realized he was a man obsessed with revenge. Apparently, he had been waiting days for me to return. When I did, he attacked me. I did the only thing I could think of; I pushed him down the stairs and ran back to the time machine room." Albert sat down on a stone and held his head in his hands. "I was just able to make the jump back into this time…into this apoplectic body."

"Why do you keep saying that?"

"He has some sort of epilepsy. He was having a fit when I entered him the final time. It wasn't usually like that… sometimes, I controlled the body, and sometimes, he did, but the last time I came, I assumed complete control."

Maeve nodded to Jessie that this was, most likely what had happened.

"More than likely, that last fit killed him, leaving you stranded."

"Stranded? Is that why he never returned? I…I had no idea."

"Of course you didn't. You do not know what you are doing. You are a child handling something well out of your abilities, and this is what happens."

"I don't care. I just want out."

"I understand that. Before we can help you, I need to know what happened when Townsend tried to kill you."

"My cheating wife had plans to run off with my double-crossing partner, and they had designs on taking my gold with them if they could find it. All my work and *she* thought she somehow *deserved* some of it! And Townsend acted like he was my best friend, when all he wanted was my life. My *life*! I thought he wanted my wife, my family, my money and my fame as an archaeologist. He wanted to take from me all the things he was too inferior to get for himself."

"So you think he killed you?"

Albert shrugged. "He must have. What else could he *do*. In the end, I wound up with a new family, riches beyond desire and—"

"And you're dead."

Albert pinched the bridge of his nose. "So you say. But I've given it a lot of thought. If I can escape back to the time just *before* Townsend killed my family, then all will be well. Don't you see? If you are the big Guardian, then you must know how to send me back to the time before I died, right?"

Jessie didn't have to look at Maeve to know this was exactly the opening they had been waiting for. "Yes, Albert, I believe we can do that. All will be well." Turning to Maeve, Jessie nodded. "It's time."

Maeve strode over to Albert and beckoned for him to stand near her. "You must close your eyes and do not open them no matter what you hear."

"But you're just a—"

Maeve held her hand up to his face. "I am many things, priest, and I am the *only* one who can send you back home."

"Home—" Albert whispered softly. "I have been gone far too long. You send me home, then you are free to go yourselves. I think that's a fair trade-off."

"Close your eyes," Maeve commanded. "Do not open them no matter what you hear." Maeve glanced over at Nefertiti and whispered to Jessie, "Take her to the temple around the bend. *Keep* her there. She need not see this."

Jessie nodded, moving over to Nefertiti.

"There is much I do not understand, isn't there, sister?"

"More than you want to know, yes."

"This thing we do tonight. It is a charade, is it not?"

"In a manner of speaking, yes." Jessie approached the temple ritual area and motioned for Nefertiti to do what she came to do. "Pray," she whispered. "And do not look up."

"Then the man...that priest was *not* in love with me?"

"He was in love, Nefertiti, but not with you. Now, please,

pray to Aset and leave your offerings to her. We will dispose of the priest first and then Tarik will take you away from here to safety."

"Then everything is a ruse but that? I still must go?"

Jessie nodded. "I'm afraid so. Once you get where you're going, Tarik will explain how it is you can return. I'm sorry, Nefertiti, but it is the only way."

Suddenly, there came a howling the likes of which Jessie had never heard. It sounded like a dozen keening females going through some sort of labor. It was a horrific cacophany filling every nook and cranny of the cavern. It was deafening.

Nefertiti, who was just beginning to kneel, rose. "What is that wretched sound?" she yelled.

Jessie yelled back, "I'll go see! Please. Finish your prayers! I'll come back to get you!"

As Jessie came back around the bend, the shrieking grew louder and louder. It was piercing, and she had to clamp her hands over her ears as she made her way back to where she'd left Maeve and Albert.

Albert.

Jessie felt nothing but disdain and disgust for the man who had been Albert Gibson. What he had done with his life made her sick, and she regretted nothing that was happening to him or going to happen. He was insane, to be sure, and she was pretty sure his continued forays into her portal had been the instigator that sent his life spiraling downward.

Her portal.

What a strange thing to think. She supposed the whole Guardian thing was beginning to mean something to her in ways she hadn't really thought about. She had a responsibility to the gate and to those who used it, but this man, this killer, did not deserve to go back to *any* life, with or without his children. To think he believed he would be able to step back into his old life showed how little he understood what was happening.

The awful sound got louder, and when Jessie turned the corner, what she saw drained all of the blood from her face. The sound she'd been hearing was coming from three white-haired crones who were keening. The three women wore tattered gray robes and were swaying in front of a different portal composed of silver branches creating a doorway against the darkness.

"The Morrigan..." Jessie uttered to herself. The Nightmare who rode away with the soul—the dark angel of death who wrestled the soul from the body. Maeve had summoned The Morrigan to help her extract Albert's soul from Efru's body. She had called on the most powerful of the soul collectors to do what Jessie had only read about. Maeve hadn't called just them. She had brought with her the Bean Sidhe, or banshees.

The Bean Sidhe were the crones whose keening heralded a death, and they were signaling the death of the second soul within this body. From behind her rock, Jessie watched, hands over her ears, as The Morrigan ripped Albert's soul out of the priest's body. The Morrigan, still clinging to the writhing, twisting, blackened soul, turned and said something to Maeve before disappearing through the death portal. Once through, the portal closed up with a pop and vanished, taking the Bean Sidhe with it.

In the deafening silence of the cavern, Jessie edged over to Maeve, who was staring down at the still body of Efru. "The Morrigan? Maeve—"

"The Morrigan can do what I could not, Jessie. What you asked me to do required skills I do not possess. Do not worry. The Morrigan are Sidhe and...well...they and I have an understanding of sorts."

Jessie looked down at Efru's lifeless body, which had yet to move.

"Is he dead?"

"Not yet."

Jessie kept staring at the body. "Where did they take Albert?"

"The Morrigan was not happy about having to return a soul to a specific time where there is no body, but they have assured me he will be returned to the place where he died." Turning to Jessie, Maeve exhaled. "They will, in essence, give his soul to those who are waiting for it. They understand this will right some of the imbalances that have been littering the portal and the area between time."

"What do you mean *give him* to them?"

Maeve shook her head. "It is an area I know little about.

I've not had to do this before. The souls in your home are there because of unfinished business. There is a piece missing. Albert's soul is that missing piece and they are going to return it to the spirits waiting for it. Go back to where you left Nefertiti and stay there until Tarik returns to himself. You do not want to see what is about to happen."

Jessie looked down at the body of Efru. "Are you—"

She nodded. "The Bean Sidhe recognized how evil and vile a man Albert was. Their keening was particularly loud because they did not wish to be near his darkness. It is their way."

Jessie nodded. "That was an awful sound."

"He was an awful man, and according to The Morrigan, the priest is no better. He was vile *before* Albert entered him and took over."

Jessie nodded. "Thank you for this, Maeve."

"Do not thank me, Jessie Ferguson, for helping you do your job. It is what we do, and Cate will be most pleased to know that neither you nor Sakura were harmed."

"So, you're going back now?"

She nodded. "We all are. We have done all we can in this accursed oven of a country, and I look forward to returning once more to my lush green valleys and cool, gray climate."

Jessie stepped up to Maeve and hugged her. "Thank you so much, I'll think of you often."

"And I, you. Now, time is of the essence. You must still get Nefertiti out of here. It is not safe for either of them to stay. Tarik will make sure the three of them get to safety, but there are evil forces at work here that not even the king is aware of."

"But Tarik knows?"

"He does. Now, promise me you will go around the corner and not look back. Then you must leave Sakura and go back to your time. She knows what must be done. You should find that your angry spirits are no longer there and your life may return to normal."

"I promise. Thanks again, Maeve. Tell Cate—"

"That you won't be visiting her for quite some time. You both need to focus on your lives in your own time, Jessie. I *need* you to do that."

"Gotcha." Jessie started back around the corner, where she found Nefertiti huddled in the corner with her hands over her ears. Jessie helped her to her feet and smiled softly into her face. "I know this may be hard to understand, but we must go away from the palace for two years. Two years, Nefertiti. It isn't safe for you to come back sooner. You must do *exactly* as Tarik says and both you and your...and I...will be safe from those who would seek to harm us. Promise me you will heed Tarik's advice in this matter."

Nefertiti looked long and hard into Sakura's face, and when she finally nodded yes, Jessie returned to the twenty-first century, and Sakura regained control over her being.

"Come now, Nefertiti. We have stayed here too long. It is time for us to make haste away from the palace and the eyes of the city."

As they came around the corner, Sakura drew in a breath as she watched Tarik pull his sword out of the belly of Efru. When Tarik saw them, he quickly sheathed his sword and took Sakura's hand. "It had to be done. If we allowed him to live—"

"No explanation necessary, Tarik Gbish," Queen Nefertiti said. "That worm deserved nothing better than a death away from his precious Aten and the sun he worships. Come. Let us get away while we still have time." Nefertiti started down the cavern to take the torch from its place on the wall.

Sakura stepped up to Tarik and looked into his eyes. When she saw her soul mate's spirit, she smiled softly.

"You have returned."

"Yes, my love, it is I. Maeve could never thrust a sword into a helpless man, but I have no such misgivings. We are free now from the tainted breath of this priest. It is time now for me to take you and your sister far away so no harm can befall either of you." Bending down, Tarik kissed Sakura's lips. "You may be my one and only love, Sakura, but that Maeve is an incredible being. I have never witnessed such power."

Sakura nodded. "You think *your* priestess is stronger than mine?"

Tarik laughed. "It is no contest, my love. Jessie may have a truly kind heart, but Maeve is gifted beyond anything either of us has ever seen. We could not have done this without her." Taking Sakura by the hand, Tarik followed after Nefertiti, glad he would spend no more time beneath the rocks outside the city gates.

21st Century AD

The first thing Jessie did when she left the portal was to run to Daniel's room and sit on his bed. She sat there for almost an hour waiting to hear anything from the spirits, but they were gone.

"They're gone, aren't they?"

Jessie started, and then saw Daniel standing in the doorway, his backpack slung over his shoulder. "What are you doing back? I thought I told you—"

"I came to see how things were coming in the spirit world. Looks like mission accomplished. They're not here. You did it." Daniel was beaming. "Can I come home now?"

"As soon as I have Tanner check it out. He…well…he *feels* these sort of things."

Daniel sat with her on the bed. "They're really gone, Jess. I know it."

"I'm sure you do, but—"

"Jess, didn't you ever wonder why it is that the ghosts came to me? Why me and not you? I mean, with all you have going on with you, why didn't they come to you?"

Jessie looked over at him as she rose. "I've wondered that at least a half dozen times."

"Have you ever thought maybe I'm special, like you?"

Jessie stopped at the door. "What do you mean?"

"I mean…what if these weren't the only dead people I hear. What if I…what if I can *really* hear them?"

A cold chill swept over her. "Can you?"

Daniel looked down at his hands in his lap. "Yeah. Yeah, I can."

Jessie came back into the room. "What do you mean, you can *hear* them?" The chills turned into something more ominous.

Daniel nodded again. "This wasn't the first time I heard

ghosts. I didn't want to say anything because I was afraid you'd think I was a kook."

"You're not." Sitting back down on the bed, Jessie studied him. He looked like her little brother in every way, but there was something different about him. Maybe he really was special as well.

"There are times when I really wonder. I've heard dead people before, but I wasn't going to tell anyone. Thanks for telling me about your gig, Jess. It's made me not feel so lonely."

"Lonely? You feel *lonely* here?"

"I feel lonely being different. We're different, aren't we?"

"Yeah, we are. Does it bother you?"

"Sometimes. I mean…hearing dead people sucks, especially when they're all mad and stuff, but it's not like I can help it. It happens when it happens."

"When has it happened?"

"Well, here, of course, and I heard one down at the coast one night when a boat came by."

"You're not messin' with me are you?"

"No. You think I'm making this stuff up? Sometimes, it's really clear, like they were still alive, and others, it's like it was in here. I can barely hear them." Daniel shook his head. "I guess I'm getting used to it."

"You want Ceara to look into it?"

"What's there to look into, Jess? We're different. Somewhere along the road, something happened to us. You do what you do and I…I hear dead people's voices. Maybe now that they're gone, I can sleep better." Daniel rose. "I'm going over to get my things. I miss my bed."

"Sport?"

"Yeah?"

"You're okay, you know that, don't you?"

"Yeah, Jess, I do," Daniel answered, walking out of his room.

Jessie started looking through the papers and books the ghosts had strewn about before they returned to hell or wherever it was they took Albert Gibson's spirit. Several of the books were about poltergeists, spirits, doppelgangers, and other spiritual phenomenon. On the back of one of the papers was an address. The address was a place near where they had lived in San Francisco. Folding the paper, Jessie put it in her pocket.

She called Tanner and Ceara and had them come up to the house. Regardless of what Daniel thought, with Tanner's empathic skills, he would be able to tell whether or not the spirits were still there.

After hugging Jessie too tightly, Tanner stepped back and stroked her cheek. "There's nothing here but us chickens. Nothing, Jess. They're gone." Tanner walked around the room, touched the walls, ran his hand across the desk.

"Are you sure?"

"Absolutely."

Gratefully, Jessie looked up at the ceiling. "Daniel is such a good kid, you know? Now he can get on with his life."

Ceara took Jessie's chin in her hand and looked into her eyes. "What is it? Has something happened to Daniel?"

Jessie looked away and sighed. "Sort of. He…he told me this afternoon he hears the dead."

"Oh dear."

"Yeah." Jessie ran her hands through her hair. "Why couldn't he have been born empathic, like Tanner?"

"Let's see…*you* send your soul across time to ancient Egypt and Celtic Rome, and you're worried about voices your brother hears? No, my dear, you have nothing to worry about. I'll spend some time with him and see if he's got anything else going on we need to know about."

Tanner nodded. "Tell us what happened."

An hour later, out back on the porch swing, Jessie finished her tale.

"So, that pretty much begs the question, what are you going to do with the bars of gold?"

"I've given that a lot of thought, and I think it's best if I gave the bars back to the Professor. It's money from his family and belongs to him."

"Whoa, wait a second, Jess. Do you have any idea how much those four bars are worth?"

Jessie shook her head. "And I don't care. It's blood money, Tanner. His grandfather raped Egypt for her relics and sold them to the highest bidder. He let his partner butcher his family while he did nothing. It's dirty money, and I don't want anything to do with it."

"Hear, hear," Ceara said.

"I did some calculations, Jess, and if those bars weigh around thirty pounds, then each bar is worth somewhere between four hundred and seven hundred thousand dollars."

Jessie stopped swinging on the porch swing. "Excuse me?"

Tanner nodded. "Today, gold is worth about twelve hundred bucks an ounce. Sixteen ounces in a pound…do the math, smarty pants. Those four bars are worth over two million bucks."

Ceara whistled. "Could buy lots of first editions with that kind of cash."

Jessie started swinging again. "It's not lost money, guys. It doesn't fall under any scavenger rules. It belonged to Leland's grandfather, and I, for one, have no intention of keeping it."

"Not even a bar for yourself?"

Jessie shook her head. "Not even a sliver. There's bad karma around that gold. He sold Egypt out from under herself, and her goddesses probably aren't thrilled. Unless the Professor does something good with that money, it could very well be the ruin of him."

Tanner kissed her hard on the cheek. "Jess, you're something else. Does this mean we're taking another road trip?"

Nodding, Jessie leaned back in the chair. "What do you think, Ceara? Let's put a period on the end of this adventure, shall we?"

"I'm all for it. I suggest you set up an appointment with him before we leave. That little meeting could take longer than an office hour."

"I will, but when we get there, I'm not planning on telling him anything other than we found the gold. There's no reason to go scab picking. I think delivering his gold to him is the best we can do."

Ceara patted her thigh. "You're a good girl, my dear. It's always good to consider what the ramifications could be with the unveiling of information like that. I'm proud of you for not feeling the need to drop a hot flaming ball in his lap."

"It's not like I have any proof other than the fact that Carolyn was having an affair with Townsend."

"Not pretty, that's for sure. In the end, nothing but tragedy centered around nearly everyone involved with King Tut's tomb, including Albert."

Jessie nodded. "Makes you wonder about the supposed curse."

"Yeah, speaking of that, when did Carter finally find it?"

"In November of 1922. Carnovan had, in fact, given Carter an ultimatum about finding the tomb. Up to that point, no one knew anything about Tut. When Carter found the tomb, it was such a big deal because it was the only intact tomb ever discovered in modern times."

"So, Al wanted to *be* Howard Carter. Sad thing is, he might have made it if he hadn't lost his marbles by traveling back and forth. Why didn't he just leave?"

"One possibility is that Carolyn and Townsend might have been trying to blackmail old Al." Jessie answered. "More likely, he just had so many screws loose that he lost his mind. Both he and Efru had mental instability issues. It was just a sad thing that happened because of greed and the desire for fame."

"And all that time, he was writing about a woman named Nefertari whom he'd had a child with?"

"Yeah. Too weird, huh? All that time, we thought he was talking about Nefertiti."

They sat there in silence for a long time, until Ceara finally rose. "Well, I'd better get the boat ready to go."

"What about us? Don't you want some help?"

Turning, Ceara grinned. "I do not. You two do whatever young kids do when they have accomplished great things. I'm proud as punch of you, my dear. You've done well."

When she left, Tanner turned to Jessie and took her hand. "I want to hear it all over again from the start, so start from the beginning and don't leave out a single detail."

The boat ride had been uneventful, and Jessie found she could barely keep her eyes open for most of the trip. Ceara explained to her that slipping across time took more out of people than anyone could accurately measure, and she ought not to fight it. Jessie didn't, and found herself taking long naps in the cabin below as Tanner sailed down the coast.

While she was sleeping, Cate came to see her.

"You're not supposed to be here," Jessie said, seeing Cate come through the mist. "Maeve made it pretty clear to me—"

"*Maeve* told me to come. She realized she had been a bit short with you before she left and wanted me to come explain why." Sitting on the rocks, Cate lowered her hood. "I am now beginning my studies in earnest and she wants me to put forth all of my energy into them and my life and not as much into lives not yet lived or already past."

Jessie nodded. "That's understandable, Cate. I wasn't upset. How could I be? Maeve really came through for me. For us. The situation was a bit dicey there for a minute."

Nodding, Cate rose and walked toward the fire. "She said you are really beginning to see your role as Guardian something to be taken seriously. For that, I am thankful. It makes me feel less…alone."

"If that's my destiny…*our* destiny, Cate, then so be it. You and the others spent a great deal of time preparing me for this. I want to be good at it. I want to do what's best and what is right and—"

Cate held her hand up. "That is a lesson you are going to have to learn on your own, Jessie. Sometimes, doing what's best is not the right thing, and other times, doing the right thing is not the best. As long as your heart stays pure and you do right by others, the best will work itself out."

"I have so much to learn."

Cate pulled Jessie to her feet. "Maeve said she felt you doubting something in your life…something important to you…something that is the very core of who you are. You just don't know it yet."

Jessie frowned. "I have no idea what that could be."

Cate tossed a yellow powder into the fire and it hissed and parted. Inside the fire, stood Jessie. She was at a podium lecturing and gesticulating wildly to a class sitting on the edge of their seats, enrapt by whatever it was she was saying. "What I have learned, Jessie, is that sometimes, the best way to learn a thing is to teach it to someone else." Turning to Jessie, who was mesmerized by seeing herself in the fire, Cate pulled her sleeve. "You have the gift of a teacher, Jessie Ferguson. You have the ability to make the past come to life for so many people. Giving the gift of memories *is* your destiny. Do not turn away from it now simply because some writer or historian got it all wrong. Do not abandon that passion which drives you deeper into books and deeper into your own soul. You will be a great teacher, someday, Jessie, and although there will be times when you question your choice, you must know you will change lives by standing in the front of students."

Jessie was staring in awe at her older self.

"Do not mention this to Maeve. She is very much against showing anyone the potential of their future."

"Potential? You mean, this may *not* happen?"

"It's entirely up to you. Free will allows us to fulfill our destiny or not. I am just showing you *one* possible outcome of your path." Cate closed the flames and turned to Jessie. "You are my dear friend, Jessie, and though I have obligations and responsibilities in this life, I also wish to prepare my soul as best as I can for you. I want you to be able to access *all* of the things you are going to need to know in order to defend the portal."

"I'm not the only Guardian, am I?"

Cate smiled. "No, you're not. There are many others out there who are Guardians, but the line of Guardians began with Sakura. She will continue to be the Guardian of the portal in Egypt until she dies."

"I was afraid…well…we sent them off to Lower Egypt for a few years…I didn't know—"

Cate nodded. "As it should be, but she *does* return, and she will guard the gates for a very long time. You saved her life, Jessie. She will repay you for that someday."

"She doesn't need to. Like Maeve said; it's what we do."

"It is, indeed. Surely you must realize it is not *all* we do, and there is much for you to do and learn in your time."

"Maeve already gave me the lecture. She wants me to leave you be. She wants us to live our own lives."

"No, she wants you to *invest* in your own life, to learn all the things you need to learn, to practice accessing all of our memories. There's much for us both to do in our own times. Maeve is just concerned for both of us. She wants what is best, and believes we are too easily distracted by each other. Do you feel she is wrong?"

Jessie shook her head. "I'm pretty sure she's never wrong."

Cate pulled her hood back up and started toward the mist. "I cannot remember the last time."

Suddenly, Jessie realized she was going to cry. "I guess...I'll be seeing you much later then?"

Cate nodded, tears welling in her eyes as well. "It truly is for the best, Jessie."

Sadness welled in Jessie's chest as she looked upon the face of someone she used to be, who was as real to her now as Daniel or Tanner were.

"And you really think I ought to be a teacher?"

"Only you can make that determination for yourself, my friend. Look deep inside. You'll know what to do." Cate hugged Jessie tightly. "I'll think of you often," she whispered, pulling back. "And remember...I am always here." Touching Jessie's temple with her fingertips, Cate turned and vanished into the mist.

When Jessie pulled the rolling backpack into Professor Leland's office, he rose from his chair and shook everyone's hand.

"I have to say your phone call really piqued my interest. I'm quite surprised to see the three of you back here so soon. Mission accomplished?"

"Well, we found a few things in our search for the truth we thought you might want."

"Please, have a seat." Professor Leland motioned toward the three chairs. "I've set aside my entire office hour for you, so, can I get you some coffee or a Coke maybe?"

"We're good." Jessie sat down in the middle chair and reached down into the backpack to pull out the leather journal. "We found this in an old trunk. It belonged to your grandmother." Jessie unwrapped the journal and set it on the professor's desk.

Professor Leland looked down at the journal without touching it. "My...are you certain?"

Jessie nodded. "It's all in there, Professor, and it's not very pretty. It's not much of a family legacy, but you knew that already. You have my word no one else has seen it and no one else needs to ever know about its existence."

He nodded as he reached for the journal and gently opened it. "You read it?"

She nodded. "I had to. But I told you you can trust us. We're not taking anything to the media or anything like that. Your family secrets are safe with us."

"Excuse me for my paranoia, but how do I know—"

Tanner leaned forward. "In less than one minute, Professor, you're going to know you can trust Jessie more than probably anyone else you'll ever meet."

Jessie reached out to touch Tanner's arm and pull him back to his seat. "What Tanner is saying is you have our word. We don't want to bring any more shame upon your family."

"Shame? How bad is it?"

"Not bad by today's standards. Your grandmother was having an affair with Robert Townsend. That in and of itself isn't awful, but, well, you know how those sorts of affairs can lead from one thing to another. When you read it, you'll see. All of your questions will be answered."

Professor Leland closed the book and folded his hands over it. "You could have mailed this. You didn't have to come all the way down here."

Jessie grinned. "I could have mailed that, yes, but these here would have cost a fortune. You see, that wasn't all we found." Reaching down into the bag, she pulled out one of the gold bars and hefted it to his desk. "We found these as well."

Professor Leland stared at the gold brick sitting on his desk. "You can't be serious."

"She's not kidding, Professor." Tanner bent over and, one

at a time, pulled the remaining three bars from the bag and set them on his desk.

"Your grandfather sold artifacts to private collectors about eight years before the Depression struck. Instead of being paid cash, he was paid with these bars of gold."

"He...he sold artifacts?" Professor Leland took his glasses off and pinched the bridge of his nose. "That...that goes against everything archaeologists are—"

"There was a lot going on at the time, Professor."

"That doesn't explain or excuse such horrific behavior."

"Nobody's explaining or excusing anything. It is what it is, and that gold is yours. For whatever reason, right or wrong, moral or immoral, this gold belongs to your family, and that's why we're here. No other way to safely transport a hundred and twenty pounds of gold."

"A hundred and..." Professor Leland stared at the bricks on his desk.

"It comes to slightly over two million dollars," Tanner offered. "Give or take a couple thousand."

Slowly, Professor Leland locked eyes with Jessie. "You're telling me you brought me two million dollars worth of gold that belonged to my gransdfather for selling artifacts?"

All three nodded, but it was Tanner who spoke. "I tried convincing her to keep some of it for herself, Professor, but Jessie isn't that kind of person. She found four bars of solid gold and insisted on bringing them to you. She has no ulterior motive except to make sure the journal and the gold end up in the right hands."

Professor Leland blinked rapidly, then slowly nodded. "I apologize for my suspicious nature. Please, forgive me."

Jessie waved him off. "No harm, no foul, Professor. The truth is, even if I could, I wouldn't be able to take anything that occurred from ill-gotten goods. He sold his beloved Egypt down the river; an act that goes against everything I believe in."

"And everything he believed in as well." Shaking his head, Professor Leland leaned back. "There's more to this than meets the eye, isn't there?"

Jessie shrugged. "The only proof of any wrongdoing comes from Carolyn's words, and we don't know how reliable those are. I just know this gold belongs to your family. What you choose to do with it is your prerogative."

"I take it you expunged the ghosts from the house?"

Jessie nodded. "I am not really at liberty to go into the details, but yes. Your relatives are finally at peace."

For a long time, Professor Leland stared at the gold bars. When he finally spoke, his voice was hushed. "I am not surprised by my grandfather's actions. According to my mother, something happened that really changed him after one of his visits to Egypt. She never said what, but she said he was never the same. He never played with her brother and sister, never took Carolyn out, never really seemed interested in their lives. I suppose something happened that sent him reeling and he never recovered. Illegally selling artifacts to the highest bidder would surely have poisoned his soul." He shook his head sadly. "The man corrupted his entire being, his family, and..." He stopped and stared at Jessie, as if all the dominoes were falling into place. "You don't suppose...he isn't..."

Ceara shook her head. "We made no assumptions, Professor, and neither should you. Other than what is in that journal, supposition is a waste of time and energy. You read that journal, take it for what it's worth, and then you'll understand as much as you can about their past." Ceara rose, and Jessie and Tanner rose with her. "We'll leave you to it. If you have any questions, here's my cell phone number. We'll be returning to New Haven in the morning."

Professor Leland rose and nodded. "I don't know how to thank you. This is...so much more than I could ever have imagined. To have my grandmother's journal? What a prize."

"A couple million bucks isn't so bad, either," Tanner added softly.

"Jessie, can I ask...how does a young woman your age walk away from millions of dollars that no one but you knew existed?"

Jessie smiled. "Sometimes, Professor, doing the right thing is the *only* option."

"There are those who would disagree."

"And they don't have to live in my skin. In my world, Professor, doing the right thing keeps your soul clean, and that's really important to me."

Professor Leland studied Jessie a minute. "You are a unique young lady, Jessie." Stretching his hand across the table, he shook hers. "It has been an honor to meet you."

"The pleasure was mine, Professor. Thank you for your help."

When Jessie, Tanner and Ceara got back to the boat, Jessie wrapped her arms around Tanner and Ceara and pulled them to her. "Like the man said, mission accomplished, boys and girls. Time to go home."

When Tanner went below to check that all engines were a go, Jessie joined Ceara on the deck. "I've made a decision about my life, Ceara."

"Oh? I didn't know there was a decision pending."

"Yeah. Remember when I told you I was thinking about leaving school?"

"Uh-huh."

"I know what I want to do with my life." Jessie turned and smiled. "I'm going to be a professor. I'm going to get my doctorate."

Ceara clapped her hands and hugged Jessie. "Oh, my dear, that's wonderful! What changed your mind?"

"Not what. Who."

Ceara smiled knowingly. "Cate?"

Jessie nodded. "Yeah. I'm going to heed her words of wisdom and follow my destiny."

"And your destiny is in the classroom?"

"Yeah. That, and being Guardian, and I'm feeling up to both tasks."

Ceara patted her back. "That you are, my dear. That you are."

Three weeks had gone by since Jessie had washed her hands clean of the whole ghostly affair. She entered the house one afternoon to find her parents sitting in the parlor with an older gentleman wearing a gray pinstriped suit. He was rummaging around in his briefcase.

"Jess, could you come in here for a moment?" Reena asked.

Jessie set her backpack down at the foot of the stairs and walked into the parlor. "What's up?"

"Jess, this is Mr. Bennet from San Francisco." Rick tried to say more and then stopped and shook his head, as if the rest was just too difficult for him to get out.

Jessie reached across the coffee table and shook his hand. "Nice meeting you."

"Likewise, Ms. Ferguson. I represent the Gibson family estate and Professor Leland has asked that I deliver this to you personally." He handed Jessie an envelope.

"Professor Leland wrote me a letter?"

"It is more of an explanation for the reason I am here." Mr. Bennet pulled a piece of paper out of his briefcase and read from it before setting it back. "As you are aware, Professor Leland came into some inheritance recently, none of which would have happened without you. He feels indebted to you for the things you have done for him and his family, and requested I come here to answer any questions about the…financial transactions that occurred this morning."

Jessie looked over at Rick. "What transactions?"

Rick swallowed hard, but it was Reena who answered. "This Professor Leland paid off all of our loans, lines of credit and second mortgage on the house. We own the inn free and clear."

Rick nodded. "He said it was the least he could do for you, Jess."

"He did *what*?"

Mr. Bennet nodded. "Professor Leland wanted the house to have a fresh slate, so he paid the debts under one condition, and that is why I had to come in person and have your parents sign this." He held up what looked like a contract. "That they leave the inn to you and only you should they retire, die or just want sell it."

Jessie blinked. "He wants *me* to have the inn."

Mr. Bennet nodded. "Apparently, it was that important to him, this being his ancestral home and all."

Rick and Reena just kept shaking their heads. "Mr. Bennet informed us that you did some research for this professor and as a result, he was able to cash in on a very large inheritance?"

Jessie shrugged. "Something like that."

"When do you have time to do this while you're in school? You *are* in school, right?"

"Yes, mom, I'm still in school."

Mr. Bennet cleared his throat. "That brings me to point number two."

"There's more?" Reena said, breathlessly.

Mr. Bennet nodded and consulted his paper again. "Professor Leland has established a college fund for you, Jessie, to carry you through to your doctorate at any university of your choice. That letter will explain the rest to you. Suffice it to say, he believes you to be a young lady of considerable merit and he feels you would make an incredible historian. He wishes to help you in that endeavor. It's all here in these papers, and if you need more money than what is in the fund, you simply contact me and I will make the necessary arrangements."

Jessie could only stare.

"No conditions?" Rick asked.

"None. As long as Jessie is in college, Professor Leland will foot the bill. It is the very least he could do and he says doing these things for your family relieves him of any guilt for being so fortunate."

"Just how fortunate is he?"

Mr. Bennet smiled as he closed his briefcase and handed a packet of papers with his card attached. "I am not at liberty to say, but Jessie can probably tell you. It was nice meeting you. I will be sure to tell Professor Leland that his old home is absolutely brilliant. You've done wonderful things with this house. I can see myself out. Thank you."

When Mr. Bennet left, Jessie was still trying to find her voice.

"Jess?"

She looked over at Reena.

"What on earth did you do?"

Gathering herself, Jessie answered, "This house used to be where our house was in San Francisco."

"You have got to be kidding."

"No. I'm not. I did some research, poked around here and there, and stumbled, quite literally, across an old journal of his grandmother's. Apparently, there was an inheritance he didn't know about, but once he had the journal, he was finally able to collect."

"Just how much did he collect?"

Jessie turned the envelope over in her hands. "A little over two million dollars."

"Two...*million?*"

"Give or take."

Rick looked over at Reena. They were speechless.

"He's a really nice guy. I never expected him to do anything like this. This is..."

"A miracle, Jess. Your father and I weren't sure we were going to able to keep the inn going for much longer. We've been barely able to break even after all the repairs."

For a moment, they all sat there staring at each other.

"Jess...is there something we should know? You haven't done anything illegal, have you? Why didn't you tell us about this place or any of this?"

She could only shake her head. "Because I knew you guys have been working so hard to get this place solvent. Everyone in town still calls it the Money Pit, and I just wanted to prove them wrong."

"This is life-changing, Jess. Do you have any idea the weight this takes off our shoulders?"

Jessie nodded. "I guess the professor just wanted to pay it forward." Jessie stared at the letter. "He was awfully generous, wasn't he?"

"That's why I ask. You don't even really know this man."

"Actually, I've met him twice, but those are long stories, and I have a ton of homework. So, if you don't mind...I'm going up to my room. I'll fill you in if you spring for a pizza."

Rick laughed. "That's the least we could do."

Grabbing her backpack, Jessie started for her room. When she got there, she chucked her bag on the floor and jumped up on her bed. Tearing open the envelope, she read the letter inside.

Dear Jessie-

It isn't every day a man of letters has the opportunity to meet someone with such incredible integrity and moral fiber as you possess. Your act of pure honesty deserves more than a card or a trite thank you. My inheritance amounted to nearly two million three hundred and fifty thousand dollars; more than a man like me wants or needs. I have donated some of it to a library fund in my grandmother's name, and am having Mr. Bennet invest the rest. You are part of that investment. It is with great joy that I am able to give you the gift of an education beyond your wildest dreams. You have the passion to be one of those rare instructors who have the capability of changing lives. Go out and change lives, Jessie. There is no better job in the world.

As for the inn...I thought long and hard about how I could best help your family make the most out of a home that once had such heinous activities occurring in it. It struck me that you were meant to have that house, to live in it for a long time because only you, out of all the people who have come and gone, only you found the chest and the trap door and the journal. Only you took the time to get to know her and her history. She belongs with you, Jessie, and it is my wish that you stay connected to her for as long as you can.

My inheritance not withstanding, I am using some of the fund to take a sabbatical so I can write my own Great American novel. With that money, I no longer have to worry about tenure or retirement, and for that, I thank you yet again.

If you are ever in the Bay Area and want to stop by for coffee, I would love to see you. Until then, I will be keeping my eyes on the history journals and will expect great things to come flowing from your pen.

Thank you, once more, for all that you have done for me and my family. May the wind always be at your back.

Sincerely,

Professor Gibson Leland

Leaning back on her pillow, Jessie sighed loudly, thinking what a pleasant ending it was to a very eventful quest. She had managed to rid the inn of ghosts, save Nefertiti's life, capture the soul of a portal trespasser, and figure out what she wanted to be when she grew up.

"All in all, it was a pretty good day's work."

Closing her eyes, Jessie knew being a Guardian and a Professor would go hand-in-hand, and that her knowledge of history would only strengthen her powers as a Guardian. "Wonder where we'll go next," she murmured, feeling her eyes getting heavy.

As she closed her eyes and felt her head getting heavy on the pillow, she saw two shirts hanging on a clothesline. One shirt was blue, the other shirt was gray, and when a slight wind blew them up, she saw two people laying on a blanket in a grassy field, unaware of anyone or anything else except for each other.

She would have that kind of love someday.

Of that, she could be certain.